Make You Mine

RUNNING IN CIRCLES

E.M. LINDSEY

Make You Mine

E.M. Lindsey

Copyright © 2023

2nd Edition

All rights reserved.

This book or any portion thereof may not be reproduced or used in any manner whatsoever without the express written permission of the publisher except for the use of brief quotations in a book review. This book is a work of fiction.

Any resemblance to persons, places, jobs, or events is purely coincidental.

Cover by: Ari with Red Hatter Book Blog Design

Editing: Susie Selva

Content warnings and information: ableism, homophobia, traumatic loss of parents and grandparents, on-page anxiety attacks.

MAKE YOU MINE

"To love and be loved, it's all that matters. In the end."

Socially awkward Noah Leib knows he wants more from life than being a forty-year-old virgin who's got a failing bakery, a strained relationship with his brother and sister-in-law, and an empty apartment. He just doesn't know how to change things. Living in Savannah, trying to keep his head above water, Noah is single-minded and plans to stay that way.

And then Noah's favorite Deaf adult film star's life falls apart in a very public spectacle on Twitter.

Noah doesn't expect anything from the ASL message he sends to Adriano Moretti, but when a shadow appears in his bakery doorway one afternoon, he finds Adriano standing there with a small smile on his lips and a hello on his hands. It's at that moment Noah realizes his life is about to change forever.

Adriano is a force of nature, and Noah is quickly swept up in his wake.

But fantasy has never been Noah's reality, and there can't be a happily ever after on that horizon.

Can there?

FOREWORD

Running In Circles is the former series On The Market, and this novel was previously titled Love Him Free. It has been completely revamped and re-written with names, places, characters, and major plot points changed.

Please see the FAQ section of my website for any questions about audio and my blog for information on the upcoming Running In Circles re-writes.

PROLOGUE

It happened on a Tuesday.

Noah was still in shock that he was actually at a university, let alone a university two thousand miles from home. There had been a time in his life when he didn't think he was ever going to get out of Savannah. Not that he didn't love it there, but sometimes—even with the ocean bracketing him on one side and the rest of the country on the other—he felt like he was surrounded by four walls that were constantly closing in.

He supposed that grief did that to a person. Not just losing his parents but the grief his mother brought with them when they moved to the States. It was fresh off the heels of his father dying, and she'd spent all her days clinging to Noah and his infant brother, making him swear in his little voice that he would never, ever leave her.

And then she left him.

It took him until high school to feel brave enough to step outside the bakery walls, and it took him until the last half of his senior year—damn near too late to even apply for school—to decide it was something he needed to do.

And in spite of the vicious look Adam had given him

when he'd gotten his acceptance letter to school in California, he was happy. He was thrilled.

He felt free.

"Who is that?"

Noah looked up at the one single friend he made—his freshman roommate in the dorms. They didn't live together anymore, but Chris had stuck around, which meant something to Noah. His anxiety had aged him into a crotchety, eighty-year-old man in a twenty-year-old's body—complete with joint pain and an intolerance for people's bad attitudes.

It also didn't help that he was socially awkward and a raging virgin with zero hope that he'd ever rectify that because the only meetups he ever attended were services at the Hillel on Friday nights. It wasn't pathetic—except well, it sort of was, and Noah was just ready to accept that about himself.

He'd die a virgin, working at his bubbe's old bakery in Savannah, and he'd have to live vicariously through Adam, who'd made it his life's mission to be everything Noah wasn't.

Noah bit his lip, following Chris's line of sight and eventually settled on a guy he most definitely recognized. His name was Adriano Moretti, and at first, Noah had known him as the TA in his ASL 4 class. And now, thanks to a viral email that had swept through their dorm building, he knew him as Sylent—the amateur porn star.

And the guy had the nerve to just be sitting there at the café like the entire world—including Noah—hadn't seen him screwing some undergrad into literal oblivion.

Noah had watched the video like sixteen times before rutting into his sheets and coming all over them, and he'd only just managed to get himself in order and pretend he was asleep before his roommate had come home.

His ears felt hot, and he swallowed thickly. "Uh. Why?"

"I feel like I know him," Chris said.

Noah bowed his head and stared down at his croissant. "He was in that video everyone was freaking out about."

"Vide—oooh. Shit."

Noah sighed. "Yeah."

"Well, he keeps staring at you. Do you, like, know him?"

Noah's heart gave a heavy thud against the inside of his chest, still refusing to look up. "There's no way he's staring at me. He's the TA in my ASL class, but I'm a thousand percent sure he has no idea who I am."

"Cool, cool, cool. Well, he's coming over here right now, so…"

Noah had just enough time to look up before Adriano was literally at the table. 'Hey,' he signed, flicking the salute off the top of his forehead.

For whatever reason, Noah always forgot everything he'd ever learned about ASL when he stared into Adriano's eyes. His hands trembled as he tried to pull himself together. Why did he have to be so awkward? 'Hi. What's up?'

Adriano's smile was soft and warm. 'I wanted to invite you to this Deaf event on campus. I know Prof P. wants everyone to attend one this semester, so I thought it might be fun.'

'Will you be there?' Noah asked, then promptly wanted to chop off his own hands.

But Adriano just smiled. 'Yeah. Come find me tonight? It's at Heller Hall. Nine o'clock.'

There was no way in hell Noah ever left his building after six, but he felt a sudden burst of courage. 'Okay. I think I can make it.'

'Cool. Save me a dance.' And then he was gone.

"Holy shit. I'm writing that romance novel right now. What did he say?"

"Stuff about class," Noah muttered because he'd done this once before with a guy who…well, it ended about as badly as a date could end, and that was the last time Noah had ever put himself out there. The last thing he needed was Chris trying to convince him this was meant to happen.

Adriano was tall, muscular, gorgeous. He literally had a fan club of students that took ASL just because he was Deaf. And they were all California tens. He was a Florida six on his best day. There was no way in hell Adriano meant it as anything other than the fact that Noah was a nerd who studied.

"Well, that's boring," Chris said, then launched into his latest story about the girl he was crushing on in his chemistry lab, and Noah did everything in his power not to think about what the night was supposed to be like.

Or about the little flicker of something that felt too much like hope dancing around in his chest.

"Noah?" Adam's voice sounded far-off like he was speaking from another room instead of directly next to him. "Noah."

He turned slowly, his body moving as if he were under water. "Mm?" His gaze fixed on Adam's face, and he slowly felt the threads of shock start to snap.

"What do we do? What…what am I going to do?"

Reality crashed in. Noah wasn't floating in some void between fantasy and reality. He was sitting in a hospital room beside a bed where his grandmother's machines were beeping out a symphony, keeping her alive because nothing else would. Her doctors had been honest and brutal about it.

She wasn't going to wake up.

Noah opened his mouth to say something, but his throat felt like sandpaper. He swallowed a few times, then squared his shoulders and reminded himself that this was it. He was twenty, he was an adult, and there was no one left to save them from the harsh truth: they were alone now.

"What do you mean?" Noah asked.

Adam blinked, then gave a harsh laugh. "She's..." His voice cracked, and he stopped for a long minute. "She's going to die, isn't she?"

"Yes," Noah said. He wanted to curl his arms around his brother and protect him from the pain this was going to cause. Adam had been too young to remember the weight of losing their parents, but it was seared on Noah's ribs like a brand.

Adam's chin trembled. "What am I going to do? Where am I going to go?"

It was the sound of Adam's panic that finally caused Noah's dissociation to crack entirely. He turned, putting his hands on Adam's shoulders and squeezing tightly. "You're not going anywhere."

"But you—"

"I'm coming home," Noah said. He ignored the stabbing pain those words caused, and he met his brother's gaze. Adam might be nearly as tall as him now and filling out. He was losing the baby-round softness in his cheeks, and he had the rough hands of a boy who would be a man soon. But in that moment, he seemed so damn young. He was the little toddler climbing into Noah's bed because he was scared and their mom was never home to take away his fear. "I'm going to take care of whatever happens next."

Adam licked his lips. "Are you...I mean. You're not done with school yet."

Noah shook his head. "It doesn't matter."

"But you—"

"It doesn't matter, Adam," Noah said, not meaning to sound harsh, but he didn't want to think about how much that hurt. Not yet. He'd mourn later after Bubbe's last breath.

If he thought about how, just hours before, he was standing outside a building trying to find the courage to walk up to a gorgeous man who wanted him around—how he was finally on the cusp of being his own person and shaking off the trauma of his past—he'd collapse.

"Why don't you lie down," Noah said. He reached over and grabbed one of the spare pillows from the little shelf behind Bubbe's hospital bed and laid it on his lap. "You've been up for almost twenty-four hours."

Adam looked like he wanted to argue, but after a beat, he just twisted his body and tucked his legs up, then laid his head on Noah's thighs. He let out the smallest sigh when Noah started to stroke his curls. "Promise you won't leave."

"I'm not going anywhere," Noah murmured. He laid his head back, and the moment his eyes closed, he found himself standing in the middle of an empty field. His parents were gone. Bubbe was gone. Adam had been taken from him.

He sat up with the smallest gasp and realized he'd dozed off. His vision was blurry, but he stared down at Adam's sleeping form resting on him, and he knew then he couldn't lose him. He couldn't.

I know bargains rarely work out for people, Noah prayed, closing his eyes and bowing his head forward. *I know it usually ends in disaster, but I have to try. No, I have to beg. I will do anything so long as you keep him safe. You will have all of me without compromise so long as this never happens to him. Please. Please. Please.*

His prayer ended, and he opened his eyes staring at the floor by his feet. For a split second, Adriano Moretti's face appeared—his sunny smile, and broad shoulders, and perfect hands. It was a sign he decided. It was a moment to say goodbye. That had been a life of fantasy. Of pretend.

This was his reality, and there was no better time than now to accept that he would never have anything more. But it was worth it. For Adam to live a life happier and longer than his own, it was worth it.

CHAPTER 1

THE FORTY-YEAR-OLD VIRGIN thing was an accident. Noah Leib hadn't planned on reaching his *twenties* without having an orgasm at the hands of another person. He certainly didn't plan on making it to his midthirties in that same state. Maybe it was an ugly twist of fate that he went from a happy-go-lucky kid running the streets with his friends while his bubbe sold bread at her little stall at the Forsyth market to this anxious, disaster of a man who couldn't keep it together for ten minutes on a date let alone enough time to get laid. And maybe it was always meant to be.

Noah was young when his ema and bubbe packed up everything they owned, swaddled his brand-new brother, and boarded a plane for a place he'd only read about in schoolbooks. It was terrifying at first to be ripped from his home and settled in a little apartment above a bake shop, where no one spoke his language. He didn't understand why he was there, just that his mother was crying a lot, and Bubbe woke up for all Adam's feedings, and Noah had to spend hours and hours with a stranger trying even harder at English because he hadn't been any good at it in school before they'd left Tel Aviv.

It was six weeks before he understood that his father was dead. His mother appeared in his doorway in the middle of the night, staring at him until she realized he was awake. She looked haggard, hair a mess and unwashed for weeks. Her eyes were red-rimmed and dry only because he was pretty sure she didn't have tears left.

She didn't say anything right away. She just stared at him, then padded with soft, bare feet across the worn carpet and climbed into his small bed. There wasn't space for the two of them, but she took him into her arms, and there was the tiniest sliver of the mother she'd been before everything was turned on its head.

"Ema," he whispered.

She shook her head and sniffed. "He's not coming back, *boychik*." She stroked the top of his curls with shaking fingers.

"Who isn't?" he asked.

Her voice cracked, and she cleared her throat. "There was a raid. Abba didn't get out in time."

That was all she said, and Noah was barely eight, but he knew what that meant. Most of the kids his age there knew what that meant. Noah was born into violence and turmoil. He was born into the strangest juxtaposition of peace and love and violence and death. He knew what bomb drills were, and he knew what it was to be carefree on the beach thinking he would live forever.

But life was fleeting, and it was a hard lesson for a small boy to learn so quickly. His father had been a good man. He was tall, larger than life, with an infectious laugh he used against his mother whenever she was angry. Later, she'd remember it. She'd tell him, "I could never stay mad at your abba. He'd just smile at me, and wink, and chuckle, and my anger would fly away like a little finch."

Noah stopped missing him so hard by the time he was nine. Adam was just starting to walk, and his mother was starting to stay out all night. The kids at school still mocked him because he hadn't lost his funny accent, and he had to count in Hebrew to remember his multiplication tables. Bubbe was working to keep their family going, and when his mother did come home, she was like a storm cloud.

He forgot quickly what it meant to be a kid. He forgot what it was like to have real friends or real freedom. His mother was never around, but when she was, all she'd do was scream. "I don't want Noah all alone here!" Her voice would rise and carry through the house, and Adam would whimper, and Noah would hold him a little tighter like he could protect him from the wrath of the grieving woman.

"You leave Noah alone all the time," Bubbe would shout back. "You go out, you drink, you sleep around. What's next, Maya? Another baby? Some goyishe seed growing in your belly?"

His mother swore at her, something shattered on the floor, and then she was crying again. She was always, always crying. "I can't let anything happen to him."

"And what about Adam?"

She never had any answer to that.

Late at night, she'd come into the bedroom, and he'd watch her stand over the crib and stroke her fingers through Adam's baby-soft curls.

"Do you love him, Ema?" he'd ask her.

She wouldn't look over, but she would pull her hand away and curl it against her heart. "He looks just like your abba." That's all she'd ever say. *He looks just like your abba.*

Noah thought Adam looked like a baby—chubby cheeks and wide dark eyes and drool on his chin. Noah thought he'd like his mother to be there in the mornings to feed him his oatmeal or at dinner to make sure he ate his smashed vegetables.

But she never was.

Six days after his twelfth birthday—one year before his bar mitzvah—his mom was taking him and Adam to Atlanta when everything changed again. Hashem—or the universe, he wasn't even sure anymore—decided to rip everything apart again.

He didn't remember the crash. He just remembered his mother yelling at him because he'd mouthed off. He remembered her crying—and she was always, *always* crying. He remembered her saying she wished he was more like his father, braver, kinder, able to make everyone smile.

He didn't remember the way she swerved into oncoming traffic because she'd turned around to yell instead of paying attention. At least not until much later. All he knew was fear and exhaustion. Then tires squealed on the pavement, and there was a horn blaring. And then he knew pain. And then darkness.

Noah woke in a hospital bed—aching from every inch of his body. Bubbe was there when he first opened his eyes. She brushed back hair from his forehead, and he could tell she'd been crying. He knew that look. He knew that expression of grief and loss. She had never gotten along with her daughter, not after Elisha died, but she had loved her, and Noah knew in that instant she was gone.

"Where's Adam? Where's…" He tried to sit up, but his body wouldn't obey, every inch of him screaming with an unrelenting pain.

Her warm hand on his forehead soothed him but only just. "He's fine. He was in his car seat, and he was fine. Not a scratch."

Noah swallowed, his throat painfully raw. "Ema?" he croaked.

"I'm sorry. She never woke up," was all his bubbe told him. "It's just us now, *boychik*."

Noah closed his eyes again and hoped the pain wouldn't last as long as it had when his father hadn't come home. He wasn't sure he'd miss her, though.

Adam asked for their mom a couple of times after Bubbe

brought Noah home, but he was more fascinated by the cast on Noah's leg and the places along his arm, jaw, and eyebrow that had been stitched together with ugly black thread.

Noah was on crutches during the funeral, the ringing in his ears from trying to manage the pain in his leg and in his heart overwhelming him. He barely heard the rabbi speaking over the din, barely understood what was going on, only that it was almost over. Strangers from the temple kissed him on the cheek and hugged Bubbe and promised to be there if they ever needed anything, but Noah didn't really believe them. He was young but not so young he couldn't hear the polite lies in their tone.

It was easier to just go home. To sleep above the bakery and wake to the smells of fresh things baking and know that this was his life. He'd sit at his window at night and work on his Hebrew because his bar mitzvah was coming the same time as the anniversary of her death, and he'd tried not to think about how small it would be. None of his friends wanted to come—and he didn't blame them, not that he had many he could have blamed. But the affair would be quiet, and somber, and a little cruel because it wasn't just the ritual that was making him the man of the house but that God was slowly but surely whittling away at his family until there was nothing left.

A small tug on his pant leg roused him, and he let Adam clamber into his lap. His soft curls tickled the underside of Noah's chin as his chubby fingers curled into the front of Noah's shirt.

"Are you sad?"

Noah almost laughed. He felt too old for such young bones. "I'm just tired, Adam."

"Wanna sleep in my bed?"

Noah clung a little tighter, and a part of him did. A part of him fought back waves upon waves of crashing anxiety that if he let Adam or Bubbe out of his sight for even a second, they'd be taken from him. Then he remembered Ema had been sitting just an arm's reach away when her life ended, and he knew then it didn't matter what he did.

Nothing was permanent.

"I'll be okay. Do you want a story?"

"The rabbits," Adam told him with a sleepy yawn.

He took his brother's hand and walked him to the room next to his. Adam's bed was covered in *101 Dalmatians* toys with matching pillowcases, and he tugged his Pongo close as he burrowed into the covers like a small nest. Noah selected *Watership Down* and fought back a sort of anguished laugh at how morbid and sweet his brother was, all wrapped up in bright, wondering eyes and wild curls.

He sometimes wondered—more than he wondered about himself—what Adam would be like when he grew up. He was so much like their bubbe—free spirted and without fear. He rushed headfirst into anything, and he had tiny burn marks all over his arms that he didn't care about because they were the marks of his early baking triumphs that he'd accomplished at Bubbe's knee since he was old enough to walk. Adam was still so young, but already Noah could tell this was where he thrived.

The last thing in the world Noah wanted was to be stuck here—in this little apartment, sweating in that kitchen, toiling his life away.

Bubbe said it was his legacy, though, and every time she said it, it felt like someone pressing a pillow to his face. But he'd do it if she needed him to. He'd do it if it meant that Adam got to race headfirst into the wildness of real life and free himself from the chains of this small town.

He cleared his throat and started to read, and six sentences in, Adam's breathing turned even and deep. Noah was pretty sure they'd never get through the book. Adam could never keep his eyes open when Noah read to him, but it was worth it. He set the book back on the shelf and leaned in to kiss his brother's forehead. Adam murmured and turned over, and Noah wondered what it would be like to sleep without the heaviness of life pressing in on him.

It was two days after his eighteenth birthday when his college acceptance letter came. He almost hadn't applied out of state, terrified of the cost because Bubbe wasn't exactly raking in millions with her small bakery. But when he'd hesitated, she took him by the cheeks, and kissed him on the nose, and let her eyes convince him as much as her words.

"Do something that makes you happy, Noah. It's not forever. It's just for a little while."

He understood she mistook his fear of leaving this place for fear of being alone. That wasn't it, not at all. Adam was heading into middle school, and he was wild and had grown from curious to reckless, but Noah knew it was just the age. All the same, he craved silence. He craved a space where all the corners were filled with him and not the echoes of dead parents, and a struggling grandmother, and a brother who was just growing wilder by the day.

In the end, he turned in four applications, and the one acceptance letter took him two thousand miles to the West Coast—a journalism program with a vague idea of working with words, something he'd been good at as long as he wasn't speaking out loud. Bubbe couldn't afford to take time off for the campus tour, but she presented him with a set of keys, and his first tuition check, and a warm kiss the day he set out to leave her.

On the first stretch of empty miles, he cried, but by the time he made it through New Mexico, it felt like the entire world was ahead of him. If he'd known that it was all going to crash down in three years, he might have stopped to appreciate it more. Or hell, he might have just stayed home and not tried to seek freedom at all.

But it was what it was, and that was something he was coming to learn with a ferocity that consumed him. No matter what he did, what bargains he made, Hashem had plans for him. Even if, deep down, Noah wasn't sure He existed at all.

CHAPTER 2

SITTING IN THE DARK, Adriano stared at the faint glow of his laptop screen. His Twitter feed was stale, the little alert at the top telling him to refresh, but he couldn't bring himself to do it. His verified account offered him the ability to ignore tweets and retweets weighing in on Eric's infidelity and their separation, but he didn't want to deal with sympathy or blame from strangers.

His fingers shook, and he reached for his bourbon, the easy burn as he swallowed only slightly distracting him from the fact that he wasn't hurting the way he probably should have been—not after this many years. His dad would laugh himself stupid if he was there. After all, he'd looked Adriano right in the eye fifteen years before and said with both words and sign, "That man is not right for you."

Adriano had spent so many years doing what his parents told him not to—or vice versa—that it was habit. He no longer knew if he was with Eric to piss them off or because he really liked him. Eric had become something like a bad habit after a while. Eric had become his blind spot and his excuse. He was a shitty interpreter and a shitty advocate, and for some reason, Adriano had come to his defense when the man needed to be dragged.

He'd cut off Deaf friends and hearing colleagues all because his boyfriend was kind of a dick, and he'd allowed it. He let out a frustrated groan, feeling the way it ripped at his throat, and he dragged a hand down his face. He didn't really expect to be crying, but he expected a little more than this vague apathy that settled in his bones.

"Don't eat where you shit," had been his dad's sage advice once Adriano was old enough to get a job. At the time, none of them had really considered that porn would be on the table. His dad was merely trying to warn him that fucking an interpreter not only crossed moral lines, but it would cause complications Adriano wouldn't be able to handle.

And maybe Eric really had been a fuck-you to his parents who would never know what it was like to need someone like Eric in his life just to communicate with the outside world. But Eric was also…different from most people he'd worked with. He was smaller, and he was pretty, and he didn't turn his nose up at the fact that when he was hired on, it was to provide director interpretation on a porno set. Eric's hands never hesitated when the director told him to thrust harder, or to use more lube, or to turn his head slightly to the left so the camera could see when his tongue sank into the other man's asshole.

He thought maybe Eric was the exception in interpreters —or maybe he was the exception to the rule that you can't mix business and pleasure, but thinking back, Adriano wasn't sure he was ever happy. He loved him—in whatever way you love someone who had been in your life for that long, but in love?

He never really did wonder when Eric started to change. It was years later and subtle in a way. It started with Eric answering questions for Adriano instead of interpreting them. It seeped into meetings where Adriano found he was agreeing to terms and shoots and movies he wasn't quite sure he had the time for.

'You're not my agent,' was the one time Adriano brought it up. 'You're trying to make decisions for me, and you have no right.'

But Eric had pouted and seemed genuinely hurt by the accusation, and Adriano gave in because, in truth, he was a sucker for those baby blues and full lips.

Though, in reality, Adriano was just a sucker. He let his graduate degree gather dust the way his bank account gathered zeros, and though Eric never pushed for a marriage, they shared everything else. A nice house in Malibu and one on Coronado. They had three cars they both used freely, and Eric's expense account never ran out. They lived like celebrities with the bonus of most people being too nervous—or maybe ashamed—to approach them in public. And he was fine with that.

It let him order his Starbucks from blushing baristas who wouldn't ask for his autograph with everyone watching. He got to grocery shop, and walk his dog in the park, and make sure his siblings and parents didn't want for anything. And he got to come home to a nice guy.

And that nice guy decided to leave Adriano one Tuesday afternoon during a rainstorm and publicly announce it before talking to Adriano about it first.

On *Twitter*.

Thunder crashed. He knew it by the way the table rattled under him. Storms this bad were rare for their little seaside cottage, and he held his breath, but the power indicator on his laptop didn't blink. It probably would, eventually, not that it mattered. He was nursing the raw, fragmented edges of his shattered relationship, and the dark felt appropriate.

His phone buzzed, and he saw his brother's name on the screen. He had half a mind to just turn the damn thing off— too many people wanted information—not just reporters but people he'd barely call acquaintances. He was ready to shut down his social media, and his technology, *and* his brain if this kept up. Having a life that allowed for the public consumption of who he was—it was difficult most days. Today, it felt impossible.

> Pietro: Do you want to talk?

He thumbed a reply, then changed his mind and slammed the phone down on the table so he couldn't see it. He scratched the empty spaces behind his ears. His hearing aids were long dead, and he had no intention of changing out the batteries. He didn't want a single excuse to be able to hear the way people were clawing at him for more, for everything, for every last drop he had to bleed.

He finished his drink, the buzz humming in his veins, then he clicked on the faint letters that read *What's Happening* on his Twitter feed and stared at the blank space he wasn't sure he had a hundred and forty characters to fill.

@SylentOfficial: The best revenge is living well. That's the way I try to live my life. Tell me how I can live better.

Asking that question was asking for trouble, but he felt like if he didn't say something—do something—he was going to explode. He didn't have the strength to watch the replies yet, but he would. Maybe. When he was drunker, and a little sadder, and steps from sleep.

His Skype alert began to flash, and he nearly ignored it, but when he saw his agent's name, he knew he wasn't going to have much of a choice. He clicked the Answer button, and immediately, Xander's mouth was flying faster than his fingers on the keyboard.

Adriano had freely and often admitted how much it annoyed him that Xander wouldn't even learn the basics of sign, but he had been good at making sure Adriano was making some of the top money in his field, and he figured trading cash for that peace of mind was enough. But Xander was clearly losing his shit and waiting for the chat bubble to post wasn't great for his state of agitation.

> Meeting tomorrow. Shit hit the fan.

For the sheer amount of time he'd spoken, Adriano was annoyed that's all he'd managed to type out. He considered typing back, but it was just to annoy Xander, so he didn't bother. "I don't have my ears on, and I don't plan to get them, so I didn't catch anything you just said."

Xander scowled at the screen, and it was too easy to make out the word, "Great," on his lips.

"I'm drunk as shit right now, and I'm going to be drunker before I fall asleep. Text me the details, but don't make it too early."

With that, he signed off, knowing he was leaving his agent swearing up a storm at his blank computer screen. Another call lit up his laptop, so Adriano slammed the lid down, then sat back in the chair, leaning as far as he could toward the counter where the bourbon was resting at the edge of the polished marble. His fingers scrabbled for it before it fell against his palm, and he didn't bother with a glass this time.

Who the fuck was he trying to impress now?

He took three more shots into his mouth before pulling out his phone, and he swiped away all his text alerts before opening up his Twitter again, hating that he'd left it right there on Eric's words that had flipped his world upside down.

@ChaddicusRex: I hate the phrase newly single and ready to mingle but that's my entire mood. Where's a brokenhearted guy go to get some rebound dick? Last night wasn't enough.

There was a text waiting for him too. Three long pages of Eric's endless words explaining why he was leaving, but none of them explained why he'd decided to take to Twitter ten minutes after everything ended. And none of them, really, explained why, after fifteen years, Adriano suddenly wasn't enough.

Maybe it was just because Eric was falling in love with someone else.

> Eric: I don't know how to explain it. I guess maybe he makes me feel the way you used to when you appreciated me. I want to be sorry, but I don't know if I can be. Not when it feels this good. I know this has probably hurt you, but I bet it doesn't hurt the way it should. Am I right?

He wanted to throw his phone against the wall and watch it crumble to the floor in pieces because that son of a bitch *was* right, and it *didn't* hurt the way it should. But he wasn't going to give him the satisfaction. He wanted to get away, to do something new and different and maybe completely off brand for him, only because he wanted to shed the outer layers of himself that were all imprinted with the man Eric was.

He hit the Home button, Eric's tweet disappearing into the void of time and space, and he tried not to look at his DMs because he knew they were full to bursting. He had a few celebrity friends—and a few old real-life friends—who were probably watching his life implode on itself, waiting for the supernova to consume what was left.

He wouldn't let that happen.

Probably.

He would live well, God damn it.

Maybe.

Dragging a hand down his face, he tried to stand, but a wave of vertigo caught him so hard he stumbled sideways and just managed to hit the couch cushions instead of the floor. He felt himself groan—it was probably loud, not that anyone was around to hear it. On his belly, his drunk-heavy limbs reached for the throw pillows that still smelled like that asshole, and he buried his face in them before closing his eyes.

When had he stopped loving Eric? Or more importantly —had he ever?

ADRIANO STROLLED into his agent's office refusing to take off his sunglasses. His double-shot Americano was cooling against his palm, and he was just barely starting to feel like a person again after a greasy plate of hash browns and two mimosas. He felt coated with grease and liquor sweat in spite of an extra-long shower, but it was hard to care when he knew something was going on.

He hadn't bothered opening his texts yet. The ones from Eric had stopped somewhere around nine the night before, and two of his brothers had tried to get him to respond, but they were easy enough to ignore. None of them had really liked Eric, so at best they wanted to gloat, and he wasn't in the mood.

Mostly, he was just stressed. He'd lost both his boyfriend and, more tragically, the interpreter he'd been working with the longest. The last thing he wanted to do right then was get in touch with the agency that employed Eric—and not just because he'd have to explain, though it was likely they already knew. But they hadn't turned out the best interpreters in the past, and once upon a time, Adriano had felt lucky to have Eric.

A bitter, sharp-edged laugh threatened to slip out, and he took a sip of coffee to wash it down as he tipped a little hello to the receptionist. If she tried to get his attention to stop him from pushing the elevator button, he wasn't aware of it, and he was inside and riding up before she could follow.

Adriano knew he approached his agent with swagger that came from his own notoriety. He was unique—the fact that he was as big as he was and had a body that required massive amounts of protein and a huge number of hours spent in his gym with his trainer. He was attractive, which was a given for his industry. He had a nice, big, uncut cock that was sought after for close-up shots even when he wasn't a headliner in a film. He was Deaf, and he knew both fetishists and the curious alike watched for that one single line at the end of every movie where he let himself voice.

Part of him hated that people got off on it, but the bigger part appreciated that his new Gucci loafers didn't put a dent in his credit line. Those people existed anyway—might as well profit.

Pressing two fingers to his temple to ward off his lingering hangover headache, Adriano managed most of his coffee before he reached Xander's office, and he didn't bother knocking as he walked in. There was a woman sitting in the corner of the room with her hands set primly on top of a grey wool skirt. Her hair was a soft blonde, pinned back, and her shirt was high-collared. He hated making snap judgments, but he was fairly sure she was the interpreter, and he was fairly sure she was going to walk out before the conversation got fully underway.

She was at least polite enough to make introductions before he had to address Xander, who remained seated with the edge of his foot hooked on the corner of his desk. He looked arrogant as ever with his silk button-down and tight jeans. He was a wannabe, which was why he was an agent and not a star, and Adriano knew there was some level of bitterness with every job he booked for his clients.

'Hi,' Adriano signed, then offered her his sign name.

'Mary,' she spelled, and didn't offer hers, which was interesting, but he didn't much care.

He knew he looked like hell, and the fact that he kept his

sunglasses on was twenty shades of rude. But fuck politeness when his ex had confessed to boning a guy he supposedly met at Trader Joe's and was now going to live with him or…whatever.

'What agency are you from?' he couldn't help but ask, and he braced himself for the answer.

'Sun Valley Interpreting Services,' she spelled.

He knew them. They mostly dealt with public events and church services, which really didn't bode well. He looked past her, then gestured for her to step back before he addressed Xander. 'Did you hire her?'

Xander never really did have any tact, even with Eric who had become actual friends with him over the years, and he stared at her over his shoulder as she spoke. "Uh, yeah," he said. "Why?"

'Did you just google interpreting services or something?' Adriano could tell her inflection didn't match the rage in his fingers, but he didn't have the strength to correct her in that moment.

Xander gave him a bland-faced shrug. "Does it matter what I do now? Eric moved on to greener pastures, right?"

And really, if there ever had been a glass-shattering moment, that was it. Not because of Xander's blasé attitude, but the reason why. And maybe it took Xander being an absolute dick for him to connect the dots that had been there the entire time, but now was that moment.

'You fucked him. He left…*You're* fucking him, and he left me for you!'

He watched Mary's lips form the first half of the word fuck before she stopped. 'I can't say that.'

Fury—a sort of burning, consuming rage—coursed through him, and he hit the desk so hard they both jumped. 'You say what I sign! I am paying you for this!'

'I can't say that,' she repeated.

Adriano's lips curled back in a snarl. "Get out," he voiced, and she took a startled step back. Her hands went up, but he shook his head. "Get the fuck out."

Somewhere in the back of his mind, he'd remember to feel bad for making someone that terrified. He knew what he looked like. He knew that his size was intimidating, and that despite his accent, his voice was a deep rumble in his chest. He knew it made people uneasy, and he'd used it against her right then. But it was so hard to care when his life was being ripped apart and the woman hired to help him communicate refused to do it.

When the door shut, the slam reverberating through the bottoms of his feet, he slowly turned his gaze back to Xander. "You fucked Eric."

His lips were moving too fast for Adriano to read them, but it didn't matter. The furious blush creeping up his neck said enough. He fucked Eric—he'd *been* fucking Eric. God only knew how long it had been going on.

"Stop," he demanded after Xander said his piece into the silence between them. "You know I can't understand you, and I don't care. You're fired."

He turned and started for the door, not anticipating how fast Xander would be or how bold. His thin fingers wrapped around Adriano and spun him, but the look on Adriano's face sent him taking a few steps back. "You can't fire me. The contract." The words—at least most of them—were easy enough to read.

Adriano sneered again. "If you think I care about the goddamn contract…" His lips fell silent, and his hands rose. 'I'm going to make you sorry. I don't care what you're threatening me with or what Eric promised you. This isn't over.'

He slammed the door behind him and didn't make eye contact with anyone on the way down. It was a blessing when he got to the street and didn't see Mary anywhere. It wasn't *her* fault, but it was just another symptom of a bigger fucking problem, and he was running out of fight.

By the time Adriano got to his car, he was trembling, his throat tight and on the verge of tears he hadn't cried in so many years he couldn't remember. His phone buzzed in his pocket again, but it was either Eric, Xander, or someone from the agency trying to reach him.

Enough was enough. He wasn't sure what he was doing next, but all this was going to come to an end, even if he had to bring it crashing down in flames around him.

ADRIANO SQUINTED off into the distance, staring at the rows of still-ripening grapes. His older brother's pet project had turned into a little something more with the cash he'd supplied them over the years. He didn't mind it. The wine wasn't half bad—hair of the dog more than anything he'd serve at dinner, but at this point the burn of any alcohol was welcome.

It was nice to take sanctuary away from Malibu where the city was huge but the circles he ran in were small and impossible to avoid. It was likely Eric and Xander were holed up in his apartment fucking and scheming because there was no way he fired Xander without consequence.

He was prepared to pay it, of course. His accountant and lawyer were both on standby to issue whatever check they had to in order to terminate his contract and get Xander off his name and out of his business for good. It had been radio silence, though, and it was making Adriano uneasy.

And Pietro was also being a little too attentive, which was also getting under his skin. For the first time in his life, the temperate spring weather of Southern California was not a balm. It felt suffocating like the wind was made of invisible walls pinning him in one place. He ached to get away, but he had no idea where to go—and frankly, he knew he couldn't go until Xander made a move.

Adriano dipped his shades down his nose when a shadow fell over his face, and a thick-fingered hand plucked both the bottle and glass away from him.

"*Hey*," he voiced with a scowl.

Pietro dropped into a chair and clasped his hands on the table. He was the eldest brother and the fussiest over all his siblings. He was almost sixty and wore his grey with charm. He would have been great in the industry too—built just like Adriano, though he looked far more like their mother than their father with his sharp black hair and narrow blue eyes.

Pietro was a lawyer, though, not one that represented Adriano, but his firm did. And it was of some comfort to know that his brother could help sort shit out so he didn't have to leave this little fake slice of heaven until he was good and ready.

'You okay?'

Of all the siblings, Pietro had been the most resistant to sign and only gave in when his years of pushing Adriano to voice and read lips yielded very little. His kids and his ex were both better than he was, but since Adriano had shown up on his doorstep a drunk mess with two Louis Vuitton suitcases and an annoyed Pomeranian in a cloth carrier, he'd been trying.

'Been better,' Adriano replied. He reached for his glass, but Pietro held it farther away and ignored his irritated grunt. 'I'm not five.'

Pietro lifted a brow and signed more in English than ASL, 'Stop acting like it.'

"*Bah!*" Pursing his lips, Adriano waved him off, turning his attention to the vineyard until Pietro's hand waved in his periphery. He turned to look as his brother hooked a finger over his ear, asking about his hearing aids for the hundredth time since he'd gotten there.

Adriano scoffed again. 'Why bother.'

Pietro, like so many others, wanted to think they made a

damn difference beyond making babies crying in planes a little sharper and the occasional ability to pick up some of the harder consonants. Mostly, he knew, Pietro wanted this to be easier on him, and Adriano was in no fucking mood to hold his hand through communication.

'What are you going to do after this?'

At that, Adriano felt a little bit of the blood drain from his face because he didn't know. He'd just wrapped up a three week shoot that was set to come out of post in June, and he knew there were two other films on the books he'd given a verbal promise, but nothing had been signed.

Mostly, Xander had been up his ass about branching out. "People want new content, and you're stagnating. Do something unexpected."

At the time, Adriano had almost considered it for the hungry look on Eric's face as he interpreted.

"Bottom, fuck a virgin, play boy to a Daddy. Do you know how fucking much money any of those would earn you?"

Adriano didn't need to worry about money. He wasn't just rich. He was smart. He had expensive designer taste, but he also had an eye for numbers, and it was easy to start investing when he realized he was raking in the cash because he was a commodity. He could sell both houses, buy something new, and live off the interest from his investments if he really wanted to. He'd never have to work again, and wouldn't that be a slap in the face to the people who had been profiting off his work?

But he wasn't quite ready to retire. Yes, he was ready to shake things up, but to walk away from his life entirely?

The vibration on the table under his hand made him look up, and he saw Pietro's frown as he pointed to Adriano's phone. The screen was lit up with messages from his lawyer, but he'd forgotten he'd turned the vibrate off just to get a little peace from people still trying to drag the real story out of him.

> Anthony: Need you to come to my office. Please bring someone to interpret. This is an emergency.
>
> Anthony: I'm going to be here until two, and then I'm coming to find you.
>
> Anthony: I just got the call from Blaylock Inc.'s representation.

Adriano's hands shook as he tapped out a quick message about being on his way. He wasn't quite sure why people like his lawyer thought he kept trained interpreters in his back fucking pocket, but he'd make do.

'Is Luca in the city?'

Luca was the second youngest—the last planned baby before the whoops that was Adriano—and he was more free spirited than any of the other siblings. He had a small condo near the beach, but he was rarely there when the weather was nice.

'I'll call him,' Pietro said. He stood when Adriano did, then laid a hand on his arm. 'What's wrong?'

'I don't know,' was the only answer Adriano could give. Whatever it was, it wasn't good. The stress and fury bled through Anthony's simple words on the screen. 'Anthony needs me, and I need a better interpreter than you.'

Pietro had the grace not to look offended but at least a little ashamed as he put his phone to his ear. Adriano didn't stick around for the conversation. He'd use a notepad and pen if he had to, which he'd done before. It took ten times longer, but it was better than nothing, and nothing was just shy of worse than a bad signer.

He hurried into the house, giving his niece a small pat on the head before he rushed to his room. Jude was at his heels, likely yipping for attention, but he ignored the dog as he grabbed a fresh shirt, then moved to wash his face.

He was sweaty from his morning in the sun, but he spritzed on cologne and changed into new jeans, doing up the buttons as he moved for his loafers tucked into the corner of the closet. The room was in total disarray—as it often was when he had to live out of suitcases. Most of his things were still in Malibu, but they all felt so fucking unimportant now that they were tainted with what Eric and Xander had done.

With a sigh, he looked at himself in the mirror and tried not to grimace. He was the same man as before, just haggard and exhausted. He hated that Eric had this much power over him. True, it was becoming obvious he hadn't loved the other man in years, but he still had a hold over Adriano's life, and that was starting to weigh on him.

He just wanted this over.

Jude followed close at his heels, and he reached down to pick up the yapping pup before snatching his hearing aids from the dresser and using one hand to push them in. It had been a while, and the molds made his ears instantly start to ache, but he gave himself a reprieve by not turning them on.

He buried his face in Jude's soft, pampered fur before moving to the living room where Pietro was waiting, pacing in front of the sofa. 'L will be at Anthony's office waiting for you.'

Adriano breathed a small sigh of relief and nuzzled his dog once more before setting him down and grabbing his keys off the side table. 'Thank you,' he signed with genuine affection.

Pietro wasted no time in pulling Adriano into a hug, and Adriano was profoundly aware he was still the baby. Even nearing forty, he felt young and vulnerable in his big brother's embrace, and he let himself sink into his own weakness for just a moment.

When he pulled back, he felt better and gave his brother a nod.

'Let me know when it's over,' Pietro insisted.

For the first time that morning, Adriano felt somewhat comforted, and he nodded. 'I will. Don't wait up.' He didn't think his brother caught that meaning, but it didn't matter. He slipped out the door and headed to his car, bracing himself for what was about to come next.

CHAPTER 3

Noah swiped a mixture of sweat and flour off his brow, then glanced up at the time. The bakery was closed, but morning came too quickly, and it was obvious after hiring an extra set of hands, Paxton wasn't going to be much good at anything except keeping track of the register and flirting with the customers, and he didn't think that second part was winning the bakery any favors.

His eyes strayed to the photo he'd hung on the wall—a copy of the one he'd given to Adam—of his younger brother baking with Bubbe. They both looked blissfully happy with dough under their nails and smears of chocolate on their matching aprons. Adam was barely using full sentences, but his passion was already obvious. Noah had never had that, never really felt passion for anyone or anything before.

Even when he was in school, he'd chosen writing because he was good at it. Writing had been a way he could express himself when his own tongue twisted into knots and made him sound like a fool. Writing allowed him no mockery as he tried to put his thoughts together and make sense of his raging emotions.

Not that it helped in the end.

He was there, at Bubbe's Bakery, alone as he ever was. Adam was living with his girlfriend, Talia, in the little apartment above her café, and while Noah was happy for him, a small piece of him felt like Adam's absence was nothing more than a mark of the inevitable ending of the bakery.

Adam had insisted he wasn't going to give up his time at Bubbe's, but working with his girlfriend proved to be a bigger monopoly on his time than he'd anticipated. Noah had assured him it was fine, that he'd make do, and he would. He had to. Bubbe's was a few missed payments away from folding, and he didn't see a solution. They had been in the red for over a year, and he knew as well as any accountant that there was no coming back from that.

Nothing short of a miracle, and he'd stopped believing in those the day he set his first stones on Bubbe's grave and realized any covenant he made with Hashem would probably be ignored. He was in too deep now to give up, of course, and Adam was too important to take the risk. But it was habit, not real faith.

With a sigh, Noah set the dough into the walk-in for the slow rise, then hung his apron up and moved to the sink to wash up. He looked a mess, but Adam was having his official grand opening over at the fire station where the fire chief had set up a little makeshift petting zoo for the kids in order to raise money for the local cat café and shelter.

It was going to be cute, and Noah would have enjoyed the idea more if it wasn't crushing him with social anxiety. But he was trying more—for Adam, for the things his brother was doing and the steps he was taking to bridge the gap between them. Noah felt worse about it for the secrets he was keeping. The fact that Bubbe hadn't left the bakery to them both, that Noah alone shouldered the burden of ownership and finances. That it had been on the verge of collapse since Noah was dragged back from college and forced to take her place, to play parent to an angry fourteen-year-old who had just lost the last parental figure he'd ever had.

He managed to keep them afloat for a while, and Adam's refusal to do anything with his culinary schooling besides work at Bubbe's had helped but not enough. The loan was a stopgap. It was a way for Noah to provide for Adam before it all came crashing down.

The foundation was already ruined, and the walls were starting to tremble.

He knew that disaster too well.

He could only pray at this point that he wouldn't lose his only family along with the scraps of their childhood home that were left now that Bubbe was gone.

As summer crept closer, the nights were easier to bear, and he enjoyed the breeze on his skin after being trapped in the kitchen all day. As much as Savannah felt like a prison some days, he did love it there. He loved that he could spin in a full circle and never get tired of looking at the cobblestones of old streets. He loved that the summer air was fragrant, and the winter was rich with smoke from fireplaces. As much as this place held grief, it also held joy.

It held Adam's first steps and his first words. It held Bubbe's smiles, and off-key Shabbat blessings, and the smells of home. He knew that the bakery wasn't long for the world, but he wasn't ready to roll over and give it all up. Not yet.

The walk to the fire station wasn't far, and he heard the soft murmur of voices as he got closer. Someone was playing music on a loudspeaker that didn't carry far, and he could already smell fresh baked goods on the breeze. He caught the swift tang of barn scent, which told him Fitz had already set up, and Noah felt a little better because he'd made friends with Fitz over the last few months and had enjoyed his company.

He was a friendly and massive man with burn scars all over his arm and face, which added to his rugged charm. If

Noah hadn't been such an anxious mess, he probably would have fallen for the man's flirting. But it was what it was.

Crossing over the grass courtyard, Noah stepped onto the pavement and rounded the corner to the massive parking lot at the fire station. The bay doors were wide open, kids hanging on and around the front of each truck, and off to the side was the makeshift paddock that held the goats, the duck, and a handful of cats who didn't seem at all interested in escaping the eager hands, giving them all love.

To the right of that were two food trucks—No Cilantro and the Lofty Latke—the little food truck Adam had set up since he and Talia had started to expand the café. It was the first time Noah had seen it in action. He'd missed the soft opening, which had been on a Friday night, and then Adam shut it down to work out the final kinks before the debut.

From his spot near the edge of the party, he saw Adam behind the small window—smiling bigger than he had in years. His girlfriend, Talia Cahn, was behind him, long hair pulled into a bun, wearing a t-shirt with *Latke* emblazoned across the front. She touched the small of Adam's back, making his brother soften just a fraction.

"Hey!" Noah turned to see the newest neighborhood resident, Will, approaching with a to-go cup clenched in his large fist. Will and his two lovers had caused a little bit of a stir when they'd breezed into Savannah a few years prior. Savannah had always been a more open and accepting small town, and the trio was probably safer from judgment there than anywhere else.

But they were new and different, and it had taken Will a while to wear what he had with Noah down into something like a friendship. Noah didn't mind now. He liked the trio's little farm and the way Will always seemed to know what to say when Noah felt like he was teetering too close to the edge of a cliff.

Will offered a smile when Noah looked at him, the turn of

his lips tugging at his freshly trimmed beard. He was every bit a mountain man in his faded jeans and flannel shirt, and Noah loved that about him. "You're late, you know. You missed all the drama." Will nodded toward what Noah now realized was a pile of glass swept into the corner near the Latke's back tire.

"Was someone hurt?" Noah asked, eyes going wide.

Will laughed and clapped him on the shoulder. "Nah. Just Chase attempting to make a bigger deal than he was capable." Will pulled out his phone and showed Noah the forty-second video of Talia's head server, Chase, trying and failing to break a champagne bottle against the side of the truck.

"I hope he didn't scratch the paint," were the first words that tumbled from Noah's lips when the bottle finally broke and everyone cheered, and he groaned at himself. He was such a damned killjoy. It was better that he'd missed it all.

Will didn't seem bothered, though. His smile softened, and he threw his arm around Noah's neck after tucking his phone away. "Adam seems like he's enjoying the new ride."

Noah rolled his eyes, but he also couldn't help his smile. "I think so."

"You're not hurting for help are you? With him gone?" Will dropped his arm and shrugged. "I could always come in and lend a hand."

Noah raised a brow. "Getting bored of retirement already?"

Will pulled a face, but his eyes kept his smile. "A man can only take so much goat milking and egg collecting before he starts to feel a bit nutty. But I mean that honestly, mate. If you need a hand…"

"I have Paxton," Noah said, but he scowled as his one employee's name fell past his lips, and he rolled his eyes. Paxton wasn't bad per se, just a bit useless. "It's working well enough."

In truth, he could have used the extra hands. He had no

money for anything. He was barely keeping the lights on as it was. It was worth it, but for how long?

Will looked dubious, but he clapped Noah's shoulder again, not paying attention to the way the touch made Noah flinch. "Just let me know, yeah?"

Noah nodded. "Of course. I should go say hi to my brother. See you in a bit?"

Will tipped him a wave, then made his way back to the pen where one of Will's boyfriends, Liam, was kneeling down, talking a small girl into extending a handful of corn for one of the silkie chickens to eat. It was sweet, and it stirred a longing in him he hadn't acknowledged in years. Not necessarily kids but the idea of family beyond two strained brothers who had been orphaned.

He pushed those thoughts away, then headed to the truck and waited off to the side until the line cleared. He was deep in his thoughts when he heard someone clear their throat, and he looked up to see Talia leaning out the window with a croissant on a plate.

"Here," Talia said.

Noah gave her a dubious look. It wasn't like Talia to share free food with him. It wasn't really like Talia to acknowledge him at all unless it was to say what a shitty brother he was to Adam. "What is it?"

"It's a delicious baked good that your brother worked his ass off to create. Eat it and appreciate him."

"It's kosher, I swear," Adam said.

Noah chanced a small smile. "Thanks. What's in it?"

"Mascarpone and raspberry."

Noah didn't hesitate this time. He only felt a small pop of envy because he couldn't bring himself to care enough about creating new food that he knew his customers were getting desperate for. He sighed, then bit into the pastry and groaned at the explosion of flavor on his tongue.

His own bakes were fine. But that's all they were, just

fine. Adam's were an entire universe contained in such a small thing. They were warm, and comfortable, and homey in a way only his bubbe's food had ever been. He peered at Adam's face and saw a mixture of smug satisfaction and beneath that, pride.

"It's amazing," Noah told him. He was trying his best not to withhold praise, which was a difficult habit to break. "Is everyone else enjoying them?"

"I think it helps having Enzo's truck here," Adam admitted. "I thought we'd end up competing, but people are buying from us both. Plus, his shit is so good."

Noah didn't know most of the townsfolk well. He knew of Enzo's five-star restaurant, Mangia E Zitto. He'd taken Adam there for his graduation dinner and scraped his savings account to pay the tab. It had been a better memory of Adam's younger years, and he had no regrets. But that was it. Enzo had lived in Savannah for just about forever, and Noah had never tried his food apart from that one night.

"Are you hungry for actual food?" Adam asked.

Noah felt his lips pull into a gentle smile. "No, I ate while I was finishing up the challah dough. Thank you, though."

Adam sighed, nodding once. "You look tired, Noah."

"I know what that's code for."

Adam snorted a laugh. "Well, you *do* look like shit. Why don't you just fire Paxton, and I'll come back to—"

"No." Noah didn't mean to sound so angry, so final. But there would be no point. He tempered his voice and shook his head. "I didn't mean to…I just…It's fine, Adam. This is amazing, and you look happy. Besides, it's only for a few weeks until you get the truck off the ground."

A faint blush rose on Adam's cheeks, and he glanced away like he couldn't take Noah's attempts to actually show Adam how he felt. "Well, I have time now if you need me. And I miss working there. With you," he added like it was a little difficult, but their relationship had always been tense since the day Noah had gone off to school.

"I know, and I miss you too." Noah swiped his hands on his jeans, then walked a few steps to the recycling bin and dropped the paper plate inside. "Right now, I'm tired, but I'm doing okay. I promise I'll let you know if I'm in over my head with work."

And it wasn't likely. Adam was official competition for him now, and he knew he'd be feeling it soon. But it was better that way.

After a beat of awkward silence, Adam shrugged, and the same old ghost of frustration and resentment flickered across his face. Before it got too deep, Noah reached for him, grabbing his brother by the elbow. "Come over Saturday for dinner."

"Can I cook?" Adam asked.

At that, Noah laughed. "Yes, and bring Talia."

Adam looked mildly surprised but also happy, which was Noah's own fault. He'd spent the last few years after Bubbe's death trying to keep the bakery together and had neglected to notice that Adam had grown up. Then he'd brought home a girlfriend, and Noah had just…panicked. And he'd shut down. Talia deserved better, and he promised himself he would try.

"I'll be there," Adam said after a beat. "I'd better get back to work, though."

Noah nodded, and just before Adam reached the doors, Noah called out to him. "It looks amazing, Adam. It's going to do well."

Adam hesitated, then nodded one last time before disappearing behind the metal door. It shut with a hard clang, and Noah didn't feel entirely better, but he felt like there were small changes happening. And really, that was the most he could ask for.

Noah's private ritual ending Shabbat had been different the day Adam told him he was no longer going to practice. He hadn't wanted to make Adam uncomfortable, so he'd made them almost private, and he hadn't broken the habit after Adam moved out. His blessings were barely above a whisper, lighting candles perfunctory, the ritual taking a back seat to his eagerness for distraction.

Checking his phone, he was unsurprised to find a text from Adam, letting him know that he was going to be late, but Talia was heading over by seven thirty and would meet him. Noah felt a small wave of anxiety he was determined to ignore, and he sank into his desk chair, firing up his laptop for the first time in twenty-four hours. Dusk had settled across the sky, glowing its last breath behind the tall trees, and he didn't bother with the lights just yet.

It had been a week since Noah had seen Sylent's life crumble on Twitter. His production company announced a delay on the release of his upcoming film and said he was taking a personal hiatus. All that seemed to contradict Sylent's vague posts about second-guessing life, and people, and his career path, and for the first time, Noah felt compelled to reach out.

Before he could pull his computer close, his cat jumped up on his lap and kneaded at his thighs. The cat had been Adam's subtle way of saying, *I know you're always going to be alone, and I don't want it to be pathetic.* With a sigh, he gave the cat a little scratch under his chin before shoving him away, then he tucked his knees closer to the desk.

His fingers hovered over the keys for long moments, but he wanted to give the man something more than what everyone else had offered. It was easy enough to fire up his webcam, to face it down at his hands rather than his face since he was terrified of being seen by anyone who might know him. He took a breath and hoped his skills hadn't faded much after not using the language for so long.

'Hi, Sylent,' he used his porn name in spite of knowing his real name because he didn't want to seem like a stalker. 'I just wanted to say that I might not understand what you're going through with relationships, but I know all about questioning everything you've ever known in life. I'm a huge fan of your work, and I hope we don't lose you, but you have to do what's best for you. You didn't deserve this. I hope you're okay.'

He checked it and rechecked it. His ASL was rusty and probably not entirely correct in grammar, but he remembered enough. As his fingers twisted through signs, it became like flowing water again, and he hoped reaching out to Sylent in his own language would offer him at least some small measure of comfort, assuming the man actually saw it.

His heart beat heavy with fear as he clicked a reply, making sure Sylent was tagged…and then he posted.

Before he could panic-delete the post, the buzzer rang, and Noah shot to his feet, slamming his computer shut. He rushed toward the door before he realized it was Talia and that he shouldn't be in a huge hurry to engage with his brother's girlfriend alone. Especially when his relationship with Talia could be better.

In truth, Noah had initially blamed Talia for the way Adam had walked away from their faith. He hadn't considered that maybe his brother had been drifting since they were kids, and it had taken him this long to realize he was blaming the wrong person.

And that he shouldn't have blamed anyone at all.

There was no delaying it now, though. He took a breath, then met Talia with a tentative smile. She thrust a pink box at him that bore the new label for the Lofty Latke across the top. He let out a small *oomph* as the package hit him in the chest, and he took a few steps back as Talia shoved past him to get inside.

"Make yourself at home," Noah told her softly. He moved to the table and peeled away the edges of the tape on the box. As the lid popped open, a familiar scent wafted out, and his heart clenched a bit in his chest. Nestled at the bottom of the parchment paper were several rolls of jachnun, looking perfectly crisped and glazed and exactly like he'd remembered. Bubbe had rarely made them, apart from special occasions.

They were temperamental and a pain in the ass to get right, and they took forever. So they were apology treats. They were comfort treats. They were something Noah had gotten a handful of times in his life when the grief of missing his father and losing his mother overwhelmed him. He hadn't had them since long before Bubbe died. He didn't even know Adam had the recipe.

His chest was tight when he looked up, and he saw Talia staring at him with a closed-off expression. "Adam said you'd know what those were for."

Noah had to clear his throat before he could speak. "Ah. Yes. Thank you for bringing them."

Talia nodded, the side of her jaw tense, her temple throbbing, which was easy to see with her hair pulled back so tight. She took a fortifying breath, then spread her hands almost in a surrender. "For Adam's sake, I guess we should be friends."

Noah couldn't stop his eyebrow from lifting, from the words falling past his lips. "You guess?"

Talia flushed and looked almost…curiously at him. "I don't totally get you, but Adam loves you, and I love him."

Noah softened a bit. "I'm really glad to hear that. I just want him to be happy."

Talia was silent a moment, then nodded. "I know. And I didn't make things easy on you either."

"No," Noah agreed from behind a sigh. "We were both in the wrong."

He wished he could change it, but he didn't know how to just be normal for once. Not even in this important moment.

"Adam, uh…he explained why you were so upset," Talia said, and there was just a hint of desperation in her voice. "I didn't grow up like you, you know. My parents were totally assimilated. We have a Chanukah bush every year, and I left cookies out for Santa. I didn't understand why something so archaic as keeping kosher mattered. My mom kind of talked me around, and I get it now. But you do know that it wasn't me, right? I'm not the reason Adam is an atheist."

Noah laughed softly. "Yeah, I know. He's always had a mind of his own. I just…think I got lost after our bubbe died and I had to leave school."

Talia nodded, not looking particularly kind but not looking as angry as she usually did. "I get it. I swear I do. I've lost a lot of people in my life, and your brother just makes me feel like I can breathe again."

Noah's chest warmed with understanding. Talia wasn't bitter at him for being so observant. As a Jew—even as a secular one—she still understood better than any gentile would. And Noah knew damn well Adam would never give his heart to someone who hated what they were—who they were—so he had no problem believing Talia had been acting out of ignorance, not malice. "I think he feels the same way about you."

"So I'm forgiven for being an ass?" Talia chanced.

"Forgiven," Noah offered easily and simply because he knew Talia meant it. She was a difficult woman but a good one. "And I hope I am too."

Talia smiled just a little. "I think I can manage that."

"Good," Noah answered with the same small wink he used to use on Adam to make him smile. "Do you want something to drink?"

Awkwardness settled again, but luckily, the door opened, and Adam saved them from any real small talk. His arms were laden with to-go boxes that bore the mark of No Cilantro, and Noah's eyes got a little hot.

"I hope you're hungry. Enzo basically threw all this shit at me after I made his boyfriend cupcakes."

There was a hint of dishonesty in his tone. Noah knew because Adam couldn't let things be easy either. But the unspoken truth was enough. "I'll get forks," Noah told him. "You two get comfortable."

Adam was almost a stranger in the apartment he'd grown up in now, but it was okay. That's what happened when you moved on with your life. And it stung. It was empty nest syndrome, Noah knew. It was change, and he had never liked that. It had always been forced upon him, but he wanted this to be good.

He gathered silverware and drinks, and together the three of them sat around the coffee table on the floor, and it was almost—*almost*—normal.

Fresh from his shower, Noah slipped into his room and sat at his desk. With Adam and Talia there, he'd all but forgotten about the video until he saw the envelope icon with a little number one hovering over it.

His heart beat in his throat. It could be anyone, anything. Could be a porn bot or some company advertising CBD gummi bears. His finger hovered over the icon, and then he clicked it.

@SylentOfficial: U Deaf?
@BubbesBakes: No, sorry.
@SylentOfficial: LOL y u sorry?

Noah's face burst into heat like he was on fire, and he pressed hands to his cheeks because he wasn't expecting a response. He wasn't expecting anything. What the hell was he supposed to do now? Tell this man he had seen him twice on campus before his life went to hell, and he'd spent the last few years wanting him so bad he could come at the mere thought of him?

Even that made his dick hard.

@BubbesBakes: I don't know. Sorry, I'm awkward.

@SylentOfficial: u say sorry a lot. It's fine. Thank u for ASL video.

@BubbesBakes: I thought it might be nice to have something in your language. I'm not good at it.

@SylentOfficial: better than most. Better than my brothers.

@BubbesBakes: I'm...sorry?

@Sylent Official: LOL.

@SylentOfficial: Ur Acct. Bubbes Bakes? In LA?

@BubbesBakes: No. I'm in Savannah, GA.

@SylentOfficial: 2 bad. I wanted cupcake. u run social media?

@BubbesBakes: Sort of. I own the shop. My bubbe left it to me when she died.

@SylentOfficial: Sorry. :(

@BubbesBakes: it's fine. Um.

@SylentOfficial: is a good job? Bakery?

@BubbesBakes: it's a job. It's not doing well.

He stopped. "Fuck, fuck. Fuck! Noah, what is wrong with you?" He dropped his head to the desk and took in a ragged breath. He'd spent so long keeping this to himself, and look how fast he'd cracked to a total stranger.

@BubbesBakes: please don't say anything about it on twitter. I'm trying to figure things out.

@SylentOfficial: that y u know how hard life is sometimes?

@BubbesBakes: lol yes.

@SylentOfficial: send video w ur face. ASL need expressions.

Noah flushed red-hot, but he wasn't about to deny that

request. Not just because it was Sylent, but also because he was right. He'd denied him half the language by showing only his hands. But hell, what if he recognized him and thought he was some creepy stalker?

He also knew he couldn't tell this man no. Not for all the money or risk in the world.

Pulling up his webcam, he angled it at himself and tried not to grimace at his face. He knew he'd be a disappointment. Sylent was never seen outside the company of gorgeous men with chiseled jaws and flawless skin. Noah was round-faced with a wide nose and full lips and freckles across his cheeks like someone had flicked brown paint at him. His hair hung in short, wet ringlets over his forehead, and his age showed in his eyes.

He lifted his hands. 'Sorry about the other video. Thank you for talking with me tonight. I needed the chat. I hope things work out for you soon. You deserve better.'

He felt waves upon waves of panic as he attached the video to the chat, then hit Send. His breath lodged in his chest as it loaded. It was less than twenty seconds long, but Sylent was taking triple that.

Then the chat bubbles rose and fell and rose and fell. Then disappeared.

Noah was about to close his laptop with a hard slam and regret every choice he ever made up to this exact moment when a video popped up in response. His hands shook violently, but he managed to click it open anyway.

There was loud noise in the background—kids laughing somewhere, a dog barking nearby. But none of that mattered as Sylent filled the screen with his wide shoulders and massive biceps. His lips curled into an easy smile as his impossibly large hands lifted and signed with a practiced grace Noah would never have.

'Thank you. You have a great face. Your message meant a lot to me. Can we talk again soon?'

Noah would have fainted if he'd been a man with a weaker constitution. As it was, he could barely get his fingers to cooperate as he clicked on the chat and started to type.

@BubbesBakes: I'm Noah.
@SylentOfficial: Adriano.
@BubbesBakes: I have to sleep soon, but we can talk later.
@SylentOfficial: looking forward to it. Good night.

Noah closed his laptop for lack of any other response, then slid into his bed because he knew his knees wouldn't support him. This was the man who starred in every single one of his fantasies. A man that was safe to want because he would never, ever be in Noah's orbit. But now, there he was. He obviously hadn't recognized him, but that was fine.

He knew Noah's name.

And he'd given Noah his.

It would probably come to nothing. Adriano was upset, and probably lonely, and probably tired of the drama around him. Noah was just space from that, and he couldn't blame the man for needing it. In fact, he was happy to provide it.

Turning on his side, Noah's erection brushed against his sheets, and Adriano's face appeared in his mind. This time, though, it was real. It was without stage makeup and good lighting. It was soft, and sleepy, and a little sad. And that smile was just for him.

He breathed, and he imagined those hands touching his thighs. It was all he needed, the only thing he needed. He spilled against the sheets, then gulped down the breath he was holding and uncurled his hand.

Noah could not be this man's friend. He wouldn't survive it.

CHAPTER 4

ADRIANO HADN'T DEALT with this level of frustration since before Eric, and that alone was enough to send his vision blurry with white-hot rage. Four interpreters had turned him down due to the nature of his work conflicting with their personal beliefs, and he wanted to shake them all and ask them what right they had to decide who was worthy of communication and who wasn't. But it was pointless.

The best he could do was file complaints and ask Luca to keep working. Luca wasn't the most fluent, but he was by far the one who had worked hardest out of all the siblings. No brother wanted to talk about fucking in front of their siblings, though, even if it was for work, but that was the position Eric had put him in.

Especially now that Xander had filed his suit.

"They want to retain exclusivity rights on your filming career for the duration of your agreed-upon contract," Anthony told him, brow furrowed behind his desk. Luca stood at his shoulder, and Adriano appreciated that Anthony, at least, gave him the benefit of eye contact.

'What the fuck does that mean?'

"It means," Anthony said, and took a deep breath. "It

means they let you out of the contract, but they retain a percentage of your fee if you do work. And it means they prevent you from working outside of the studio for pay."

Something niggled in the back of his mind. 'For pay?'

Anthony sneered. "Yes."

'So I could work for free?'

At that, Anthony's face fell into something like shock. "Why would you work for free?"

Well, he wouldn't normally. He didn't do shit for free. Not conventions, not appearances, not photo shoots, and certainly not films. He'd never worked for free in his life. But he'd been lining both Eric's and Xander's pockets since he'd started in the industry. First Eric, then Xander when Adriano signed him as his agent, had benefited from his film career, and they wanted to see that he continued to provide. The thought made him sick with rage.

'What if I just pay the fee and refuse the rest?'

"He'll take you to court," Anthony said. "It would prevent you from doing any work until it settles, and that could take…"

'Forever,' Adriano signed with frustrated hands. He knew Xander's legal team was capable of it. He'd seen it happen more than a dozen times. It wasn't always just about throwing money at a problem, and there was every chance they'd offer it so long as it broke Adriano, and he wasn't going to let that happen.

His phone buzzed in his pocket, and for the first time in a week he didn't feel frustrated. Maybe it was a text from some website trying to get an interview. Maybe it was a co-star trying to capitalize on all the attention he was getting right now.

But more than likely, it was Noah. More than likely, his sweet, freckle-faced baker, two thousand miles away, was saying good morning because that was a thing that was happening now. If this had been just days prior, Adriano's entire attention would have been fixed on the situation and how to make sure Eric couldn't take any more from him, but that message from Noah had changed everything.

He wasn't even sure why he'd watched it. He'd seen hundreds of fans over the years fumble their way through YouTube ASL trying to get his attention, but something about Noah caught his eye. Maybe it was Noah's slender fingers or the way his pale skin was marred with dark scars that looked like burns. Maybe it was the way his signs were sweet but classroom formal and a little shaky on grammar.

Maybe it was the way Noah looked just slightly familiar—from a long-dead past he tried not to think about.

Maybe it was just that Adriano needed to reach out to someone, and Noah was convenient.

And that could have been it. At first. Then he'd seen Noah's wide, soft eyes, and the way he smiled shyly like he wasn't quite sure he belonged in the world. It was obvious Noah was a fan, but he didn't treat Adriano like a character or some internet personality. He just talked to him like he understood.

He knew a little about him now. That he was working in a failing bakery, that he was trying to get his brother set up before he had to shut the doors.

A hand waving at him regained his attention, and he rolled his eyes. 'I need time to think.'

"You have some," Anthony replied, "but not a lot."

Adriano's jaw clenched, but he nodded and rose, extending his hand for a quick shake before storming out. Luca was quick at his heels, but he didn't attempt to say anything until they were in the parking lot by their cars.

'Are you going to stay at Pietro's?' Luca asked.

Adriano dragged a hand down his face, then rolled his eyes up toward the low roof of the parking garage. 'I don't know.' In truth, his brother was so far up his ass that if Adriano stayed any longer, he might explode, and he didn't need that over his head while dealing with Eric and Xander. 'I might head out of town for a few days.'

'Do you really think that's a good idea?' Luca challenged, but at the look Adriano gave him, he backed up and rubbed his fist over his chest in a circle. 'Sorry. I just want you to be okay.'

Adriano softened a little, and he let his hand rest on his brother's shoulder for a moment. 'I'll be fine. I just need space.'

Luca nodded and let Adriano go without a further fight.

Adriano felt some measure of relief when he got back to Pietro's house and found the place empty. He wasn't sure where his brother or the kids were, but he wasn't going to look a gift horse in the mouth. He gathered Jude to his chest, then laid down on his bed and pulled his laptop up on his knees.

When he had it situated, he opened his phone and found two texts from Noah. The first was a photograph of him—a selfie holding up a bit of something that looked like darkly toasted pastry, and there were crumbs on his cheek.

> Noah: This is the last of the jachnun my brother made me. I'm eating it all, even if it's stale and disgusting.

Adriano laughed to himself and stroked his thumb along the side of Noah's image. He liked him—God help him. He'd never inflict this life and this stress on a sweet man like Noah, but the more they talked, the closer he felt to him.

> Adriano: I need 2 get hell out of here.

> Noah: you should come to Savannah. Sea air will do you good.

> Noah: I'm kidding, you don't need to show here. You'd be mobbed.

> Adriano: if it mean seeing u, would b worth it.

He set his phone aside, then opened up his maps and tracked the journey from Santa Monica to Savannah. His eyes widened when he saw three damn days without any real stops—an impossible drive but an easy flight. But he didn't think he'd go unnoticed at the airport, and a part of him thrummed with the possibility of a road trip.

He could make it if he pushed himself. With food stops, bathroom breaks, and walking Jude, it would be almost thirty-five hours, but it wasn't like he hadn't done it before. He'd road tripped with friends and slept in back seats and eaten shitty roadside diner burgers. Once upon a time, his routine didn't depend on protein shakes and hours on the treadmill.

He didn't realize the decision was made until Jude licked his face. "Road trip," he said aloud to the pup.

Jude licked his nose again, and Adriano smiled.

Easing the dog to the side, Adriano rolled off the bed and began packing without thought. After all, he had nowhere to be. Anthony would take weeks to sort out the issue with Xander, and chances were high Xander would win. So why stick around for nothing? Why subject himself to the constant fear that Eric might come looking for him.

No, he needed this. Even if Noah was just being polite and didn't want to see him at all, it would be worth it. He zipped up his case, then grabbed Jude's travel crate, his leash, and his supplies. It took him three trips to fill up the car, but an hour after his decision was made, he was behind the wheel.

> Noah: flattery will get you nowhere.

> Adriano: lol I guess we'll c.

He sent a smiley face, then a heart, then threw his phone

onto the seat next to Jude and turned the car on. It rumbled to life beneath him, his foot hit the gas, and then—without another thought—he was on his way.

ADRIANO HAD NEVER BEEN SO exhausted in his life by the time he pulled up to the Airbnb closest to the bakery. Most of the hotels in the downtown area were fully booked since tourist season was in full swing, but the historic house with the two apartments for rent had offered him not just a room but a discount.

He knew he looked a mess as he stepped out onto the pavement and stretched his back. He'd caught a few hours of sleep at truck stops, then he'd pushed it all the way to the coast.

He thought he was going to fall asleep at the wheel, but as he twisted and turned through the dawn-lit roads that wound around the tall trees, he found he had a second wind. Savannah itself had a timeless, historic feel to it. Adriano had traveled enough that he could easily compare it to little Dutch cities that were forgotten in time, and he liked it.

In spite of the old-world buildings, it was modern enough, and he passed by a couple of parked food trucks and a fire station. There were school zone crossings, which were just starting to flash when the clock hit seven thirty, and a couple of gas stations along the way.

He tucked Jude into his carrier before grabbing his suitcases, knowing the poor dog needed some time to exercise after being stuck in the car. But everything hurt, and he wanted to sleep for a year. The other half of him, though, wanted to comb the town for Noah, but he found himself wanting to make a good impression. It was bad enough he'd rolled into town with no notice like some kind of stalker, and he damn well knew celebrity status didn't give him that right.

A shower would help, and actual food. He just had to pray he didn't have to deal with any assholes who balked at using his phone app. He had his standard reply waiting for him that he never erased—*do you speak ASL*. For every two dozen people who said no, one said yes, so it was always worth it.

He didn't have a lot of hope for a small town like this, though. He already felt like an outsider with his sports car, small dog, and designer shades and the fact that he probably looked like some reality TV star coming off a coke binge. Places like this boasted little old ladies knitting in rocking chairs. They boasted adorable, freckle-faced Jewish bakers that he could fluster with a single text.

Letting Jude down, Adriano glanced around at the little space. It was a two-story building with a narrow staircase that barely fit his shoulders, but it was warm. The ad had warned him about how the street was loud, and he placed his palm on the frame next to the front door, and sure enough, he felt the rumble of a car passing by.

Deaf gain, he thought to himself as he grabbed his case and began the climb up the stairs. He looked behind him to make sure Jude was following, then he tossed everything into the bedroom. It was cozy and small, but the bed was big enough for two, and he tried not to think about the implications of what that could mean.

He didn't want to hope anything about Noah, despite the fact that he swore his heart was beating out the rhythm of the man's name whenever he thought about him. Adriano had definitely touched himself more than once after getting off a long texting session with Noah. He'd watch the video he sent—those long fingers and perfunctory signs like he'd learned them all in a classroom.

He'd stare at Noah's face and try desperately to remember where he knew him from, but in the end, it didn't matter.

He was there now. He was across the damn country as far away from his piece of shit ex as he could get without leaving the States. He knew it wouldn't solve his problems, but it brought him closer to something resembling peace, and that would have to be enough.

Staring at the bed, he turned back to Jude. 'Up,' he signed.

The dog obeyed and quickly got comfortable against one of the pillows. A short nap would have to do, then he could take a quick walk just a block down and see if maybe—just maybe—he really had made the right decision.

CHAPTER 5

Noah stared down at the flyer, then back up at the man standing at the counter, and he knew instantly he wasn't going to be able to tell Fitz's soft doe eyes and pouting mouth no. He knew Fitz was turning on the charm. That's what he did. Noah had known Fitz for as long as he'd been in Savannah. During his brief stint in the Scouts, Fitz and his best friend, Ronan, had ruled the roost. They weren't mean, just loud and a little too boisterous about trying to include Noah in their activities.

They were some of the few who hadn't mocked Noah about his accent or his very apparent anxiety, but they never quite made him feel welcome either. Bubbe had let him quit, though, long before a fire almost killed Fitz on a camping trip. Noah hadn't seen him for months after that, and when he finally got back to school, he was quieter.

To this day, Noah was amazed he'd become a fire fighter, that he'd stuck with it long enough to assume the role of chief, but it made sense. He'd never shied away from his scars, never hesitated when wearing short sleeves or extending his scarred hand when meeting new people.

Fitz had been the sort of man Noah had always wanted to be—the type of man he knew he never could be. The sort of charismatic, happy-go-lucky man who took tragedy with the same enthusiasm as he took joy. Noah did like that about him. He liked that Fitz had matured into a kinder, softer person. He liked that he never hesitated to try and include Noah, even when it meant encroaching on his quiet time Wednesday morning.

"My brother has a food truck, you know," Noah pointed out. "I don't need to set up a booth if Adam is going to be there."

Fitz shuffled his feet a little and gave him an imploring look. "We all love Adam's new thing." He waved his hand around in an absent gesture. "It's good. But Bubbe's stuff is part of downtown."

"I just don't know if I have the manpower to do a booth and the store," Noah admitted. Paxton would be useless at the shop by himself, and Noah wouldn't trust him anyway, but turning him loose at the Forsyth Farmer's Market would be a recipe for disaster—and a possible sexual harassment suit.

"It's in the evening. I mean, Bubbe's closes early anyway, right?"

Noah couldn't argue there. "Yes, but…"

"You can keep a limited menu. Just…cookies and maybe the bagels." He drawled the last word to remind Noah how often the station ordered bagels from them, and he fought hard to suppress a smile. "Bubbe used to do it when we were kids."

Noah's gut clenched a little because that was true. She loved it. It reminded her of the market back home, and it had been that little piece of Israel she'd been able to keep. Noah had been tasked with keeping an eye on Adam, who wanted to touch anything and everything, but he was usually content with a snow cone and Spider-Man face paint.

It had been years since Noah had set foot in the market.

"We made sure it was moved back from Friday nights," Fitz told him softly.

Noah raised his eyes, startled a little by the admission. "You…"

"Not just for you," Fitz said like he understood Noah didn't want special treatment or to be put on the spot like that. "But it's a bonus, right? Please?"

He wasn't going to say no. He'd known that the moment Fitz had walked into the shop with the familiar flyers clutched in his hand. "I just need to make sure Adam doesn't mind the competition."

"He doesn't," Fitz said. "He's the one who told me to come over here." Fitz leaned over and snagged a piece of rugelach from the dome-covered plate of samples—a batch that had burnt just enough that he couldn't sell them. But Fitz groaned like it was heaven, and Noah felt his cheeks heat. "I'll add your name to the list, and I'll come by with your booth assignment. Do you think you can start up next week?"

The market had been going on since the start of September, but it never really picked up until October when the weather got nicer and they had more visitors from around the area than not.

"That should be fine," he said quietly.

Fitz patted the counter twice with the flat of his palm, then winked when Noah looked up at him. "See you soon."

Noah sagged against the marble once the door swung shut, and he had half a mind to flip the sign to closed. No one was going to come in for end-of-day pastries anyway, and if he really was going to do this next week, he needed time to plan. Part of him wanted to send a message to his brother and chew him out for doing this, for putting him on the spot like that.

Wanting to be a little more social was one thing, but forcing him to integrate into a town that had spent the early part of his childhood ruthlessly mocking him for his differences wasn't what he had in mind.

He liked some of the locals. He tolerated Talia as best he could, and Oscar, the guy who ran the '90s-snacks-themed restaurant next door to Bubbe's, was a good guy.

He'd even started to consider himself actual friends with Will. So he wasn't totally alone, but this seemed like so much.

And yet, he also recognized it for what it was—an olive branch. Adam understood the food truck was competition with Bubbe's. This was his way of making peace and making space for him. It made the guilt worse, knowing none of this would really matter. He just wanted to stay afloat long enough to ensure the debt wouldn't totally crush him when he closed the doors for good.

Rubbing at his tired eyes, Noah crouched down, feeling an ache in his knees as he set the flyer under the register. He heard the small chime of the bell as he tucked the paper into the corner and fought back a groan as he stood up.

And then his world narrowed down to one single thing, one single sight.

Sylent—no—*Adriano* Moretti was standing with his hands shoved into the pockets of tight-fitting sweats, his lower lip between his teeth like he was nervous, eyes searching Noah's face.

Adriano was there.

Adriano was…

"What are you doing here?" The words slipped past his lips before he remembered, but Adriano seemed to understand because he took long strides with powerful legs and closed the distance between them.

Noah's entire body reacted, a visceral thing. His cock was so hard he could have cut steel, and the only thing that saved him was the counter between the two of them. He pressed his hips against it, then said a small prayer he wouldn't come because he was close.

God. He was close.

"I hope this is okay." Adriano's voice was a deep rumble, a bit lighter than his videos, and he knew a lot of that was the mics and the affect. But it was so much the same that Noah's cheeks flamed, and he just barely fought back a moan.

"You...Of course," he managed to get out. Then he shook his head and lifted his hands. 'I didn't know you were serious. It's, like, a thirty-hour drive from LA!'

Adriano laughed, and Noah's dick throbbed, ready to spill. 'I had a bad day. A...very bad day.' His emphasis on the word bad was enough to at least pull back on Noah's raging want—the weariness in his eyes, the way his lips turned down at the corners. It must have been damn near torture if Adriano had gotten into his car and driven two thousand miles.

To see *him*?

He was too terrified to assume.

'Where are you staying?'

'An Airbnb up the street,' Adriano signed. 'Nice place. Very cozy.'

Noah's lip twitched at the corner, and he watched Adriano's eyes trace the movement. He swallowed thickly. 'Have you eaten?'

Adriano shook his head, then gestured at the door before turning back. 'I have my dog outside.'

Noah's eyes widened. He became aware that for as much as they talked, they didn't know hardly anything about each other, and yet, there Adriano was. 'I'm about to close. We can have dinner at my place, and you can bring the dog.'

'Jude,' Adriano spelled, and Noah froze, a frown marring his brow. 'My dog,' Adriano clarified, then offered him the sign name for the animal.

A slow smile crept across Noah's face. His erection had calmed enough that it wasn't visible under his apron, so he walked around the counter and beckoned Adriano to follow.

Just outside, he saw the little thing—a small, orange ball of fluff like a round little marshmallow tied to one of the benches just outside the shop.

He heard an involuntary coo rip from his chest as he knelt down, and the small thing trotted over to sniff his fingers. He wasn't entirely sure he believed this was a dog. It seemed like a science experiment to create a living ball of fur rather than an animal, but a wet tongue laved across his knuckles, and he sighed as he sank fingers into the soft fur.

'Cute,' he signed when he turned back to see Adriano watching him with heavy eyes.

Adriano chuckled, then walked over and unlatched the leash, scooping the thing into his arms and giving it a nuzzle. Noah's heart beat rapidly against his ribs at the sight of a man Adriano's size holding something so small and so delicate. And Noah knew the power in Adriano's hands. He had been watching them for years.

'He's spoiled,' Adriano signed with one hand.

Noah laughed as he realized that for as down to earth as Adriano seemed, he was spoiled himself. He had no doubt everything Adriano wore was designer, that his shoes probably cost more than Noah's monthly loan payment on the shop. And it made him a little bitter, but he also knew Adriano worked hard in an industry that usually didn't make room for men like him.

'My door's around here,' Noah told him, and they walked around the side of the building to the second entrance he never used. The key stuck in the latch for a second, but it eventually opened, and he propped the door with his foot. 'It won't be locked. Help yourself, and I'll be up after I close the shop.'

Adriano looked a little bit startled at how readily Noah had accepted him into his space, but he didn't complain. He just signed a quick thanks, then took the steps two at a time with a heavy thud. Noah let the door shut, refusing to watch the flex in his thighs and ass any longer, and he rushed back into the shop and turned the deadbolt.

Before he could reach for the closed sign, someone gave the door a shove, and he looked up to see Will's other boyfriend, Isaac, staring at him with frantic eyes as he tried to get it open. Noah heaved an annoyed sigh but undid the latch. "Please God, tell me you have those fudgy cupcake things," Isaac said in a rush.

Noah's brows lifted. "Uh. I might? Not a full batch."

"That's fine. I'll pay you double. Triple," Isaac said in a halting staccato.

Noah beckoned him over with a shake of his head. "Calm down. What happened?"

"Well...I'm the worst boyfriend in the world. I'm just stressed, you know? Because of this damn cat café, and Liam is struggling to keep up, and I know I'm not the easiest person to get along with, and..."

Noah held up his hand to calm Isaac's ranting. "You upset Liam?" He knew a little about their dynamic—how Isaac was fussy and spoiled, and Liam was quick to temper. Will was an easy sort of guy, but fighting and drama usually sent him into hiding, usually at Noah's shop. It was a strange dynamic, and Noah didn't quite understand it, but he was also a forty-year-old virgin, so he was in no position to judge.

Still, he liked that it worked for them, and he felt for the way Isaac looked genuinely afraid. "Go lock the door. I have company for dinner, so I can't take any more customers, but I have cupcakes for you."

Isaac groaned. "Oh my God, I am so sorry. I'm *such* a dick."

"You are no such thing." In truth, Noah thought he was sweet, and it was no trouble to pull out the remaining cupcakes from the fridge and box them up. Adam had made them anyway—an experiment before he added them to the truck. They were never really a cupcake shop, but the demand for sweets like that from tourists was beyond his rugelach and hamantaschen and babka, and it was a perfect avenue for his brother. For him, however, he knew the place was closing and there just wasn't any point anymore.

He put a little tape on the box, and when Isaac tried to hand over his card, Noah shook his head. "Let me pay," Isaac demanded.

"No. These were either going to get eaten by my brother and his friends or tossed. So take them."

Isaac hesitated.

Noah set the box down firmly in front of the worried man and looked him in the eye. "I know you love those two, and they love you. Liam will forgive you without cupcakes, but chocolate never hurts."

Isaac swallowed thickly. "You're nice, but I feel guilty."

At that, Noah couldn't help his laugh. "Most people wouldn't agree with you about the nice thing. But I like you guys, and I'm happy to help. I wasn't going to sell these anyway. There's not enough of them, and Adam is too busy this week to bake more."

Isaac worried his bottom lip between his teeth. "If you're sure…"

Noah gave him a firm nod. "Of course I am. Will's been hanging out here a lot, so I'd prefer him in a good mood."

Isaac calmed down considerably, and though it took effort to get him out of the shop, eventually Noah was able to lock back up, set his closed sign, and turn the lights out. He was going to have to get up long before dawn to make up for the morning prep he was missing for this dinner, but the man waiting upstairs for him—he was pretty sure—was totally worth it.

Noah trudged up the steps one at a time in order to delay having to face that Adriano Moretti was in his apartment, and his brain flitted between trying to scrape together his mediocre cooking skills and calling for delivery. The last thing in the world he wanted to do was offer the man pizza, but the thought of showing off his subpar omelet skills made him feel like the floor was falling under his feet.

"*Get it together, Noah*," he hissed at himself as he reached for the door handle.

Inside, the apartment was almost totally silent save for some sort of low murmur in the back room. Adriano was nowhere to be found, but his small dog—Jude—was sitting on the floor at the foot of the sofa while Marshmallow perched on the top, staring unamused at the interloper.

"Be nice," Noah warned the cat before he set his keys and phone down, then went in search of his guest. As he slipped down the short hall, the sound got a little louder, and it only took a second for him to recognize what it was.

In all fairness, Noah hadn't expected the star of the fucking movie to be in his home, and he also hadn't expected that stranger to make himself comfortable in his bedroom with his porn. All the same, Noah blushed so hard he felt dizzy, and his hands shook as he threw his bedroom door open and found Adriano standing over his laptop, arms crossed over his large chest.

Adriano didn't notice Noah had come in right away, and Noah had no idea how to alert him without fainting out of sheer mortification. The laptop's screen was small but not small enough to conceal the image of Adriano as Sylent, holding a man in bondage as he pounded his ass.

"Fuck. Fuck my *life*," Noah hissed. He took another step in, and the vibrations must have been enough because Adriano looked over his shoulder, his mouth spread in a *cat who ate the canary* sort of grin. "Um," Noah said.

'You're a fan,' Adriano signed.

Noah swallowed heavily, and he knew his humiliation was written all over his face. 'I *did* tweet your pseudonym account.' He was on the cusp of defensive, and he knew when he got defensive, he got mean, and that was the last thing he wanted with Adriano.

After a beat, Adriano's long arm stretched out, and he flipped the computer shut. Noah's breath of relief was short lived because only a second later, Adriano had closed the distance between them. Noah took involuntary steps backward, hitting the wall, but Adriano didn't seem to mind.

'You like my work?'

A thousand responses flitted through Noah's head from a simple, *'B'ezrat Hashem*, yes,' to a lie like, 'I find porn disgusting, and I was praying for you.'

None of that came out. He just let out a single whimper and a nod.

Adriano's smile turned a little dark. 'I like you.'

Noah laughed. He didn't mean to. He didn't even really think it was funny. Just the idea that someone like Adriano Moretti—Sylent, the adult-film star, who could have literally any man he wanted—thought he was worth anything had to be a joke. His stomach twisted because what if it was?

He didn't think Adriano was cruel, but...

His thoughts fled as Adriano's large hand touched his face, and when Noah found the courage to look up, Adriano's eyes had gone soft. "I'm sorry," Adriano said aloud, and Noah jolted from the sound. "I didn't mean to embarrass you."

Noah swallowed past the lump in his throat, then shook his head. He wanted to sign, but Adriano had crowded in so close it wasn't possible. "I didn't want you to see that. I feel like a freak."

"A freak?" Adriano clarified, and Noah nodded. Adriano's brows flew up toward his hairline. "You think making porn means I'm a freak?"

"No!" Noah burst out, then turned his face away for a second to gather his breath. "No," he said again when he turned back. "I mean me." He patted his chest for emphasis.

Adriano took a step back to give himself signing space. 'You're not a freak because you like to orgasm.'

Noah shook his head. 'I...' He stopped, then decided that fuck it because Adriano deserved to know. 'We met back in college. On campus. You were the TA in my class, and you invited me to a Deaf event.'

Adriano stared at him, then his eyes went wide. 'You never showed up.'

Noah swallowed thickly and glanced away for a second. 'My grandmother died that night. I was there, but my brother called...' His hands stilled.

Adriano grabbed him by the wrists and pressed a kiss to the top of his knuckles, one after the other, until Noah felt like he was on fire. "I'm so sorry."

Noah shook his head and pulled back so he could answer him. 'I followed you after that. I had seen the video already, so I found you on Twitter. I've been a fan for a long time, but I was afraid to say anything. I didn't want to seem like a creep. I messaged you because I felt bad that you were hurting. But then we talked, and I realized I liked you as a person. But I still...like your work,' he finished, his hands shaking a bit.

Adriano's smile returned, and he reached out, taking Noah's hand back in his, squeezing with a gentle strength Noah wanted to curl up in and never leave. "It's okay."

Noah drew his bottom lip between his teeth, then his eyes darted toward the window before he looked back at Adriano's face. 'Pizza?'

With a hearty laugh, Adriano tugged Noah away from the door, but he didn't let go. Instead, he slung an arm around his waist, and Noah's entire body went hot, on the knife's edge of orgasm. It was only his sheer panic that kept it at bay, but Noah knew it would be a damn miracle if he didn't come in his pants before the night was out.

As they moved into the living room, Jude marched away from the sofa and right into Adriano's arms, and the familiar, soft feeling of watching that big man cuddle the small dog was back. Noah's flush hovered around the base of his neck, making it hard to talk, though he supposed that didn't matter at all. But it was wholly distracting and probably going to be the death of him if he couldn't get himself under control.

Adriano was sweet, and he said he liked Noah, but...

Noah couldn't let himself think like that. Adriano's life was so much more than Noah's. It was bigger, and chaotic, and beautiful, and free in a way Noah couldn't begin to understand. Noah didn't envy what Adriano did, but he envied the way life seemed to pour off him, even in times of heartbreak.

He took a deep breath, then grabbed his phone. When he looked over, he found Adriano on the sofa, legs up on the table with Jude against his side. Noah had an unwilling, unwanted flash of the future. Of Adriano being here as a partner—as more than just a fly-by-night guest who left town on a whim.

Stop, he ordered himself. He bit his lip, then waved his hand until Adriano looked over. 'What do you like on your pizza?'

'Whatever,' Adriano signed lazily. He grinned, then winked, and when Noah flushed, Adriano looked triumphant.

He knew what he was doing, Noah realized. He didn't know if Adriano was toying with him or if maybe he actually liked him, though it was damn near impossible to assume the latter. Noah had seen what Adriano's ex looked like, and Noah did not measure up. He was round and soft, on the chubby side. Eric had been cut from marble with a million-dollar smile and baby blues that someone could get lost in for days.

His hands shook harder as he fumbled with his phone. "Hi, I need..." Noah struggled with the words and closed his eyes. "I need pizza for delivery."

Eventually, he got his head together enough to order cheese, olives, and peppers, then set his card out before taking hesitant steps toward the sofa. He was still painfully hard, but it was mostly confined to his jeans behind his baggy shirt. It made walking with any grace impossible though, and he flopped down with the dog between them and reached out tentative fingers.

Jude didn't hesitate to nuzzle in, to absorb every ounce of affection, and Noah heard Adriano scoff. "He acts like no one loves him."

Noah lifted his eyes. 'I can tell he is very spoiled.'

Adriano's laugh was deep and genuine, and he shook his head with a grin so wide his ears lifted with it. 'So is your cat. What's his name?'

'Marshmallow.'

Adriano's smile widened. 'Cute. How long have you had him?'

Noah glanced away for a second, steeling himself. 'Since Adam moved out. My brother got him for me. Our friend runs a cat café in town.'

Adriano's eyes were soft and attentive, and he nodded for Noah to go on.

'Adam brought him home for me.' He pointed at Marshmallow, who was primly grooming his paw.

Adriano reached over and gave the cat another scratch.

'He was already named when Adam gave him to me.' His fingers trembled. 'But my brother tried to change it. To Sylent.'

Adriano blinked, then threw his head back and startled both dog and cat with his booming laugh. 'Because of me?'

'No,' Noah hurriedly signed, then dropped his hands and shrugged. 'Yes. Maybe. I don't know. I thought it was a coincidence, but he probably knows how much I...' He forced his hands to still.

Adriano leaned in. 'How much you what?'

Noah wanted to look away, wanted desperately to be anywhere else not having this conversation with the object of his obsession. 'Enjoy you.'

Adriano's tongue darted over his lower lip. 'You enjoy me?'

'As much as you seem to enjoy tormenting me,' Noah said. He had to spell tormenting—he had no idea if there was even a sign for that, but he watched the way Adriano's eyes followed the shapes of his fingers, the way they darkened even more.

'I don't want to make you feel bad, N.'

N—for Noah. 'I'm embarrassed. Of course you knew I was a fan, but I...I enjoyed talking with you.'

'Don't you think it's okay to be friends and a fan?' Adriano challenged. He sat back a little, and Noah felt just a bit more air fill his lungs. 'I don't mind.'

Noah wanted to explain better how all this made him feel, but he supposed Adriano wouldn't be able to understand what it was like to be a terrified virgin baker trapped in this small town.

'You didn't ask me to come,' Adriano said, interrupting Noah's thoughts. 'I showed up. If anyone should feel bad, it's me.'

Noah's eyes widened. 'No...'

Adriano's hand darted out, touching his wrist, quieting his response. 'I liked talking to you too. There was so much going on, and you were the first person that made me feel like more than just a public figure. Everyone wanted details. They wanted to make me bleed emotions.'

Noah's heart twisted for him. 'I'm sorry.'

Adriano shook his head, his smile soft. 'You just asked me if I was okay. So simple but just what I needed.' He reached out again, his big hand cupping Noah's cheek, thumb tracing his jaw. Noah's dick throbbed so hard it was a miracle he didn't spill right then. He was on edge, though—too close—but Adriano pulled away just in time. "Thank you."

Noah shifted. The weight of his jeans against his dick was too much. 'I need...toilet,' he spluttered. He was on his feet and racing for the bathroom before he could see Adriano's response. The moment the door slammed, he ripped at his zipper. He got his dick out seconds before his balls went tight, and he shot, missing the toilet and hitting the edge of the sink. His moan was loud, ripping from his chest, and he panicked only for the second it took to remember Adriano wouldn't hear it.

"Hell," he said, the swearing too common since Adriano had shown up in his doorway. His sweaty hand dragged down the front of his face, and he forced himself to straighten up, to look in the mirror. His cheeks were so splotchy his freckles stood out like tattoos against his skin—dark and far too visible. His nostrils flared as his erratic breathing fought to go back to normal, and he wondered if losing his virginity was even possible at that point.

He'd spent years coming without touching himself, losing all restraint at the thought of Adriano's hands on him. He laughed, the sound anguished and bitter because it would be absolutely no surprise if Noah had ruined himself for anyone else. After all, ruining everything was what he did—whether he wanted to or not. His limp, come-covered dick hanging out through the slit in his boxers was proof enough why he had no chance with Adriano, why Adriano shouldn't even be there.

Noah took his time cleaning up the mess and washing his

hands, and he was mostly put together by the time he stepped out. The pizza would be there soon, and he found Adriano on the sofa holding Jude on his lap. The cat was nowhere to be found, but that didn't surprise Noah given the way he'd raced out of the room.

He gave a sheepish smile to the other man, who beckoned him to sit back down, and Noah appreciated being able to lower to the cushions without the weight of his erection between his legs.

'Sorry,' he started, but Adriano waved him off.

'Are you okay? You looked like you were going to be sick.'

Noah shook his head. 'No, I'm not sick. It's been a long day. Long week.' *Long life*, he thought, but he didn't add that. It felt wrong to drop his angst and frustration on this man who had come seeking some peace from the mess his own life had become. 'Pizza will be here soon.'

Adriano hummed quietly in the back of his throat, then he pushed Jude off to the side and shifted closer. Noah felt the familiar stirrings of want heating up in his belly but not enough to be a problem, not yet.

'So your brother used to live here?'

Not the question he'd been expecting, but if anything was a boner killer, it was talking about his relationship with Adam. 'Yeah, but he moved in with his girlfriend, Talia.'

'Do you like her?'

Noah worried his bottom lip between his teeth. 'I guess.'

'You guess?'

'I love my brother, and I just want him to be happy, but he's had a rough life.' That was the easiest answer. 'My parents died when we were pretty young. Adam was a baby when our dad died. He was barely four when our mom died.' Noah was surprised at how steady his hands were, but he supposed all the years between then and now tempered his grief. 'It was a car accident. We were heading to Atlanta, and she swerved into the wrong lane. I woke up in the hospital.'

Noah rubbed at his sternum where he had a thin scar that had never totally faded. 'She was brought in with me, but she never woke up.'

'I'm sorry,' Adriano signed, the sympathy on his face genuine and without the sort of patronizing air most people used when offering condolences.

Noah waved him off. 'It was a long time ago. We lived with our grandmother, but she died when Adam was a freshman.'

The truth dawned on Adriano, and it flared in his eyes with empathetic pain. 'You had to leave school for good. Not just that night.'

Noah nodded, giving a small shrug. 'She left me the bakery, so I took care of Adam and ran the place. I had no idea what I was doing, but I've lasted this long.'

Adriano winced. 'Is there no way to save it?'

'Money,' Noah answered with a harsh, frustrated laugh. 'It's always money. I had to take out a loan, and I'm not making enough to pay it all back along with the other expenses. Adam has a food truck now, and his girlfriend owns a café, and they're doing well. I'll probably close at the end of summer.'

Saying it like that—even with his hands—was profound. Noah had known it. In the back of his mind, he'd known. He wasn't hiding from the fact that Bubbe's legacy was coming to an end all because Noah was nothing more than a failure. He had been a terrible parent to Adam—had never quite figured out how to be anything other than an anxious mess. He had been a dumping ground for his mother's grief, and he'd been little more than a disaster for Bubbe to take care of.

None of it was a surprise, but it hurt. It hurt that he couldn't do this one thing, even if he truly didn't want it. There was no point in trying to turn it over to Adam either. Even if his skill and willingness to give up their restricted kosher certification could bring more people in the door, it wouldn't be enough. It couldn't save the hole Noah was in.

He'd find a way to tell Adam, and then it would be done.

A warm hand touched his cheek again, and Noah's breath rushed out of his lungs. He turned his eyes up to find Adriano holding his gaze, his look as firm as the caress of his fingers. His heart thudded against his ribs, want pooling in his belly. He ran his tongue over his lower lip, and then… he leaned in.

The knock startled him back before Adriano could respond, to either accept or reject the offered kiss. He'd forgotten about the pizza, and his face was so hot he thought he might burst into flames as he scrambled to his feet and hurried toward the door.

He clutched his card between his fingers, but as he reached for the doorknob, he felt a hot, firm body behind him. Adriano's chest pressed against him as his large hand grabbed the handle and wrenched the door open. Noah's ears were ringing with shock, loud enough he couldn't hear the pizza delivery woman who was holding the two boxes in one hand.

Noah stood there, wordless and still, as Adriano thrust cash at her. He took the pizzas with one hand, signed his thanks with the other, then shut the door. Noah's senses were flooded, overwhelmed. The smell of spices, dough, and cheese took over and below that, the undercurrent of Adriano's cologne. The hot press of his body remained against his back, the slow puffs of his breath brushing the back of Noah's ear.

And then, a steady hand turned him. Adriano's eyes were still dark, but Noah couldn't get a read on his expression.

'Eat,' Adriano finally signed into the space between them. 'Talk after.'

It seemed an offering, and Noah would be a fool not to take it. He was resigned to his fate—whatever it was—as he let Adriano take his hand and drag him back to the sofa. He was at some sort of turning point, but as Adriano opened the first pizza box and gave him another one of his unreadable looks, Noah was well aware he had no idea what was coming next.

CHAPTER 6

HE KNEW HIM. Shit, Adriano knew him. The memories were a little foggy after so many years, but he remembered the shy, wide-eyed man in the ASL 4 class Adriano was using for his TA hours. It wasn't even related to his degree, but the college had insisted it was the only place suited for him, and he was too damn tired—and frankly too caught up in starting his porn career—to give a shit.

But God, he'd had such a crush on Noah, and knowing after all these years that Noah had followed him? He didn't let himself think about how different life would have been if Noah had shown up that night, but a small part of him wondered.

Of course, he would have lost him in the end. Noah's grandma died, and he was forced to be a parent to a young, grieving sibling. Adriano knew himself too well to assume he would have stuck around for something that heavy.

Maybe it was fate. Maybe they needed this time and distance to grow into two men who could be good for each other.

His head was a mess as he stared at Noah, who'd jumped up from the sofa like his ass was on fire. He realized it was the door after a beat, and he couldn't stop himself from following, though he knew better.

But it was entirely due to his job that Adriano had been able to hold back giving in to his desire to draw Noah into his arms and take him apart until dawn. He was hard. Not as hard as he could have been, but Adriano had learned to restrain himself on command after years and years in the film industry.

Helpful, he supposed, but Noah was testing his abilities like no one ever had. Maybe it was because he was so unrestrained with his feelings and the way they played into every expression on his face, and every motion of his body, and the tremble in his fingers as he signed, and the way he looked at Adriano. Or maybe it was because he was nothing like the men Adriano had been surrounded by since he'd started his work.

And he loved his job. He did. He loved the lifestyle it provided, and he loved that he was good at it. He even enjoyed most of his colleagues and the friends he had. But he was growing tired of the fear that everyone around him was just waiting to see what they could get. He once thought Eric had loved him just to love him, but that idea had been shattered without mercy. In the weeks he'd wallowed after his breakup, his heartache wasn't for the love he'd lost but for the sudden realization that no one might ever love him for the man he was.

The person beyond his body, and his skill, and the number in his bank account.

But Noah was *different*. It wouldn't be the first time Adriano had fucked one of his fans. He didn't do it often, but he'd given in to the temptation a time or two when he was just getting started. And after Eric, there had been parties where the two of them had devoured shy men who had managed to get an invite and spent the night pressed against the wall, trembling with need.

He hadn't hated those moments, but Noah was not like any of those men. His concern after finding Adriano at his laptop was genuine. He looked afraid—and maybe a little hurt—that Adriano might think Noah's friendship was anything but. Noah was a sea of complications. Adriano knew that much. There was a pain in his eyes Adriano didn't understand, though knowing about his parents and grandmother, it made sense.

He couldn't imagine what it would be like to have his entire life decided for him, to be thrust into the role of guardian at such a tender, important age. To have whatever dreams he was following, whatever freedom he'd fought for, snatched by the hands of death.

It sounded like a prison sentence.

Noah was sad, and he was resigned. His bakery was failing, but he wasn't asking for help. It was water cupped in his hands. Adriano fought back the urge to throw money at him, to just solve the problem with a check. He could do it. He wouldn't have a single regret, even if it turned out Noah had befriended him for that reason alone.

How could he? The way Noah's flushed skin felt against his palm when he touched him was worth more than he could say. He was soft, and sweet, and Adriano wanted to devour him.

When Noah had rushed off before the pizza arrived, Adriano was more than aware of what was going on. He didn't need to hear the thumping, or the moans, or the sharp cry of orgasm to know that Noah hadn't been able to hold back. He closed his eyes and could too easily picture Noah standing over the toilet, hand flying over his dick, spilling ropes of seed into the water below.

Adriano's mouth watered. He was often tired of sex, but he never got tired of genuine want, genuine desire in the form of a man's hot breath, and warm cock, and thick tongue that wasn't being paid to be there, that wasn't getting something out of it. He wanted Noah, and maybe coming here had been a spur-of-the-moment decision, but he didn't regret that for a second.

He did feel resentment when their kiss was interrupted—at least at first, but it was too obvious to see how lost Noah was. He didn't know Adriano well, and it was unfair to take advantage of him like that. Adriano wanted to woo him, to seduce him with more than just his name, his reputation, his body. He wanted every inch, every *molecule*, of Noah to be desperate for him.

He wanted Noah so wrapped up in him that he begged Adriano not to leave.

Or maybe he'd beg Adriano to take Noah with him. That idea had some appeal.

He had no timeline right now. He was in limbo, waiting for Anthony to sort out whatever the hell was going to happen with his film career and Xander. He had three years left on a contract—three long years to potentially not film a single scene. That might have been a death sentence to other stars, an easy way to become irrelevant. Adriano didn't want to lose his life, but as he looked across the sofa at Noah delicately picking at his pizza, he didn't think it was the worst one in the world.

'Tell me what's good to do around here,' Adriano asked after waving to get Noah's attention. 'I need to head back to my place soon. I'm exhausted. But I have no plans after tonight, and I want to spend as much time with you as I can.'

Noah's cheeks pinked beautifully, and Adriano wanted to drag his teeth over those freckles. 'There's a ton to do if you like shopping. Or eating. Or walking.'

Adriano raised a brow. 'I can do that in LA.'

At that, Noah laughed and shook his head. 'There's a farmer's market tomorrow night in Forsyth Park. Tons of people show up, and most of the shops around here have a booth.'

Adriano leaned forward. 'You?'

Noah glanced away, then shrugged. 'Normally, I don't, but Fitz,' he spelled the name slowly. 'Fire chief. He asked me if I would set one up, so I told him next week.'

Adriano studied his expression. 'You regret it.'

Noah looked pained. 'It won't help the bakery. It just means more baking, and I have no help, and Adam is busy with his truck.'

Adriano worried the inside of his cheek, then gave a firm nod. 'Teach me.'

Noah startled in his seat, almost knocking his plate off his lap. He gingerly pushed it to the table, then looked back at Adriano. 'Teach you what?'

'Baking. I'm from a huge Italian family. I was born to be in the kitchen. I'll help you get ready.' He waited, and Noah's hands lifted to protest, so Adriano grabbed his wrist lightly and squeezed, shaking his head. 'Let me help.'

The wet, pink tip of Noah's tongue dragged over his bottom lip, and Adriano fought the urge to lean in and taste it. God, he wanted him. 'Maybe.'

'You have a better idea?' Adriano challenged. And maybe Noah's hesitation was right. Maybe it would be damn near impossible to keep his hands to himself if they were in a kitchen together, but that part was far more than seduction. He wanted to ease a few of Noah's worry lines, wanted to soothe the way his soul was all twisted up into knots with more than just fucking.

He had never been so gone so fast before, but Adriano was also the kind of man who followed his heart, even when his heart was wrong.

'Okay,' Noah finally said, and Adriano felt his grin stretch wide enough it nearly split his face.

'When?'

'Wednesday night after close.'

Adriano felt the vibration of his throat with his hum as he

nodded. 'Tomorrow, you can show me the market. I'll come over when you're done.' He made sure it was a statement, not an offer. Noah's anxiety was obvious, how he'd say no, how he'd run, even when he didn't want to. Adriano didn't mind applying a little firm hand where it was needed, especially knowing Noah wanted him, and more than that, he liked him.

After a beat, Noah's shoulders moved with a laugh, and he shook his head, but the delight in his eyes wasn't a rejection. 'Fine. I can close early. Come by at six.'

That settled, Adriano knew he had to get out before things got carried away. He pulled the thin leash from his pocket and clipped it to Jude before rising, then held a hand out to Noah. His palm was warm and a little slick from the pizza grease, but he clung tight as Adriano pulled him to his feet.

'Walk me out.'

Noah nodded, and he stayed close enough that Adriano could feel his body heat as they approached the door. He twisted the leash around his palm just before they stopped, and he spun fast, gripping Noah by the waist.

Noah's mouth parted with a puff of air as Adriano spun him, then pinned him to the wall by the door and nosed along Noah's cheek, right over a smattering of freckles that looked like the night sky. His lips were open, grazing Noah's cheek, and he pulled back.

'I like you,' he repeated.

Noah's swallow was heavy, his Adam's apple bobbing. 'I like you.'

Adriano's mouth quirked in a half grin. 'Kiss me good night.' Yet again, not a question. He saw war waging in Noah's eyes, fear with need with hesitation with raw desire. He let it go on only a moment more. 'Kiss. Me.' His signs were sharp and demanding, and eventually, Noah nodded.

Adriano was kind enough not to torture him more, not to

make him work too hard for it. He closed the distance between them, tucking his hand behind Noah's short curls, burying his fingers in the soft locks, twisting them around as his lips parted and he took the thing he'd wanted since he'd set eyes on the man.

The kiss was hot. It was sloppy. It was unpracticed. Noah seemed unsure what to do with his tongue, with his mouth, but Adriano didn't mind. He nudged Noah's lips apart with his own, then dragged his tongue in gently, slowly. Noah tasted of oregano and tangy sauce and something else that was uniquely him.

Adriano groaned, pressing his body hard against Noah's. He felt him hard and throbbing, felt the way his pulse rocketed. He was close, Adriano realized. He was on the edge of coming. He thrust his tongue deeper, let his own erection just barely graze Noah's, and he felt it when it happened. He felt the blaze of a flush shoot through Noah's skin, felt his body stutter, felt the way Noah's fingers dug into Adriano's arms, painful and present.

When he pulled back, Noah's eyes were shut, but there was a look of hesitant shame on his face. Noah had come in his pants like some teenager who had never been kissed, and something niggled at the back of Adriano's brain. But this moment was fragile and delicate, thin ice across a lake, and Adriano didn't want to crack it just yet.

He dropped another soft, careful kiss on Noah's lips, coaxing him, urging his eyes to open. When they did, he smiled. 'Goodnight, beautiful.'

Noah nodded. He didn't move, and Adriano deliberately didn't look down to see if the wetness had darkened the front of his jeans.

'Tomorrow?' he added.

Noah nodded again, his limp arms falling to his sides.

Adriano let out a small breath, then caressed the side of Noah's face before reaching for the door. He didn't break eye contact until he was in the hall, then he pressed the tips of his fingers to his mouth, offering Noah a last breath of a kiss, and then he was gone.

He didn't look back, didn't let Noah know he was aware of what happened. He just put one foot in front of the other…and started to make a plan.

Adriano had never been big on sleeping in. His routine had him up at dawn for a morning run, then weights since he decided to make film his career. So even on vacation, sleeping until seven was a luxury. His body still ached from the drive and from sleeping in his car, but he threw on track pants and took Jude for a walk around the neighborhood. He had forgotten to ask if there was a gym nearby, but he decided a few days off wasn't going to kill him.

Hell, if it came back that he wasn't going to be able to film for three years, what was the point anyway? Trying not to let frustration seep in, Adriano went back to the house and set Jude up in the little crate before deciding to check out the café next door for breakfast.

He snatched his phone from the nightstand, then tapped out a good morning to Noah before ignoring the texts from his brother and heading back out into the chilly morning.

The morning air felt good on his heated skin, even if it was more humid than he was used to, but he felt like he could live there comfortably. And fuck if that wasn't a thought he wasn't expecting. He liked Noah—maybe not enough to propose marriage, but even that didn't seem like the wildest notion for a future.

He wasn't sure what it was about the guy that had him so captivated. He was the opposite of everything Adriano had ever looked for in a partner, but maybe that was just it. Adriano's usual taste for spoiled twinks had gotten him nowhere except hiding out across the damn country, and Noah was the first person to show genuine concern about him and not the figure he was to the public.

The thought calmed him a little as he made his way through the café doors and followed the smell of bacon to a dining room where a bored looking man who couldn't have been older than his early twenties was leaning on the counter. He offered a smirk as he gave Adriano a once-over.

If Adriano hadn't been utterly consumed with Noah, he might have taken more than just a quick notice of him, but he had no room for anyone else in that moment. He approached with a smile, then pointed to himself, and held up one finger.

The guy didn't try to talk, so he'd either seen Adriano signing to someone around town the day before or recognized him for his work. And by the look in his eyes, Adriano assumed the latter. He tried not to smirk a little as the guy led him to a table near the front of the buffet, and when Adriano sat down, he realized the guy was waiting for his attention.

'Coffee, tea, juice?' his hands signed, not quite right but close enough. Adriano appreciated it more than he could say when servers actually took the time to learn.

'Coffee,' Adriano signed.

The server nodded, then pulled out a notepad and gestured for Adriano to write on it.

He took a second to scan the menu, then jotted down: *egg white omelet w/ turkey and cheddar, side fruit, OJ.*

The server read it over, then nodded and gave him a thumbs-up before turning on his heel. Adriano watched the guy walk away with a bit of a sway to his hips and appreciated the view and the attempt to communicate. He hadn't expected to feel any sort of warm welcome at all there, but all these people were quickly changing his mind.

It only took a second for the guy to return with the large

glass of juice and the pot of coffee, and he set it down next to the little bowl of creamer pods.

'Be back soon,' the server said, mostly through pantomime.

Adriano gave him a nod, then filled his mug, gulping down the hot, bitter liquid before adding a couple packets of sugar and a single creamer. There were a few people who came in right after him, and Adriano fell into his favorite habit of people watching. He liked when he was somewhere new and got a glimpse of the locals.

Coming from LA, even the people who grew up there never seemed to belong. They were all just getting by and dreaming of somewhere with less chaos. It was why all his brothers, except Luca, had moved out of the city and why he was now dreaming of a life along the East Coast.

Lost in his thoughts, Adriano almost didn't notice someone appear at his table until a plate moved in his periphery. He startled and almost knocked it out of the poor guy's hand, then quickly tried to offer an apology, but it died in the air between them as he stared at a man he didn't know…

But he *knew*.

It was the eyes mostly. The same color and the same sort of soul-deep anguish of a lonely childhood that Noah shared. The man had a sharper face, skin a little bit darker, and without the freckles across his nose and cheeks. His hair had the same tight curl, but it was a few shades lighter, shorter, and styled rather than the wild curls on Noah's head.

More than just knowing this was Noah's brother by the look of him, it was the recognition in his eyes when he stared at Adriano.

"Adam?" He wasn't even sure he had the name right with the movement of his lips and tongue, but the man's eyes widened, and a wash of color crept over the tips of his ears.

Adam dipped his head, his lips twitching like he wanted

to speak, but he wasn't sure. Adriano regretted leaving his hearing aids in his room, but he still planned on trying to make something of an introduction.

"I'm Adriano. Nice to meet you."

Adam took his hand, balancing his plate on the other, then looked over his shoulder at a woman who had slid up behind him. She had long dark curls and was wearing a dirty apron and a curious scowl. She put a possessive hand on Adam's shoulder as he gave Adriano a look up and down.

Adriano watched as Adam's lips moved in explanation, watched as the woman's scowl melted into something like amusement. Her eyes lifted to Adriano's, and he extended his hand. Her lips curved, and though Adriano had never been great at lipreading, he was pretty sure this was Talia.

"Nice to meet you," Adriano said. He pointed to the empty chair at his table and shrugged. "You want to sit?"

Adam's smile went from friendly to a little bit nervous, but Adriano took it with a grain of salt. The invitation was out there, and they could take it or leave it. Moving his chair back, Adriano pulled his plate closer, then reached for his coffee and took several swallows now that it had cooled to a reasonable temperature. He jolted a little when the chair opposite him was filled, Adam looking a shade nervous, but Talia joined him a few moments later with a pad of paper and a pen.

Adriano took it and saw scrawled across the top in neat script, *I'm Talia. I own this place. This is Adam Leib. Neither of us really sign. Sorry.*

Adriano waved them off. "It's fine. I don't read lips well. Thanks for the paper." He studied them to see if they were put off by his speech, but Adam only looked relieved, and Talia was scribbling again.

You came to see Adam's brother, right?

Adriano glanced down, then he thought of Noah. And then he smiled. "Yes. I had dinner with him last night."

He didn't miss the way Adam choked on his drink so hard his face went bright red. Talia said something, rubbing his back, but Adam pushed her away with a gentle hand, then grabbed the pen from her.

You know my brother? Like, know *him?*

Adriano frowned, and instead of speaking Noah's business to the whole restaurant, he took the pen for himself. *We're friends. He never mentioned me?*

He saw the way Adam dragged his lip between his teeth, the way he looked nervous. Noah was right. Adam had known Noah was a fan. He just hadn't known Noah had kept their friendship to himself. It stirred something in him, something warm and kind of wonderful. Proof in the softest, best way that Noah had meant what he'd said. He hadn't gone parading around, sharing who Adriano was, hadn't spread his personal business, not even to his brother.

It was a wonder, and he wanted to go find Noah right then and kiss him, then kiss him until he couldn't breathe, then kiss him until he came. He fought back a shiver before looking down at Adam's messy script. *He doesn't tell me a lot. It's nice of you to come visit.*

There was something in Adam's face now—maybe hurt or confusion. Adriano hadn't meant to cause a problem. He appreciated that Noah had kept it to himself, but it was possible that was a symptom of a bigger problem between the brothers. He couldn't understand it, of course. He came from a family who overshared to the point of rage. But he hated knowing he might cause a bigger conflict.

"We met back in college, but we just connected again. I… had some personal problems, and he was kind. I didn't expect a friendship. I like him."

Adam's face softened again, and there was the spark of something more. Pride, maybe? Adriano wished he knew these people a little better. Adam took a breath, then nodded and wrote a bit longer. *Noah's a good guy. That doesn't surprise me. Anyway, I hope you don't think I'm rude, but I was getting breakfast to go. Talia is helping me with my food truck today, but if you come by the farmer's market tonight, stop by, and I'll give you some pastries to try.*

'Thank you,' Adriano offered, fingers tipping from his chin.

Adam knew sign enough to respond with, 'You're welcome,' before he gathered himself and left, Talia following close at his heels.

Maybe he really had fucked something up, but he liked Noah too much to care. There was a long day ahead of him before he could see Noah again, but knowing it could be measured in hours made all the difference in the world.

CHAPTER 7

ADRIANO WAS NERVOUS. It was a new experience for him—or at least it had been a damn long while since anyone had given him sweaty palms and butterflies in his stomach. But Noah did. He'd texted him a couple of times that day, had even gotten a selfie of him with flour dusting his cheeks and a golden glow of afternoon sunlight creating a halo around his short curls.

Adriano wanted to kiss him again. He wanted to press Noah against the wall and feel the way he groaned, the way his breath made his entire body heave, the way he seized and trembled with an untouched orgasm. Adriano didn't entirely know what it meant that Noah was so worked up over a single kiss. Even his biggest fans had more restraint than that, and Adriano didn't think it was obsession.

It felt like something bigger.

He distracted himself by passing Jude off to the guy who ran the cat café, then perusing downtown. Nearly everything was accessible on foot, and he found a little blacksmith shop that was closed for the afternoon but had some of the stuff on display in the front window. It wasn't lacking in kitschy little tourist shops either, but a lot of the places looked homegrown like they'd been around since the start of Savannah.

Even the old building with faded stucco and cracked roof tiles that bore a sign for the Savannah newspaper seemed to fit. Behind the foggy glass, he saw the hustle and bustle of people, and he wondered what it would be like to call a town like this home.

He didn't think there was much Deaf community to speak of, but in all honesty, he hadn't really integrated much himself back in LA either after getting into film. He wondered if he could find some sort of peace in this little oasis on the shores of the Atlantic. He didn't want to hope, but he couldn't help it.

He was careful to avoid the bakery's storefront, knowing he wouldn't be able to resist going in, but knowing Noah was close was a comfort to him. And he enjoyed that people didn't just stare. The staff at the little trailer-park-themed diner on the corner didn't bat an eye when he used his notepad to order food, and later in the afternoon, the Forsyth Park coffee cart barista knew enough for *thank you* and *you're welcome*.

He got back to Noah's brother's café and found a new server who hadn't been there at breakfast. He had a look on his face like he'd been told about Adriano, but he smiled, and it seemed genuine. Adriano wasn't a stranger to dealing with hearing people who had no background in sign, but he was starting to feel a little tired.

'Coffee?' Adriano signed, trying to exaggerate the word.

The guy nodded and gestured to the cups until Adriano nodded to the large. "Hot?"

Adriano nodded again and waited for him to fill the cup before waving at the guy, then tapped out on his phone and handed it off. *What's your name?* He gestured at the guy's apron to show he wasn't wearing a name tag.

The guy grimaced in apology. 'C H A S E.'

Adriano spelled it back, then made a C, which was easiest. *Where's a good place to take someone on a date?* he typed on his phone.

Chase's mouth formed a very faint smirk, and he grabbed a bit of receipt paper to write out his reply. *Is it Noah?*

Someone around here has a big mouth.

He liked how Chase laughed with his entire body, his eyes crinkling, showing both age and youth all wrapped up into one man who looked like he had the weight of the world on his shoulders. *Yes, she does. Talia likes to start drama. But she's also dating Noah's brother. Anyway, there's a couple of decent restaurants that aren't too far from here. Five-star dining if you're into that sort of thing. One of them is co-owned by this guy, Tristian, who has a YouTube channel. It's mostly Italian food. It also has a kosher menu that's certified if you're taking Noah out.*

Adriano wasn't a fan of the American interpretation of his culture's cuisine, but he had a feeling he'd struggle to find a place that Noah could readily eat at, so Adriano grinned and signed, 'Great. Thanks,' mouthing along.

Chase offered, 'You're welcome,' that looked like he'd been trying to brush up, and Adriano didn't hate it.

Maybe by the time he was done, some of the town would be proficient. Hell, it was more than most of the people he'd been working with for over a decade had done. The thought was a bitter pill, and he walked off with a wave before his thoughts could turn dark. He had a date to go on, and a farmer's market to peruse, and an adorable man to seduce.

IT FELT like Savannah got darker faster than most of the places around the state, but Adriano had a feeling it was the way the tall trees loomed around them from all sides. He didn't mind it. It had a sort of romantic feel to it when he pulled his car into the single curbside spot that was open in front of the bakery. The neon open sign was off, but he saw the door was cracked open, and he swiped sweaty palms as he reached for the handle and stepped in.

He never liked being in stores past their closing. His mom used to take him shopping for hours, and when the overhead lights started to dim, his irrational child's brain convinced him they'd be locked in until morning. He'd cry and scream loud enough to humiliate her, and after the fifth time he'd lost his absolute shit in a Dillard's, she stopped taking him.

Even now, even knowing it was Noah's place and being locked in a kitchen with him wouldn't be the worst idea in the world, he felt that small rush of fear at the dark shadows and unlit, empty pastry windows.

The kitchen door swung open after a minute, and Noah popped his head out, grinning widely against the backlight of where he was baking. 'Lock the door?'

Adriano nodded, giving him a thumbs-up before turning to do just that. He felt the heavy click of the deadbolt under his fingers, and the fear thrill turned into something else. His mouth watered, his cock plump behind the zipper of his jeans. He dragged a hand through his styled hair, then grimaced and tried to set it straight before gathering his courage and pushing through the swinging doors.

Adriano had worked in a kitchen once. His mom knew a restaurant owner willing to take a chance on a Deaf kid who hated voicing. He didn't do much beyond bussing tables and washing dishes, and it wasn't easy. The kitchen had been chaotic and loud, and the sounds that got through his hearing aids were piercing and unkind to his sensitive ear drums. But he loved that he was doing something on his own, earning his money, proving to himself he was capable, even if it was just cleaning up the messes of the LA middle class.

This kitchen was nothing like that. It was tidy to the point of pristine apart from a long wooden baking table that was covered in flour. Noah was nowhere to be found, but the evidence of his recent work was all over. There were trays stuck inside a tall rack that were filled with cookies and unbaked bread dough, and an industrial mixer was whirring and kneading a massive lump of what he assumed would probably be bread.

He felt a faint vibration under his feet, and he saw Noah coming out through a side door that he realized probably went up to his apartment. He wasn't covered in flour anymore, and he looked nice in jeans and a button-up. His hair looked damp, his curls in ringlets that just barely touched his forehead, and there was a faint dusting of color on the apples of his cheeks.

'What are you baking?' Adriano asked, pointing at the mixer.

'Challah. I like to make extra because it sells well Friday afternoons before I close.'

Adriano raised an eyebrow. 'Is there something special about Friday afternoons?'

Noah shrugged. 'It's for—' Adriano didn't recognize the sign, and Noah blushed furiously as he spelled it out. 'Shabbat. Sabbath,' he clarified when it still didn't make sense.

Adriano took four steps closer, hands fighting to reach for him, wanting to kiss the shy smile off his face. 'I didn't know those words.'

'I didn't know I'd ever be able to teach *you* ASL.'

Adriano laughed. 'Living language, always learning.' He finally gave into his urge—just a little—and brushed the backs of his knuckles over Noah's heated cheek. Adriano felt the way Noah's entire body shuddered, the way he leaned into it like he was starving for touch. 'Do we need to wait until it's done? I want to take you to dinner.'

Noah dragged his bottom lip between his teeth and shook his head. 'No. I just need to wait until my timer goes off. I'll put it in the fridge after.'

Adriano nodded and wondered if maybe he could convince Noah to kiss him more while they waited. If Noah came again, they weren't in the ideal place to get spunk everywhere, but at least they were close to home. He stepped a little closer, saw the way Noah responded, saw the way his cock began to bulge.

Adriano's hand had just started to reach out when Noah jolted, and it took him a second to realize something had made noise. The timer. Noah ducked his head and moved around him to tip the massive bowl onto the table. With a large cutter and quick, proficient movements, Noah separated the dough, then slapped them all onto baking sheets and added them to the rack.

He moved precisely, like it was in his blood, but Adriano could see the discontent in his eyes as he pushed the rack into a massive fridge and slammed the door. He ached to make Noah feel better, to take some of the burden away. He liked watching Noah in this place—in this kitchen—but he hated that it seemed to suck the life out of him.

'Where are we going?' Noah asked after he swiped his hands on a towel.

Adriano spelled the name of the restaurant and saw the way Noah's mouth quirked into a half smile. 'The server at Talia's café said it was a good place to take a date who needed a kosher menu.'

'Is this a date?' Noah asked. His lips were parted like maybe he was having a hard time breathing, and *fuck*, Adriano liked that.

'Yes. If you want.'

Noah looked terrified, but only for a moment. It melted into something more—curiosity and desire and need all at once. 'Yes.' His answer was steady.

Adriano offered his arm, and Noah laughed as he took it. He turned the lights off as they headed for the door, and Adriano swore he had never, ever been so charmed.

CHAPTER 8

Noah sat across from Adriano in the dimly lit restaurant and tried not to reflect back on the one, single, disaster date he'd been on in college. Three days after midterms his sophomore year, a guy who had been sitting across from him in his Chaucer lecture approached him near the elevators and had nervously asked him out.

"I've been staring at you for the last six weeks," he said, face a little pink. He wasn't unattractive, but Noah didn't have the heart to tell him he hadn't ever taken notice. "Do you want to maybe go get dinner or something?"

Noah's heart rammed hard against his ribs as he said yes, as he gave the guy his number and his dorm room. He had sweaty palms as they walked together—not close enough to hold hands—to the little Irish pub down the street.

They spent half the night talking about how much they hated Chaucer and how much they hated their professor. They laughed a lot and drank too much. Noah ordered a cheeseburger with bacon and indulged in every single sinful bite.

He thought it was *the* moment. He thought maybe he wasn't some anxious, lonely nerd. He thought he was worth something. Every single smile he dragged out of the guy fueled his courage, and he'd gone in for a kiss. Their lips never connected. The guy pushed him back, and laughed, then asked Noah if he wanted to suck his dick.

"Uh…"

"Dude, I'm not going to kiss you. Jesus, I just wanted to get off, and you looked like a willing mouth." He looked Noah in the eye…and then he laughed. He laughed hard enough to double over, and Noah ran. The guy quit showing up to the lecture, and Noah didn't think he'd ever have the courage to try again.

Never, in a million years, did he think he'd be sitting across from Adriano Moretti at a restaurant. He never thought he'd be sitting across from him after having been kissed so hard and so thoroughly he'd come in his pants the night before. Twice.

Noah's only saving grace was that Adriano didn't know. He hadn't heard the way Noah had groaned as his cock spilled, and he never looked down to see the wet spot spreading across his jeans. He'd just looked Noah in the eye and told him he'd see him later.

And now they were on a date. At a kosher restaurant that Adriano had researched just for him. No one, not even his brother, had ever bothered to check before, and he wasn't sure how to process that knowledge.

Noah's head was spinning, and he wanted more, but he knew he couldn't do that without telling Adriano the truth first. They'd come close to kissing in the kitchen, but the timer had saved his jeans from another embarrassing mess.

Part of him half wished it had just happened. At that point, he'd have been forced to explain, and chances were, Adriano wasn't going to want to deal with some forty-year-old virgin who couldn't hold his come. But the selfish part of Noah, the part he was used to ignoring and refused to indulge, wanted this. Even if Adriano walked away at the end of the night and never looked back, at least Noah would have this. That last kiss—which had been his first—and the vision of the man himself smiling sweetly across the table at him.

'Dessert?' Adriano asked.

Noah's lip quirked. 'My brother would kill me if I took you anywhere else but his truck.'

Adriano chuckled, then signaled for the server before handing off his card. It was an easy exchange, and before long, he was scribbling his name beneath a tip, then holding his hand out for Noah. As he accepted, Noah felt eyes on him. He knew how the people of Savannah looked at him. The weird, anxious, hermit baker who rarely set foot out of his apartment unless it was to shop with his head down and rush out before anyone could make conversation with him.

He was the inevitable shadow of the boy who had slowly whittled down into this mess. The boy who had never been brave enough to stand up for himself or to do anything besides turn the other cheek. And there was so much irony in that it almost made him laugh.

Noah hated being a spectacle, but Adriano seemed to thrive on it. He grinned wider at all the people watching, tugged Noah closer, walked with shoulders straighter. How he envied him. What he wouldn't give to just have the bravery to not give a single shit what people thought.

The night air was cooler than expected, but he appreciated the chill as they turned the corner and followed the bright streetlamps toward the park. He heard the fountain and low murmur of people milling around. He smelled the sweet scent of kettle corn and heard faint music from some live cover band competing with the street musicians.

It gave him a thrill to share this piece of himself with Adriano, even if he hadn't been part of it in years. He would be again, though, and soon. The following week, he'd show up early after closing down the shop and force himself to smile politely and not shrink back from friendly attempts at small talk.

His stomach rolled with unease at the thought, but then Adriano squeezed his hand a little tighter to get his attention. 'Tired?'

Noah laughed and shrugged. 'Yes, but I'm always tired. I had to get up earlier than usual this morning.'

Adriano's brow furrowed. 'Why?'

'Because I had dinner with a certain someone last night and missed my evening prep,' Noah told him, then winked. He led the way toward the bustling market as it came into view and paused as Adriano took it in with wide eyes and a growing smile. When he looked back, however, his gaze was concerned. 'Don't worry about it. It's fine.'

'I don't understand,' Adriano insisted.

Noah let out a small sigh, realizing he'd have to tell Adriano several truths tonight. 'I usually work late and get prep done because, since my brother took a few weeks off to get his food truck established, there's just me. The dough takes hours to get finished, so I don't have time in the morning unless I get up at three.'

Understanding dawned on Adriano's face. 'And you missed prep because of me.'

Noah's look was stern. 'It was worth it. I promise.'

Adriano hesitated, then nodded, and Noah appreciated that he didn't fight, didn't try to make light of what Noah had sacrificed to spend time with him. 'We'll get back early. How much did you skip tonight?'

'Just a little,' Noah attempted to reassure him, but Adriano shook his head.

'I'll come with. I'll help.' He took Noah's hand after that, silencing his attempt at a reply, and it was just as well. Noah would have argued, but he didn't want to tell Adriano no. He let the other man lead him right into the crowd, and Adriano kept him close. He walked next to him with shoulders straight, and for all that this was Noah's town, he felt like Adriano was trying to shield him. 'Are they staring because I'm Deaf?'

Noah wanted to roll his eyes, not at Adriano but at himself and how he'd done this all on his own by being such a damn mess. 'No. It's me.' When Adriano gave him a dubious look, Noah led him to an empty picnic bench, and he propped up against the table. 'It is me. I don't…I mostly grew up here, but things with my mom were bad, and I didn't make friends very easily. They didn't like my accent.'

Adriano reached out for just a brief second, brushing his thumb over Noah's bottom lip, and that was almost enough to make his cock explode. 'You have an accent?'

Noah laughed to cover up how loudly he wanted to moan. 'Not anymore. Not really. I only spoke Hebrew when we moved here, but I learned English pretty quick.'

Adriano looked curious now. 'I thought you enunciated'—he spelled the word slowly for Noah—'differently. Not accent.'

Noah shrugged. 'It was bad when I was a kid, and I didn't know how to fight back, so I didn't. They thought I was a wimp.'

He braced himself for Adriano to laugh—or even smile a little—but he didn't. He heaved a sigh, and there was understanding all over his face. 'Kids are assholes.'

From behind them, someone burst into laughter, and Noah turned his head to see Birdie there. Birdie was the captain of the fire department, working under Fitz, and was one of the nicest people Noah had ever met, though he didn't know him well. He was always kind, though, when he came to pick up bagel orders. His smiles for Noah were soft, his voice easy like he didn't mind Noah was an anxious mess on Sunday morning. He ran a little blacksmith booth at the farmer's market, and on his display table he had an array of jewelry and sculptures that were strange but beautiful in a chaotic way.

Birdie looked a little sheepish at being caught, but he beckoned them over and leaned on his table as they approached. 'Kids *are* assholes.'

Adriano looked startled, then lifted his hands. 'You sign?'

'I'm CODA. Single Deaf mom,' Birdie supplied, and Noah startled because he hadn't known that. Of course, after refusing to leave his house after being dragged back when his bubbe got sick, he didn't know these people well at all. 'It's been a few years since she died, so I'm probably rusty.'

'You're fine,' Adriano insisted.

Noah felt a wave of ugly jealousy hit him for just a moment because Birdie was nothing like him. He was almost as large as Adriano, and gorgeous, and friendly. He had been the quiet one of his friend group, but he wasn't a shy mess like Noah.

No one was like Noah.

He was dragged out of his twisting anguish when Adriano tugged him closer. 'We're on a date.'

Birdie's eyes went wide, his lips turning up at the corners. Noah expected to see something mocking, but instead he saw genuine pleasure. 'That's amazing. You know ASL?'

Noah nodded. 'I took it in college. Three and a half semesters.'

'Four got to be too much?' Birdie teased, and it didn't mean to land hard. It was obvious by the look on his face he was treating Noah like he would anyone else.

But it just landed wrong, and he winced.

Adriano shook his head. 'We have to go. It was nice to meet you.'

Adriano turned his back, taking Noah with him, and he heard Birdie's apologetic voice call after them, "It was good to see you, Noah. I hope you come by next week."

Noah didn't turn around. He didn't even look up from his

shoes until Adriano sat him on a bench, and he realized they were at the outskirts of the market. They hadn't even seen anything before he had to be rescued, not even from the crowd but from a single, friendly man. He curled his hands into fists and squeezed, wanting to feel the pain.

His breathing was a little labored, and he didn't calm until Adriano pressed strong thumbs into the strained tendons of his wrist. When his hands uncurled, Adriano swung his leg over to straddle the bench, and he waited for Noah to look up.

'When your grandmother died, you knew you weren't ever going back.' It wasn't a question, but he could see Adriano's concern.

'I probably could have taken Adam with me and shut down the bakery,' Noah admitted. 'Finished school then. But I didn't even know what I wanted to do. I was one semester away from graduating, then I got that phone call, and...' Noah's hands dropped for a second, and he swallowed back tears he hadn't cried in so long. 'After that, I just didn't want to do anything except get by and keep Adam from spiraling out of control. He was so angry at me for leaving him.'

Adriano cocked his head to the side. 'He loves you now.'

Noah couldn't help a bitter laugh and shook his head. 'Mostly. He resents me a little bit too. We spent the last few years on opposite sides. He thinks I'm too rigid in my beliefs.'

With a soft grin, Adriano reached out and traced the edge of his jaw. 'You feel soft to me.'

Noah choked back a sob. He wanted to lean in and lose himself in the strong arms of the man who seemed to want him in spite of all the ways he was a disaster, but he couldn't let himself. Not yet. Maybe not ever. 'Losing my dad was hard, but he was in the military, and he was gone a lot. My mom lost herself to grief when he died, and I think...' He glanced away and rubbed at the scar on his chest. He didn't remember when during the accident he'd gotten it. He didn't remember feeling pain until days after he left the hospital. He had seventy-three stitches there, and he remembered every eternal minute it took to pull them out. 'My mom's car crash was ruled an accident, but I don't know if I believe that. Sometimes I wonder if it was on purpose. It was a miracle I survived, but I think Adam blames me for living when she didn't.'

Adriano's face fell. 'That's probably not true.'

Noah gave a small shrug. In truth, it didn't matter. 'I was anxious, and my grandmother didn't know how to deal with it, so she just…hovered. Adam resented me for that. I think he believes things with my mom were better than they were, but…she couldn't stand him.'

Adriano's eyes widened. 'When he was a *baby*?'

'He looks exactly like my dad,' Noah told him with a tense smile. 'She couldn't look at him. So I took care of him when my bubbe was working. But I had nightmares all the time of her dying, of him dying. Of being left all alone in this place to rot.' He closed his eyes and breathed out. 'After my bubbe died, I made a bargain with Hashem. I would live as strict of an orthodox life as I could manage, and He would keep Adam safe.'

'Noah…' Adriano spelled his name in slow, careful letters.

'I know. It's stupid. I know that's not how it works. I know that Hashem probably laughed in my face when I tried to make a deal with Him. But I was too afraid to go back on it. And Adam felt like I would have lost it on him if he told me about how he'd lost his faith. And he was probably right. I'm not great with people, not even my own brother, and I didn't know how to live outside of my strict rules for so long.'

'But you're not like that now,' Adriano pointed out.

Noah bit his lip, then shrugged. 'I'm trying to find the path that works for me. The path that isn't a bargain or me living in abject fear that one wrong move and my brother will die. But I think it made me a difficult person.'

'Maybe a little difficult but not unkind.'

'No,' Noah agreed, 'but I'm hard to love. My entire life, everyone has made that very clear.'

Adriano cocked his head to the side. 'I don't agree with that either.'

Noah tried not to laugh. 'You don't know me well enough yet.'

'Well, I'm here, and I'm willing to give it time.'

Noah bowed his head for a second and took in a shuddering breath before looking up. 'You deserve better than the mess my life is. I still don't know what I want out of life, and my business is falling apart. I don't know what I'd do with myself if it went under, but I don't know that I have the passion or the want to keep going.'

'Could you…give it to Adam?' Adriano offered.

Noah shook his head. 'It's too far in the hole even for him to save, and not enough people want what we sell. There's way too much competition. Besides, Adam wants something of his own, even if he thinks he wants Bubbe's. He needs to be himself—new and trendy and bright. He's the lightning in a storm, and he needs to be bigger than this sky.'

Adriano bit his lip. 'Maybe…'

Noah touched his wrist. 'No. Even if I can pull myself out of this debt, the bakery has been losing money for years. It's just…time. The city outgrew it.'

Adriano bowed his head. 'I'm sorry. I wish I could help.' He reached for Noah then, but Noah rose, stepping out of his grasp.

He was letting loose now, letting it all come out, and he wasn't going to stop there. 'Sorry,' he said when Adriano looked almost hurt. 'I'm sorry. Just…There's more.'

Adriano blinked, then nodded. 'Okay.'

'I like you,' he said, and he both loved and hated the way

Adriano's bright smile could make his stomach swoop, could make him feel like he was hovering inches above the ground. 'But there's stuff you don't know about me. About who I am that might be too messy for you to want to deal with.'

Adriano laughed at that, loud and unexpected. 'Noah, my boyfriend of almost fifteen years has been fucking my agent, and now my *ex*-agent is trying to force me into paying his usual percentage for any film I do for the next three years. And my lawyer thinks he might have a case. It can't possibly be worse than the mess I'm in right now.'

Noah blinked at him. 'Oh, no.'

Adriano nodded miserably. 'I wasn't in love with my ex when he left me. I was angry that he lied, angry that he put me at risk, angry that I lost my interpreter because of him. But I haven't loved him for years.'

Noah took in a breath. 'You deserve better.'

'Yes,' Adriano signed firmly. 'Yes, I do. And I like you.'

Noah shook his head and took a step back. 'You don't know what I have to say.'

Standing, Adriano tried to close the distance between them, but Noah was worked up now, and he knew if Adriano touched him, that would be it, and that's not how he wanted Adriano to find out he was a walking disaster virgin who couldn't hold his come.

'Wait,' he begged, and Adriano stopped. 'Last night,' his fingers shook, and he had to stop for a second. 'Last night, when you kissed me…that was my first kiss.'

Adriano's hands hovered in the air between them. 'With a man?'

Noah bit his lip almost hard enough to draw blood and shook his head.

Eyes going wide, Adriano's fingers almost shook when he asked, 'First kiss ever?'

Noah nodded, feeling his stomach sink at the way Adriano's expression shuttered, going impossible to read. 'Ever.

I've never kissed anyone, never touched anyone. I'm a virgin, and when you kissed me, I came in my jeans. I'm a sad, sorry, pathetic…'

He didn't get to finish the rest of his sentence. Adriano was on him, taking him by the wrist, by the mouth. Noah's back was against the wall of the building, and his entire existence came down to the points where Adriano held him—by the hands, a thigh between his legs pressing against his groin, a tongue sliding along his.

"Mine," he rumbled against Noah's lips. "Mine."

Noah groaned, arching into Adriano's grasp, but he couldn't speak for lack of air in his lungs.

He let out a rough moan when Adriano pulled back, but before he could chase the kiss, he heard a deep, rumbling voice in his ear. "Noah. Come. *Now.*"

And he did.

CHAPTER 9

ADRIANO FELT NOAH, felt the way the orgasm ripped out of him. Noah hunched into Adriano's grasp and shuddered all over, and Adriano held fast. He used the size of his body to block Noah so no one would see. At best, they'd think their make-out session was hot and heavy. No one would know Noah had just given Adriano this gift.

And that's exactly what it felt like—a gift. The fact that Adriano could coax orgasms out of Noah just like this with the bare taste of his lips, the stroke of his hands, the command of his voice. It was more power than he felt like he deserved, but he didn't want to let go. He felt wild and possessive.

As he felt Noah starting to come down, Adriano took hold of his chin and tipped his head up. Noah's eyes were squeezed shut, so Adriano nudged at his lips with his own, pressing soft, chaste kisses until the tension in Noah's shoulders began to unwind.

He didn't tell Noah in words but with touch that he adored every second of what they had just shared. Time ticked by, Noah held tight to his arms, and neither of them moved.

"Noah," Adriano said eventually, and he felt the other man stiffen, felt him start to pull away.

Adriano allowed for just enough space between them that he could move his hands freely, and he waited for Noah to open his eyes and straighten back up on his own two legs.

'I'm sorry,' Noah began, but Adriano shook his head firmly.

'I wanted that.'

Noah let out a small scoff, his mouth grimacing with it. 'You don't understand. It's more than just the kiss.'

Adriano squared his shoulders. 'Okay. Tell me. Tell me all of it.'

Noah's fingers had a slight tremble to them, but he did. 'I don't touch myself. Ever. I've had an orgasm but never because I got myself off. I'm a virgin in almost every way it's possible to be a virgin, and I'm so wound up. Hell, I can't even kiss you without losing it. It's pathetic.'

Adriano's eyes narrowed. 'It's not pathetic.'

'It's embarrassing.' Noah looked like he wanted to turn his head away, but he had also learned enough about Adriano's language to know he couldn't—or shouldn't.

'I like it,' Adriano reiterated, and he took another step back. 'I like you.'

Noah's face scrunched up like he wanted to argue, but he didn't seem to have the strength for it. He looked exhausted and wrung out, and Adriano knew walking around with come in his boxers wasn't comfortable.

'Do you want to come back to my place with me?'

Noah blanched and shook his head. 'I don't know if I should. I have to be up so early.'

'I can wake you,' Adriano pointed out, but his assurances didn't seem to matter. Noah still looked utterly and completely panicked. 'Home, then. Your home,' he clarified. 'But I'd like to stay with you for a little while.'

Noah glanced to his right, then nodded. He started to pull

away from the building, but Adriano saw the way his legs wobbled, so he slung an arm around his waist and bore some of his weight. Neither of them said anything. Noah just let Adriano help him, and they headed back the way they'd come.

The walk to the bakery wasn't far, and Adriano waited patiently behind his new lover as Noah got the door open and began to ascend the stairs. It was dark, save for a faded bulb at the very top, and everything smelled like bread. He was reminded that Noah still had work to do, that Noah had put off work for him.

Noah was exhausted and had lost sleep just to eat pizza and share a small kiss at the door. If Adriano thought Noah would regret this—regret him—he would have walked away. But he didn't believe that. He followed close behind, and he let his hand rest at the small of Noah's back as they entered the apartment.

'Make yourself comfortable,' Noah told him, then grimaced as he pulled at the crotch of his jeans. 'I'll be right back.'

Adriano wanted to follow him, to touch him more, to see how worked up he could get the other man. He wanted to see if he could drag it out and delay the inevitable, but he also knew Noah needed to process. Right now, they were friends. They had kissed, Noah had come twice, and there was nothing between them that meant anything. No promises, no vows.

Adriano hadn't felt this way about Eric when they'd first met. He'd been thrilled to have an interpreter who'd work on a porn set, and he'd been happy Eric didn't seem judgmental. He liked that Eric was okay with his work and didn't try to get him to quit.

He hadn't realized the price for all that.

And he certainly had never been so smitten.

Flopping onto the sofa, he kicked one foot up, then pulled out his phone to send Liam a text, checking on Jude.

> Adriano: Won't be all night. I hope Jude is behaving. Will pay overtime.

> Liam: Better than the humans in town.

Adriano chuckled, then set his phone to the side and startled when he felt the cushion to his right move. He glanced over to see the cat getting comfortable near his thigh. Pets either loved or hated him, and he had to admit it gave him a small thrill to know Noah's fur baby had accepted his presence.

He shuffled downward and patted his chest, and the cat quickly made himself comfortable on the broad expanse between his pecs. He dug his fingers into the cat's fur and felt the heavy vibrations of his purr. It was soothing and comforting in a way he hadn't expected, and he felt himself drifting just a little bit until Noah appeared in his line of sight.

He had changed out of his date clothes, now in lounge pants and a t-shirt. His hair was fluffy and disordered, and his cheeks still carried a faint blush as he worried his bottom lip between his teeth like he didn't know what to say.

Adriano took pity on him and tapped the cushion the cat had abandoned. Noah stared for just a moment—just long enough for Adriano to feel a prickle of fear that Noah might ask him to leave—before he crossed the room and settled down.

He was close but not close enough, though Adriano didn't want to push it. 'He's sweet.'

Noah frowned, shaking his head, but there was amusement in his eyes. 'He'd sell me out for five ear scratches and a can of tuna.'

Adriano laughed, probably too loud because Marshmallow stood up—claws deployed—and launched himself to the ground. He grunted under the stabbing claws but let out a breath of relief when Noah's hand brushed down his shirt.

'Sorry. He's also petty.'

Adriano laughed again but softer this time, and he closed his fingers around Noah's wrist, locking their gazes. He didn't want to let go—not now, not ever. He wanted to lean in and kiss Noah again, wanted to pin him to the sofa and exist with him there and nowhere else ever again.

Reality was cruel, though, and crept around the edges of his fantasy.

'I'm sorry if I made you uncomfortable,' he finally signed, letting go of Noah's arm.

Noah shrugged. 'You didn't. It was me.' Adriano lifted a brow, and Noah pulled a face. 'I don't want to be like this. I want to be normal. I'm not…I didn't stay a virgin on purpose. I was just too anxious, and like I said before, I'm not an easy person to be around.'

Adriano wanted to go back into Noah's past and put a fist into the face of every man who had ever made him feel inadequate. Adriano knew too well what it was like, had seen the mocking way kids had moved their mouths in mimicry of his Deaf accent, the way they fluttered their hands into nonsense shapes to make fun of his signs.

But he didn't believe his choices made him stronger than Noah. They were just different people. It was obvious Noah had a quiet, unassuming strength about him, and Adriano was falling for that. Hard.

'Tell me how I can help you,' Adriano said.

Noah flushed deeper. 'With my…' He gestured to his crotch, and Adriano chuckled.

'I meant your life. The bakery, what's going to happen after. Though, if you want help with that too…' He crept his hand up Noah's thigh until Noah pushed it off with a laugh.

'There's nothing to be done about my shop. When Adam

moved out and started to work with his girlfriend, I knew it was the beginning of the end. We have a couple contracts with some of the restaurants here, but we're still taking a loss every month. I haven't told Adam. I don't want him to think everything he worked toward was for nothing.'

Adriano bit his lip. 'He's going to be angry.'

'Yes.' Noah's fist nodded and his face showed nothing but resignation. 'Maybe. He's got Talia now, and their future. But there's nothing I can do to change things. All I want is to know I can get out from under this loan and close the shop without having to sell everything I own and live in my car.'

Adriano would have turned over every cent in his savings right then—or at least most of it. But he knew men like Noah. 'You could make porn.'

Noah's eyes widened, and the blush spread to his ears and throat. 'You can't be serious. I can't even kiss you without coming!'

"*Bah!*" Adriano waved him off. He'd meant it as a joke, just something to lighten the mood, but it occurred to him that's how he'd gotten started. A random frat boy at a college party said gay porn made good money. At that point, Adriano was broke and more than happy to try getting off for a little cash. Adriano started out in amateur videos, but it wasn't long before people took notice, and suddenly he'd become Sylent.

Adriano had been doing this a long time now, and he damn well knew people would pay to watch Noah get off, to come all over himself without being touched. For a brief, furious second, he pictured another man touching Noah, and he felt his entire body grow hot as fire with possession and jealousy. He didn't want anyone touching Noah other than himself, and he didn't care that his job made him a hypocrite.

'Wait,' he signed, and Noah stared at him. 'Make a video with me.'

Noah blinked. 'With you?'

'There are amateur sites all over the internet. We could

film here. People would pay a ton of cash to watch you come just from being kissed.'

Noah's blush was so deep he almost looked tan. 'I can't.'

Adriano held up his hands in surrender. 'Okay. That's fine. It is. I'd never push you into doing something you find wrong.'

Noah's eyes went wide, and he shook his head. 'No. No. I don't think porn is wrong. I...I've been your fan since'—he glanced away and looked vaguely embarrassed before looking back and giving Adriano a stern frown—'for a long time. I don't think what you do is wrong. I just don't think anyone wants to watch someone like me. I mean, look at me.'

Adriano felt heat creep into his eyes. 'I am. I want to watch you fall apart under my hands.'

Noah's swallow was thick enough that Adriano saw it stick. 'Why?'

Unable to stop himself, Adriano traced just beneath Noah's lower lip, watching the way his mouth opened to let breath escape. He felt it, hot and humid, against the pads of his fingers. 'You're beautiful.' Noah lifted his hands to protest, but Adriano wouldn't let him. 'You *are* beautiful. And you deserve to be worshipped.'

He wasn't sure if that was blasphemy to Noah. His family was staunchly Catholic, but Adriano had never put much stock in religion, and he didn't understand a lot of Noah's. But it was hard to care when he wanted him this much.

'What would...what would the videos be like?' Noah finally asked. There was a faint tremble in his fingers, but he held unexpected determination in his eyes.

Adriano didn't need to think about what they'd be like. He knew. He'd been fantasizing since the night he left Noah, come in his pants, standing in his doorway. 'I'd lay you down and strip you slowly. I'd kiss your neck and nowhere else until you let go.'

Noah shuddered. 'Just that?'

Adriano shook his head. He ached to put his hands on Noah again, but he refrained. 'I'd touch you. I'd drag fingertips up and down your thighs until you couldn't hold it in. Maybe in another, I wouldn't touch you at all. Maybe I'd just speak to you.'

Noah's head fell back, and his lips were parted as he took several breaths. 'I'm close.'

'I know,' Adriano said when Noah opened his eyes again. And he did. It had only happened twice, but he already recognized the signs in Noah's body. 'I can stop.'

Noah looked him directly in the eyes, then shook his head. 'Don't.'

Licking his lips, Adriano shifted closer. 'Maybe I'd teach you restraint. Maybe I'd get you worked up and get you coming over and over until you can't anymore.'

Noah's eyes were nearly all pupil now. 'Is that all?'

Adriano's hand landed on his thigh and squeezed just for a brief moment. 'No. For the last one, you would fuck me.'

And with his lips parted on a cry, Adriano watched Noah let go once more.

CHAPTER 10

Noah wasn't consciously aware of where he was going, only that he had to get away. His apartment felt like it was closing in on him. Adriano's offer, and his kisses, and the heat of his hands felt both erotic and terrifying, and he didn't know what the fuck to say.

So many things warred inside his head that he started to lose grip on reality. He had a mountain of work waiting for him in the bakery kitchen, and for the first time since before he left for college, he didn't care. He found himself winding through the dirt path that led to a massive, open stretch of land on Tybee Island. He knew where Will, Isaac, and Liam lived. He just hadn't ever been out there.

Will had given him a half dozen invites out to their place since he'd started coming into Bubbe's to visit with Noah, but Noah had never taken him up on it. Even now, he felt waves of guilt that he was there to unburden himself rather than to visit a friend, but he knew Will was the sort of person who wouldn't mind, even if it was late.

Noah had tried the market first. After Adriano left, he'd tried to clear his head with a long walk, but Will's booth looked like it had been closed up for a while, and Noah eventually gave in to his urge to just...go.

Now he pulled into the drive and saw a light on in the front room and prayed he wasn't interrupting anything. His palms were sweaty with anxiety as he made his way up the steps. They creaked, but in the sort of brand-new, house settling way since the place had only finished being put together over the last two months. Noah had sent over a massive basket of welcome goodies when they had their house-warming party, and he regretted not showing up, but it had been a Friday night.

Will always forgave him, but Noah knew he couldn't blame Shabbat for everything.

With a breath, he rang the buzzer, then waited. Only a minute passed before the door opened, and Liam's face peeked out, his face dropping into a startled smile as he realized who was standing on his porch.

"Noah? Hey."

Noah offered a sheepish smile. "Is Will home?"

Liam chuckled, shaking his head as he swung the door wider. "Yes, he is. Do you want to come in?"

"I," Noah started, but Will appeared just then, setting a hand on Liam's shoulder.

"I've got this, cariad. You look like you could do with a walk. I need to check the paddock gates anyway. Want to come with?" Will's soft Welsh accent was soothing to Noah's frayed nerves, and he let out a grateful sigh as he nodded.

"Yes, thanks. Sorry, Liam. I'm...I don't mean to be rude."

Liam waved him off. "It's fine. You boys play nice."

Will leaned in and kissed his cheek, whispering something into Liam's ear that made him blush. Noah didn't ask, didn't want to know. He hated intruding, but he did like knowing that his one and only friend in Savannah was happy.

Will took off ahead of him, and though they had flood lights, he struggled to keep up in the dark. He heard the waves crashing gently on the shore in the distance, and he took in a deep breath of ocean air.

The paddock wasn't far, and Noah managed not to fall on his face as they reached the fence and two of the smaller kids came running up, excited for the attention.

"You alright, mate?" Will asked after a bit.

Noah loved how Will knew that he needed time to gather his thoughts. He'd never been impulsive, though right then was the closest he'd ever felt to it. "I think I'm seeing someone."

Will chuckled. "Deaf bloke, eh? The porn-star guy who's been visiting everyone's shops? Super tall. Super fit."

Noah was glad the dim light hid his blush. "His name is Adriano. Uh…you know who he is?"

Will turned to him, and Noah could just make out a frown on his face. "Isaac might have shown me a handful of his videos. Seems like he's quite famous."

Noah laughed with some relief. He knew that enough people were aware of who Adriano was and what he did, and it was nice to have a clean slate with Will. "Uh. Something like that." Noah stopped and cleared his throat. "Is there somewhere to sit?"

Will's face grew more concerned, but he reached down and flipped the latch on the paddock before beckoning him inside. They made their way to the barn before Will froze and narrowed his eyes at Noah. "You're not allergic are you? To goats or ducks?"

Noah laughed until he realized Will was serious. "No. No allergies."

"You sure? We had a bit of an issue a few weeks back with Isaac's mate. Got carted off to hospital, and I'm not looking for a repeat."

Noah reached out and squeezed Will's shoulder. "Just grass and pollen like the rest of the world, I promise."

Will seemed a bit dubious at first, but eventually swung the barn door open and led the way inside. It smelled of animal and hay, and though it was probably offensive to some, Noah found it oddly comforting. It was warm in there, and a bit humid, and there were benches along the wall, which Will dragged out.

The goats were happy to bounce around their feet, but after a few pets, they got bored of Noah and hurried off as the pair took seats. "It's nice in here. Do farm animals like living at the beach?"

Will chuckled. "Goats adore it, and I think Florida has more beach chickens than the Midwest has farms. But I feel like you didn't come to talk about the sunbathing habits of farm fowl."

Noah laughed, but it was strained. "Yeah, no. My bakery is closing, and I think I'm freaking out."

Will blinked in surprise, then sat back. "For good?"

Biting the inside of his cheek, Noah fought back a fresh wave of grief and anxiety as he shook his head. "I think so. It's been hemorrhaging money for years. I was making ends meet—mostly—when I first took over, but each year just keeps getting worse. When Adam moved out and started the food truck, I realized we were dead in the water."

Will's brow dipped into a deep frown. "That's the thing with him and Talia, is it?"

"Yeah," Noah said quietly. "He's so happy, and I didn't want to rain on his parade, so I took a loan out to help with the shop, but I'm about to default on my first payment, and I don't want it to end like that."

Will swallowed. "Mate, I can lend you money. If you need…"

"No! I didn't come here to borrow money," Noah said a little harshly, though he didn't mean to. Dragging a hand down his face, he took a breath. "And it wouldn't help even if I had. One month, two months—even six more wouldn't matter. I can't keep this up. It was on the verge of failing when Bubbe got sick, and I didn't have the skill to resuscitate it. This was just borrowed time."

Will looked down at his feet. "I'm sorry, mate."

With a shrug, Noah leaned forward over his thighs and steeled himself for the rest. "Adriano had an idea. It's…I don't want to give you details. But it could work. Not to save the bakery, but to pay off the loan. It'll be enough that I can walk away and not worry."

"Is it illegal?" Will pressed.

Noah laughed and rolled his eyes up toward the ceiling. "No. It's not illegal, but it does…maybe cross some lines I'm not sure I'm ready to cross."

"Is it a religious thing?" Will asked.

At that, Noah's lip curled up in a half smile. "A bit? In all honesty, Judaism is so diverse it's impossible to say yes or no. It's not the same as other faiths. But I'm not sure I'm brave enough to talk to my rabbi about it."

"I get that," Will said with a smile.

"Anyway, my hesitation's more personal." Noah paused. "It's something I've been avoiding for years, and Adriano makes me want to branch out, and…I don't know, find freedom? Not be so damn strict with myself?"

"Is it because of him or because it's something you want for you?" Will asked.

Noah loved that about his friend, loved that he'd find the nuance in what Noah was struggling with. "Both. I want it for both reasons. I'm lonely."

Will made a soft noise and shifted a little closer. "You have people who love you, you know."

"I'm starting to accept that," Noah admitted softly, "and I'm trying."

Will set a hand on his shoulder. "I know."

Noah remained silent a long moment, trying to gather his thoughts. "I'm scared if I abandon everything I know, more things will fall apart. I'm scared Adam will get hurt by this and never speak to me again." He swallowed past a lump in his throat. "I don't think I could live with that. He's all I've got left."

"Noah…"

"I *know* it's irrational. I knew years ago when I was practically on my *knees* begging Hashem to keep Adam safe that it was irrational. But I've been doing this for so long now that I don't know how to stop." He only realized his hands were in fists when his knuckles began to ache, and he forced himself to uncurl his fingers. "I probably need a therapist. And…and I need to trust that Adam can take care of himself and that he'll understand the reason why this has to happen."

"He seems happy, and happy people don't cut their only living relatives out of their lives. And therapy is good. I had a good one after my divorce. I didn't go long, just enough time to get my head back on straight."

Noah glanced over and saw actual kindness in Will's eyes, not pity. "I'm afraid once Adriano knows what an actual mess I am, he'll end things. Which is a ridiculous thing to worry about. I mean, I barely know him."

Will laughed and shook his head, hanging his hands between his knees as he leaned forward and looked at Noah. "I fell in love over the span of three weeks, starting at my sister's wedding in Maryland."

Noah's eyes widened. He knew the way Will, Liam, and Isaac had fallen in love was unconventional, but he hadn't realized how unconventional. "Were they already together?"

Will laughed. "They were exes who were trying to find their way back to each other, and then they did. They burst into my life when I needed them the most. I was lost, I was divorced, I had buried my father a year before that. I had no idea what I wanted in life. All I had was a small nest egg in the bank and the desire to do something different with my life." Will smiled wistfully. "I didn't go on some backpacking trip to find myself, but in exchange, I got two men who I will love for the rest of my life."

"And a cat café," Noah offered.

Will laughed, shaking his head. "And the sodding cats. And a goose and our four bloody goats. And two men who love me back just as much as I love them. People will always tell you not to rush. They'll tell you to be careful, to take it right, that love at first sight doesn't exist. They'll tell you that there's a way to fall for someone, but they're not always right. Sometimes, mate, you really do know when you know."

Noah was warm all over, soft inside, and desperate for Adriano. Adriano had offered his hand, and Noah wanted to take it. More than just for filming, though he didn't know that he wanted to reject that idea either, but he needed more. He needed to know Adriano would be willing to give him that.

"This helped," Noah told him.

Will grinned widely. "Good."

"I should, um…" Noah nodded toward the door, and Will rose, following him out and not saying anything until they reached his car.

"Promise me you'll be back. For proper dinner," Will ordered, and Noah laughed.

"I will."

"No more hiding?" Will pressed.

Noah took Will's arm by the wrist and squeezed. "No more hiding. I'll bring Adriano."

"I'll look up some sign language videos," Will vowed. "The American sort. I know the British one, but I don't think that'll help."

Noah laughed. "No, and I think he'd appreciate that." He got into his car and started it, pulling onto the main road and heading back into town.

On the drive back, he didn't feel as awful. He had a few hours to sort this out, and he was ready.

He found parking in front of the café, a block from the address Adriano had sent him, locking up before he glanced down at his phone. He wasn't sure if he was breaking the rules or not, but he needed this to be a surprise. He didn't know if he was really brave enough to do it, but he needed to try. Adriano deserved someone who didn't hesitate.

It felt like an eternity before he was standing on the front porch of Adriano's rental. He could smell chlorine from somewhere, and he heard people talking a few houses down. He poised his fist to knock before he realized his mistake, then he pulled out his phone and opened his texts.

> Noah: I'm outside your door right now. I hope you're home.

A minute passed that felt like an eternity before the door swung wide, and Adriano was there, filling up all the spaces between them. His eyes were a little wary, a little nervous, but also a little hopeful. 'Are you okay?'

Noah bowed his head, breathed, then nodded. 'I'm good. I'm more than good. I like you, Adriano.'

Adriano's expression went soft. 'Yeah?'

'Yes. And...I think I want to take you up on your offer.'

Adriano beamed. 'Okay.'

Before Adriano could reach for him, Noah put up a hand. 'I do have some conditions. Deal breakers. Can we talk about them?'

Adriano stared, intense and captivating, then he put one hand at Noah's waist and pulled. Noah's feet moved without his permission, and the door slammed shut behind him like a benediction. It was over before he could even start to fight, and really, he didn't mind. Adriano's body was against him, eyes drinking him in like he hadn't seen Noah in years.

It was heady.

It was addicting.

Adriano leaned in, brushing a breath of a kiss to Noah's jaw, then he stepped back, just out of reach. His long, thick fingers rose, and he signed with absolute purpose, 'I'm ready to negotiate.'

CHAPTER 11

'AND WE CAN DO *this any way you want, but I'm glad you trust me. I'm glad you want to do this with me. It feels different with you. Better. Like...'*

"Noah!"

Noah snapped back to reality, back to the bakery, to the kitchen with a ball of dough in his hands that was supposed to be bread but was hard as a rock. He glanced behind him at Paxton who looked more confused than annoyed that Noah had been off in his own little world.

"Sorry, Paxton. You okay?" He swiped his hands on his apron, then grabbed the ball of dough and tossed it into the trash before turning to face his employee.

"There's someone here to see you," Paxton said, thumbing over his shoulder.

For a moment, Noah's heart leapt, though he knew it couldn't be Adriano. Or well, it shouldn't be. Noah hadn't stayed as long as he'd wanted at Adriano's place, but they'd parted with a plan. Adriano was going to spend the day in search of a place he could rent that wouldn't have the telltale signs of Noah's apartment, or the bakery, or somewhere on a public rental website. If Noah was going to do this—if he was going to be brave enough to take a step outside of his tiny bubble—he wanted at least a little anonymity. Even if it didn't last.

"Who is it?"

"Birdie. That fire department guy," Paxton said with a shrug. He glanced at the baking table and the pieces of dough Noah had separated. "You want me to take over here?"

Noah knew by the way Paxton's face fell that he hadn't hidden his grimace well enough. But his mind immediately went back to the last time he had let Paxton help and the wasted batches of cookies that had been little more than charred lumps of coal.

"Why don't you take lunch?" Noah moved to the sink to wash up, then glanced at the clock and breathed a sigh of relief to see it was almost noon. "I'll handle the front for a bit."

Paxton looked like he wanted to argue, but at the resolute set of Noah's jaw, he shrugged and untied his apron. "It's not busy anyway."

And when was it ever? Noah would wager Birdie wasn't coming in to buy anything. Apart from bread for the French restaurant and bagels for the firehouse, they only occasionally had trickle-in business. Tourist season, with the fall festival and the market opening, meant a few more customers than normal, but not enough.

And he'd seen a drop now that the Lofty Latke was parking in various spots around town. Not that Noah could blame the people for wanting Adam's bakes. They were better and more diverse. They were trendy—like brie and bacon croissants. They were everything Noah wasn't and didn't want to be.

Drying his hands, Noah finally walked out to find the blacksmith bent over the glass display. When the door creaked, Birdie straightened and rubbed the back of his neck, looking sheepish. "Hey." He looked good in his Chatham

County FD shirt and jeans, his hair tousled by the wind, cheeks a little pink.

Noah raised a brow. "Hi. Is there something I can help with? If you want anything that's not challah or almond cookies right now, you're gonna want to find Adam."

Birdie shook his head, even though he smiled at the mention. "No. I'm not here to buy anything."

Of course he wasn't. Noah followed where Birdie's eyes kept tracking—a row of almond crescent cookies—so he grabbed one and handed it over. "They're actually not bad," he insisted when Birdie hesitated.

He was quiet as Birdie took the offering, then smiled a little when the blacksmith let out a groan. "Those are amazing."

"Bubbe was go big or go home with flavor," Noah told him with a shrug. He leaned on the counter. "Is there something you wanted? If Fitz sent you about the market booth..."

At that, Birdie's face fell, and he shook his head. "No, that's not..." He stopped and let out a heavy breath. "I'm here to say sorry for being such a colossal dick at the market last night."

Noah blinked at him for a moment. He'd expected a lot of things—most of them involving some sort of favor or baking order—but an apology? "What are you talking about?"

"I upset you. What I said. I'm not sure why. I mean, I think I get it. Fitz mentioned how you came back after your grandma died. I figured that's why you had to come home, and I didn't mean to make a joke out of it."

Noah felt a fresh wave of grief in his belly, a low simmer, nothing like the overwhelming pain he felt when her death was fresh. But it was still a lot. He cleared his throat, then shrugged. "It's fine."

"It was *so* not fine. I know you never really liked me, but..."

Noah's head snapped up. "What are you talking about?"

Birdie laughed, rubbing the back of his neck again. "I know that I annoy the hell out of you when I do the bagel run. I tried to be your friend, but I mean…I'm loud and obnoxious, and I get why you'd hate me…"

Noah held up his hand. "That's not…I don't hate *you*. Everyone hates *me*."

Birdie's shy smile dropped into a frown. "Uh, literally no one hates you, Noah. Ronan and Fitz talk about you sometimes. I think they worry." He trailed off with a sigh, shrugging. "I know they gave you a hard time when you were kids."

"It doesn't matter," Noah answered softly.

Birdie laid a hand on the counter. His fingers were thick, not as big as Adriano's but close. His skin was marred with scars like someone had taken molten metal at the end of a brush and flicked it over him. But it fit. It suited him in a way Noah couldn't explain. "It obviously mattered when you came back to town and locked yourself in your apartment. I just thought you were…I don't know…antisocial."

Noah couldn't help his laugh. "I *am*. I'm a socially anxious mess."

Trying for a half smile, Birdie shrugged. "Well, that's kind of our fault, isn't it?"

"No," Noah said, and he couldn't help the hint of bitterness in his voice. "It's my dad's fault for dying and my mom's for dragging me here and dumping all her grief on me, then *also* dying. And my bubbe's for not trying harder to help me fit in when I needed to." He shrugged. "And it's my own fault for not getting help when I was older and locking myself away instead of dealing with my problems. None of you made me like this."

Birdie's eyes were soft, sympathetic, and maybe full of a little pity, but Noah felt like maybe he deserved that. He was pathetic after all. "I'd like to be friends."

Noah bit his lip, then nodded and extended his hand.

"Friends is...good. I think I can do that. Just don't get your hopes up for me being any good at it."

For all the work he did with his hands, Birdie's palm was surprisingly soft and cool. "Just be you, man."

Noah withdrew and dragged a hand through his hair. "I accept your apology. I also need to get back to work since I close at four today."

"For a date?" Birdie pressed.

Noah felt his entire body go hot. "No." Which wasn't entirely the truth. He would be keeping the Shabbat, but he wouldn't be doing it alone tonight. He just wasn't ready to share that with anyone, not even a new, self-professed friend. "Not a date. But, um...thanks for signing with Adriano. He says it's fine when people don't, but I know having someone use ASL helps."

Birdie shrugged. "My skills aren't what they should be, but I'm happy to practice. Maybe we can all get together for drinks or something."

"I'll ask him," was the most Noah was willing to concede right then.

He had a lot to think about, not just the videos with Adriano but everything Will had said. How it was okay to just know when someone was right for you. How it was okay to not be...normal the way everyone else was. How therapy wouldn't be the worst thing in the world. How being a little bit broken didn't mean he wasn't worth loving.

When Birdie was gone, Noah contemplated just giving up, locking up shop and going upstairs to wait for Adriano to get back. But he glanced behind him then, at the photo of Bubbe smiling between him and Adam when they weren't quite old enough to understand what this bakery might mean to them one day, and he knew. He knew it was coming to a close, and he accepted that, but he wasn't ready to hit the end on their legacy just yet.

CHAPTER 12

Of all the things Adriano thought he'd be doing when he got to Savannah, none of them involved perusing private luxury rentals so he could film a series of amateur porn videos where he made his little baker lover come without touching his dick. And Adriano had also started to believe that nothing could get him really and truly worked up again. A person, yes. He had been wildly attracted to Eric on and off during their relationship. The softest, quietest, most vanilla sex between them had often been the most erotic sex he'd experienced.

But this thing with Noah? It was both. It was everything. Knowing that he could get Noah off with a few quiet words and the drag of fingertips along his neck made him wild with power and want, but he acknowledged the voice deep inside him that told him he wouldn't feel this way if it had been anyone else but Noah.

In truth, he could lay Noah out and fuck him missionary style, and he'd still be out of his mind with desire. He could lay him out, strip him down, and tie him up before fucking his throat with long strokes, and he'd get off just as hard as if

Noah was on all fours, doing little more than spreading his thighs for Adriano.

It was the man. It was the man with his curls, paint-splatter freckles, soft belly, and slightly crooked smile. It was the man who didn't like himself much but wanted to, and Adriano knew he wouldn't rest until Noah freed himself from the belief that he wasn't worth any of this.

Adriano would burn his life to the ground if it meant keeping Noah in it, and he had never felt like that before. Not even with Eric, not for a single moment they had been together. Adriano had once thought about marrying Eric. He had thought about just making it official and choosing to spend the rest of his life with that man, but that seemed such an absurd, far-off idea now.

He almost wanted to send Xander a thank you note for being the piece of shit who had been sneaking around with Eric behind his back.

It was with that smile he walked into the lawyer's office, which sat next to the newspaper, and offered over a handwritten note and a blank check.

I'd like to make an appointment and pay for a retainer in order to draw up a contract.

The secretary looked like she was a hundred years old. Her arthritis-bent fingers took the note, eyes squinting behind her bifocals. Her lips moved, and he knew she was speaking, so he waved at her to get her attention, then signed, 'I'm deaf.'

It was not necessarily a universal sign, but even a person with almost no ASL usually got the gist. She stared at him a long second, then started to speak again.

"I'm *deaf*," he said aloud.

Her brows furrowed, and her finger pointed toward the

door, lips flapping. He had a feeling she was dismissing him, and his anger started to rise before the door behind her desk opened and a man walked out. He looked a lot younger than Adriano, maybe late twenties, and a little nervous and harried. His hair was light brown, skin pale, fingers soft when he extended his hand, and Adriano took it.

The man said something that looked like, "Right this way," and the beckoning gesture was enough for him to trust it.

He passed the old lady and moved into the office, finding it cozy and warm with mahogany furniture and leather sitting chairs. The man gestured to them, and Adriano got situated while he moved behind the desk, then pulled out a yellow legal pad and began to write.

Do you have an interpreter?

Adriano didn't really expect the sharp twinge in his chest at the loss—not of Eric but of communication. Of how Eric ruined everything, of his own part for not following his own damn rules about relationships with his interpreters.

No. I'm not a resident in town. I'm staying at a rental. I need help with a contract, though.

The man's eyes scanned the note, then he wrote again. *My name is Joe Garcia, and I'm familiar with some contracts, but I'm a family attorney.*

Adriano knew that. He'd looked the office up online—the best rated one within a fifty-mile radius. He knew it was a crapshoot, but he had to try. *I'm aware of that. The contract is simple. I need something to ensure that a video that will go up for sale will be the sole financial property of my co-star.*

Adriano hadn't written *porn*, but he saw when the meaning of *video* hit Joe Garcia. A faint sheen of sweat broke out on his brow, and he licked his lips three times before he wrote again. *I don't know how well it would hold up in court.*

It will be enough for now. It's for his peace of mind. I have a personal attorney, and he can sort out something more permanent later.

Joe drummed his fingers on the desk, and Adriano absently touched the wood to feel the rhythm of it. *Okay. Can you come back at three? I'll need legal names, the name of the company that will release the video, and the basic terms of the contract.*

Adriano didn't know why this gave him such a thrill, but he could guess. This would make money. This would make Noah a lot of money, even before other people realized it was Sylent who was starring opposite him. Viewers lapped stuff like this up like it was his actual come. But apart from that, apart from knowing it would pull Noah out of debt and give him something to lean on when his bakery closed, it was also a fuck-you to Xander and Eric. It was double middle fingers to the way they tried to cuckhold him and corner him and take away his ability to do anything without giving over pieces of his work.

As long as he wasn't getting paid—and he didn't *need* to be paid—they couldn't touch him. In these videos, he wouldn't be Sylent. He would be Adriano Moretti. He would be lying with his boyfriend, faces obscured, and his hands would get him off. Over. And over. And over.

Until Noah was free.

The pen flew across the page, and Adriano eventually had it all down. He watched Joe's eyes move over the names, and when they didn't flare with any sort of recognition or judgment—at least no more than a normal small-town prude's would—he felt safe that Noah's reputation wasn't being completely tarnished.

"Do you need anything else?" he asked.

Joe jumped at the sound of his voice, and Adriano tried not to scowl as he watched him write again. *This should be enough. Leave your number and I can call you when it's ready.*

Adriano read the words, then lifted a brow as he tapped on the word *call.*

With a flush, Joe scribbled it out. *Text. Sorry. I'll text.*

Adriano nodded, shook his hand, then got the amount for the meeting and the services, scribbling the number on the check before passing it over. Joe took it and slipped it into his drawer, then showed Adriano to the door.

He was annoyed Joe hadn't apologized for his secretary, but he was walking on air that things were happening. He felt like a kid again, like a student exploring the dark edges of himself he hadn't realized were there. But this time, instead of freedom from expectation and family, he was touching the freedom to love. Real and true love, not the bullshit, superficial obligation that had come with Eric.

And God, it was fucking beautiful.

ONCE HE WAS DONE with the lawyer, it took Adriano only a short while to find a place to rent after he'd gotten someone to reply to his email inquiries. He found several rentals listed, and the one he'd chosen was an eighteenth-century European cottage with a thatched roof and picket fence. It smelled a little stale, and there was a draft coming from somewhere in the house he couldn't identify, but it was far enough from the historic district that if he wanted to make Noah scream, he wouldn't have to worry about complaints to the owner or calls to the police.

There were three bedrooms, and they were all very nondescript—a typical bed-and-breakfast-style layout with a poster bed and floral covers. He liked that there were no stairs, and he liked that there was a swing on the back porch, which they could use in the mornings if Noah truly wanted to stay with him for more than just their arrangement.

Jude nipped at his heels as the realtor started reading over the documents, so Adriano motioned that he was heading outside, and he unclipped his baby and let him run off into a short grove of trees to finish his business. The sun was low in the sky—closer to dusk than not—and Noah would be expecting him soon.

Checking his watch, Adriano waited for Jack Garcia—ironically enough the brother of the lawyer who was helping him with the contract—to get the rental agreement sorted out. Adriano paid with his credit card, and he knew his accountant would eventually take notice, but so far, he'd done well in avoiding messages except from his lawyer, which had so far amounted to nothing.

He knew the situation would come to a head, but he also knew if he was forced to take this to litigation, he'd be tied up for months. He would deal with it—happily—if it meant spending more time with Noah. They had so much to learn about each other, and he was looking forward to it for the first time in…maybe ever. And that was a blow.

Adriano was due to spend the night over at Noah's. He didn't entirely understand the whole Shabbat thing, though he'd spent an hour on his phone looking up the rituals, and it seemed needlessly complicated. The last religious thing he'd ever participated in was his cousin's baptism, which had been an eternally long mass, then a garden party at his aunt's, which went late into the night. It had devolved from tea and watercress sandwiches to his mom throwing together pasta and everyone drinking out his uncle's wine cellar.

Apart from the big holidays, weddings, and confirmations, his family didn't do much in the way of God or belief. The idea that Noah was so dedicated to his faith, that he lived every day in constant adherence to it—at least as much as he could—was fascinating. It was also a little bit sexy, Adriano thought. Noah was nervous, and he was anxious, but beneath that was an underlying current of intense passion.

It ripped through him at any given moment, at any brush

of Adriano's hands or whisper of his voice. And as much as Adriano wanted to believe it was all him—and he would take credit for some—he knew so much of it was just Noah. It was just the pieces of him he'd been neglecting for so long that still existed. Those pieces were clawing their way out now, though, and Adriano was overwhelmed by the beauty of it. Watching Noah fall apart, and more than that, watching him give in to the freedom of losing control... There were no words to describe it in either of his languages.

Jude came trotting back after a moment, and Adriano lifted him to his face, rubbing his nose through soft fur. He felt the pup's chest vibrate with his little bark and pulled back for a few kisses. He knew he was a bit of a diva, knew he was a spoiled pain-in-the-ass, sort-of-rich actor with his pocket dog and sports car. He had never been ashamed of it, but now he felt like maybe he was something a little more. He'd be seeing his lover soon—his *lover*—and God how that thrilled him.

When Adriano and Jude walked back in, Jack was finished with the lease agreement and tucked the check away in his pocket before handing off the keys. Adriano had a feeling once Jack had looked him up, he hadn't bothered with his references. Or, if he had, it was simply to say he was able to speak to a few of the top adult-film stars in the industry. Adriano would unashamedly use whatever he could to get his way. He wanted this for Noah. This wasn't just for himself.

Tucking the key for the lock of their new sanctuary into his pocket, Adriano got into the car and shot Noah a text, letting him know he was on his way. He'd been instructed to bring dinner—something that didn't mix dairy or meat and no pork. That was easier said than done when his first instinct was a creamy carbonara or even a pizza. But there was an Israeli restaurant on the outskirts of town that had a kosher claim on their website, and he loaded up on shawarma and falafel and couscous.

The spices infiltrated his car, and Jude looked far too interested but rode obediently on the edge of the passenger seat, only perking up when Adriano pulled into the spot near Noah's car and turned the engine off. He probably had too much with him, but for now he grabbed the food, the dog, and Jude's little suitcase with all his things.

> Noah: It's sunset, and I've already lit the candles. Go ahead and let yourself in.

Adriano, after all his study, had some idea what this meant. It meant Noah wouldn't do a lot of things for himself, nothing that was considered work. It meant Adriano could now exist in his space, and take care of him, and fill the places Noah had left vacant until sunset tomorrow.

He hitched Jude up close to his chest, balancing the rest in one hand, then ascended the stairs and went inside. It was dimly lit, the only light from the kitchen and from two candles burning on the table. Noah was on the sofa, and he was smiling at the sight of Adriano, though he didn't get up.

'You can turn the lights on if you want,' Noah told him.

Adriano set Jude down, and he hurried over for some love. His heart went soft as Noah picked up the dog and cuddled him close. 'It's romantic like this.'

He saw Noah laugh as Adriano eased down next to him and set the food on the table. 'It isn't supposed to be romantic. I always forget to turn enough lights on.' Noah eased back, not in a hurry to eat, which was fine. Adriano wasn't ready yet. He just wanted to bask in Noah's presence for a while. 'When Adam was younger, he used to turn all the lights off when he was angry at me.'

Adriano's brow furrowed. 'That's cruel.'

Noah shrugged. 'He was a kid, and I was hard on him about not practicing.'

Shaking his head, Adriano turned more toward him. 'Taking advantage of your…I don't know what you call it. Dedication?'

'Observance,' Noah spelled.

Adriano nodded. 'You can't turn the lights back on. It's cruel.'

Noah's face fell a little, the light in his eyes dimming. Adriano could tell he was approaching a line if not crossing it. 'Adam could be mean. He spent his whole life knowing he missed out on what I had: memories of our mother and attention from our grandmother. I don't think he knew what it cost me, and I didn't know enough to communicate that to him.'

Adriano watched Noah's face as he signed, the way he half moved his lips around some words, the way he fumbled and spelled a lot but made it so easy for Adriano to just understand him. 'Did you ever tell him?'

Noah shook his head. 'I didn't want to ruin what he knew, what he thought he knew. My mother was not well, and she was not kind. She hated Adam because he looked like my dad, but she hated me more because I wasn't enough to make the pain go away. She'd go out and get drunk, then spend hours telling me how terrible her life was here. I wanted to fix it for her so badly. I wanted to make the pain stop, but I think she wanted to die miserable.'

Adriano reached over and cupped Noah's cheek, brushing his thumb over cool skin. Noah turned his head and kissed Adriano's fingers. 'You deserved better.'

'Adam and I both did. Bubbe didn't know what to do with me, so she just…She fed me and comforted me. She tried to soothe my worries by sheltering me. That just made it worse. I felt normal in college for a little while, but…' Noah's fingers hovered halfway through the sign, then dropped.

Adriano felt his heart twist. He wanted to shake Noah's brother a little bit and force him to look beyond his own nose and his own heart to see what Noah had done for him. But a part of him also knew that Noah hadn't done his part in giving Adam the opportunity to know what he was going through.

Being the baby of his family, Adriano had been sheltered from the worst of what life could throw. If his parents didn't step in, then his brothers or sisters would. Noah was complicated, and his past was so different from what Adriano had ever known.

'Do you want to eat?' Adriano asked.

Noah laughed, then eased Jude off him and sat up. 'Yes. Will you unwrap it all?'

Adriano had no trouble doing that. In fact, he wanted to do more. He wanted to cup his hands around Noah and protect him from anything else that might dig in claws and leave behind scars. He knew he couldn't, not entirely, but he could still cushion the way down from every fall. If Noah would let him.

It wasn't Noah's first Shabbat with company. Bubbe had always made it fun, even with a reluctant Adam who even at such an early age had started to push at the confines of their religion. When he was scolded, he'd shuffle into the bathroom and slam the door, flicking the lights on and off until Bubbe put him in his room.

When Noah returned from school, he tried to enforce it, but Adam would simply stare at Noah, then hit the lights and leave him in the dark. Noah didn't give up immediately, but when he realized what Adam was doing—forcing him to make a choice between keeping and breaking the Shabbat—he gave up. He wasn't going to force Adam to observe, to believe, to even care if he didn't want to. Adam's identity as a

Jewish man didn't rest on how he practiced. He was no less than Noah.

And it wasn't until years later that he realized his mistake. Adam wasn't looking to hurt Noah. Not at first. He was goading Noah into breaking his strict resolve because he was feeling unloved. The pain of the realization hit him, the pain that Adam would use his religion and faith in that choice gutted him like no other.

He had no way of explaining to Adam that choosing that path—turning away from assimilation, from what was easy, from the things that brought him some measure of joy—was all *for* Adam. It was all to hold up his end of a flimsy bargain so Noah wouldn't spend the rest of his life totally alone.

They were both a mess. They had both stripped each other of all the comfort and safety that could be had between siblings.

They were better now. Now that Adam had met Talia and found some sort of peace and happiness with whatever they had, there was room for healing. But Noah knew they could never have what they once might have been able to if their dad hadn't died, if their mother hadn't been so selfish, if Bubbe hadn't worked herself into an early grave.

But it was what it was.

Friday evening, Noah found himself with his head in Adriano's lap, with thick fingers brushing through his curls. He was full from a hot meal—something he hadn't had on a Friday since before he'd left school. Noah felt peace during the Shabbat for the first time in years. He felt safe, and cherished. He felt like himself. And Adriano seemed more than content to allow Noah those hours to himself, not demanding anything of him, just existing with him.

By morning, he felt rested and content from a long night, even though they'd done nothing besides hold each other. His sexual needs were Pavlovian trained, responding too easily and too perfectly to warm lips and firm hands. But

Adriano didn't seem to mind. He didn't push Noah where Noah didn't want to be pushed, and he respected the importance of that night.

Noah woke with the dawn, a prayer of thanks on his lips that he was able to feel Adriano's hand cupping his thigh without tumbling over the edge. Adriano didn't sleep much longer than him after that either. Noah went to the bathroom, and when he came out, he found the bedroom empty. He heard noise from down the hall, though, and followed the smell of coffee and browned butter to the kitchen.

Adriano greeted him with a kiss—quick and perfunctory but warm and now familiar—which made his head spin. Noah was falling hard, and it terrified him a little because he didn't exactly know what he meant to Adriano.

He'd been there less than a week, had known him only a few weeks beyond that through stilted chat and text messages. But he didn't feel like a stranger. Something in Noah's gut told him to trust the other man. That little voice said if he asked, if he just said his fears aloud or on his hands in his slowly measured signs, Adriano would tell him.

And he should, but there was another voice speaking softly about the glass shattering. He didn't want this bubble to pop yet. He wanted to be more than just a handful of videos that might save him from crushing debt and something to keep Adriano occupied while his lawyer sorted out the rest of his life. He would live if this whole thing was nothing more than that, but Adriano would take pieces of him when he left.

He pushed the thought aside for the quiet afternoon. Adriano didn't seem in a hurry to go anywhere, leaving only to walk Jude before he settled right back in. He kept Noah close, he petted Marshmallow whenever the cat deemed them worthy of his time, and he threw the ball for Jude when the pup started getting restless. He cooked lunch and helped prep for dinner so Noah could cook the moment Shabbat ended. Adriano looked at him with soft, fond eyes, and he kissed him a lot.

It felt too good to be true.

Noah stretched like a cat as the sun dipped low on the horizon. He felt the anxiety buzz forming around the base of his spine, that familiar, antsy hum when the sun began to set. It would be another hour or so—maybe more—before it was finished, but he was anxious to do more. Noah appreciated that his faith required these reprieves from life. He technically didn't always do what he was meant to do. He didn't always think about himself. He didn't contemplate ways to be a better person, or a better Jew, or a better brother.

Sometimes he didn't even feel grateful for this life or being alive.

Yet he always walked away feeling like the Shabbat had meant something.

Breathing in motes of dust floating in a warm stream of sunlight, Noah turned onto his side. He felt Adriano startle a little, then glanced up to see him reading on his phone. Adriano's cheeks went faintly pink, offering a sheepish smile as he flashed his screen toward Noah. It looked something like a webcomic, and Noah felt a rush of affection toward this man. This giant, stoic-faced, aloof man who also liked nerdy comics and had a pocket-sized dog and, for whatever reason, just really seemed to like Noah.

Once upon a time, he had wanted to know him beyond his personality in films. He never felt brave enough to make up stories about what he might be like when he wasn't Sylent, the imposing bear taking twinks apart one hand job at a time, but he had been curious. He wanted to know if he'd still like Adriano if he got to see deeper layers of him.

It was better than he could have expected. He was just as arrogant and spoiled as he was on Twitter, but he was also softer. He was kinder and sweeter. He was brave, and he was protective. He could read the subtle motions of Noah's body language, and he instinctively knew when to step closer and when to pull away.

Noah hadn't realized how much he'd needed that in his life, but it was hard to know those things when he'd never let anyone close. He'd spent most of his years actively avoiding attention, but with Adriano, he wanted it. He wanted that laser focus on him, those dark eyes holding him in place, the mouth devouring every single one of his kisses like he was starving for them.

Fuck.

He was falling in love.

Pushing up onto his elbow, he let Adriano take him into his arms. He didn't have to move. He just had to give in. Adriano used his strength against Noah, but Noah didn't care. He wanted it, wanted to feel overwhelmed by every inch of this man's body.

Adriano's thighs beneath him were powerful, and they spread to let Noah fit between. His head dipped, lips already parted, and Noah was ready for him. The heat of Adriano's kisses always seemed to consume him but in the best way. He let Adriano tip his head back, let Adriano nudge his lips farther apart, let his tongue fuck into his mouth in a rhythm that Noah knew—on instinct more than anything—that he wanted in other places.

"Please," he groaned, unable to stop himself. His fingers dug into Adriano's shoulders, and he spread his legs because he was close. Again. And Adriano knew.

"*Noah*," Adriano said.

The orgasm crested…

"Hey, Noah?" Adam's words punctuated the charged air between him and Adriano just before Jude began to bark.

The orgasm retreated, leaving a painful ache behind, and Noah fought to cover the space in his lounge pants that was tented and wet with come. Adam appeared only a second later, and Noah knew there was no way he nor

Adriano looked put together. He watched it all dawn on Adam's face, watched the color drain a bit, watched him take a step back.

"Oh *fuck*, did you—"

"No," Noah ground out. Not yet. But he had been too close to begging for it. "Is there something you need?"

Adam looked vaguely embarrassed as he nodded toward Adriano, then cleared his throat. His eyes held a gleam of mischief, and Noah knew this wasn't the last he'd hear of what his brother had just walked in on. "I brought over some stuff from the truck that didn't sell last night. I left it in the kitchen downstairs and wanted to let you know I was ready to come back to work. At least for prep."

Noah glanced at Adriano, who was clearly not following Adam's cadence of speech, so he quickly interpreted before answering his brother, first in speech, then in sign. "Actually, I was going to call you to see if you could handle prep tonight."

Adriano stood up and turned to Noah, laying a hand on his cheek, touching the edge of his mouth with his thumb. 'I'm going to walk Jude.'

Noah nodded. 'Okay. Sorry. He doesn't normally burst in here like that.'

Adriano quickly snapped his fingers for Jude, and the pup came to attention, primly turning so Adriano could attach the leash. 'Nice to see you again,' he signed to Adam, then headed out the door.

When it was shut, Adam turned to his brother with a sigh. "I have to learn ASL now, don't I?"

Noah bit his lip as he shrugged. "You don't have to, but…"

"Is he sticking around?" Adam gave the armchair a dubious look.

"We didn't have sex in it," Noah groused.

"Have you had sex at all?" Adam sank down but kept to the edge of the cushion like he didn't believe him.

Noah looked down at his hands. "It's not exactly your business, but no."

"No, or not yet?" Adam pressed. "He's a porn star. He's not going to be into this cute virgin act forever."

Noah fixed his brother with a hard stare. "Are you trying to hurt me on purpose?"

Adam opened his mouth, then closed it again with a heavy breath. "No. I'm really not. I'm sorry."

Noah bowed his head and shrugged. "I like him. And I don't know if he's going to stick around. I hope so, but it's new, and it doesn't feel right to put that kind of pressure on him with everything he's going through."

"Yeah, I saw." Adam sighed, and it didn't surprise Noah that he'd gone snooping. "There was that huge pile of bullshit on Twitter." He stared down at his hands, flexed his fingers, and made a few nonsense shapes with them. "Is sign language hard?"

"Yes," Noah told him because he wasn't about to lie. "It's just like any other language."

Adam picked at the edge of his nail, then put his hands back in his lap. "Is he worth it?"

"I don't know." It was the most honest answer he could give. "I think being in customer service, it's a good language to learn. You never know who might need it." He swallowed thickly, then said, "I hope he is."

At his quiet statement—raw with truth and fear—Adam looked up at him. His eyes were softer than usual, his tone quieter when he spoke. "I hope so too. And I'll take prep tonight. Do you want me to open the store tomorrow?"

Noah opened his mouth to tell Adam no, to tell him it wasn't his responsibility any longer, but he knew that wasn't the case. He'd been working hard and standing in Adam's way to protect him from the truth about Bubbe's. Adam knew the bakery was in trouble, but he didn't know how much because Bubbe believed Noah could shoulder the pain of debt and loss better than Adam could. And it was Noah's fault for still believing that this many years later.

He had a moment of anger, of desperation, of wanting someone to go soft on him just because. Everyone in his family had laid their problems on his shoulders because he had been strong enough to take it, but he didn't always want to be strong.

Sometimes he wanted to be able to break under Adam's anger, under his mother's refusal to live for her children, under Bubbe's suffocating care.

He knew he never would. Not now, not after this long, but he was tired.

"I wouldn't mind a day off," he admitted. "Will your truck do alright?"

Adam blushed and glanced away, and Noah realized it was embarrassment. "I think I'll be fine if I take a day."

"It's doing well, isn't it?" Noah asked, and though he didn't mean it that way, it sounded like an accusation.

"I don't want this place to buckle under competition, but I want to do well, Noah." He could hear the sharpness of Adam's words rise with his defense, so Noah got up and crossed the room, kneeling beside his brother.

He touched Adam's arm, felt the warmth of it under his long sleeve. "I want you to do so well that you never need to look at this place again."

Adam stared down at him a long moment. "I don't want you to suffer anymore."

"I'm not," Noah promised. "I have a plan." He knew Adam would be devastated when it was all said and done, but he'd do nothing except pray until he told his brother the truth. He had to believe Adam was old enough now, mature enough, had been around all this long enough to understand why the bakery had to close.

They were one of the oldest shops on their street. That had to be enough.

"I'm sorry," Adam said after a second. He stood, so Noah rose with him, and he took a step toward the door. "It's been kind of a week, and it's all been good, but...this is so new, you know? Falling for someone. Starting off on my own. It feels a little like I'm walking upside down."

"I know the feeling," Noah told him.

"I'm grateful that you let me go." Adam reached up absently and pulled the tie from his hair. It fell in soft waves around his shoulders before he gathered it again, and Noah recognized the anxious gesture for what it was. "I think I'm exactly where I'm supposed to be."

"I think so too," Noah offered. "Thank you for the food. I'm going to go stay with Adriano for the night."

Adam's smirk was back. "At his rental by the café?"

"No." Noah shook his head with a grin. "He rented out a beach cottage on the island, and he'll be staying there until he..." He didn't finish the sentence because he didn't know how to. He didn't know what Adriano was doing next, and he was still too afraid to wonder, let alone ask. "But you and Talia won't run into me."

"I...Thanks," Adam said, sounding relieved.

Noah laughed. "Yeah. Trust me, I didn't want that either." He opened the door, then hesitated before dropping his hand on Adam's shoulder. "Dinner soon?"

"Yes," Adam agreed. "And I'll look into the sign language thing." It was Adam's last promise before he walked out and the door shut behind him. Noah glanced at the clock and saw it was less than an hour before sunset. It was enough time to sit just a bit longer, to feel just a little more, and to do his best not to wonder what was coming next.

CHAPTER 13

Noah carried his bag, and Adriano carried the rest of the stuff. They'd made a quick trip to the grocery store, and Noah knew Adriano had over shopped, but it was fun not to care. It had been years, far too many to count, since he'd done something like this. He didn't sleep away from home, and he didn't trust the day-to-day of Bubbe's to anyone else. Not even Adam. But he had to trust his brother could handle things.

He knew Adam would keep Paxton in line. He also knew Talia would be around if Adam was spending the day with Paxton. There would be three people taking care of what was left for the short while it was still standing.

And Noah was giving himself this.

A small thrill rushed up his spine and spread warmth through his limbs as he crossed the threshold into the house. It was small and cozy, the air slightly chilled from the ocean breeze. It was surrounded by a sea of sand and very few neighbors, and it felt private, like their own personal island that no one in the world could find.

He knew this was more than just a vacation. He knew that under the cover of darkness, he was going to give

Adriano his body for public consumption. He'd make money and pull himself out of the hole he'd dug—the one his bubbe had started and left him—and then…he didn't know what. If he was lucky, he'd have something left after the sale of the building, and he didn't think he'd need to sell the apartment, but part of him wanted to.

It would be like hacking off a limb, leaving that place, but it was time. His past felt infected, and there was no other cure but to remove its hold on him.

Swiping his hand over his forehead, Noah felt sweat in spite of the fact that it wasn't hot. He was nervous. He heard Adriano in the kitchen, the heavy thud as he put things away, the way he walked hard on the floors. Adriano murmured sometimes, unconscious, quiet noises he probably didn't realize he was making, but Noah loved them. They were a reminder that he was there, that he was comfortable enough with Noah to let himself relax.

Swallowing thickly, Noah explored the rest of the house and found one smaller bedroom with a blacked-out window, and he knew instantly what it was for. His heart hammered in his chest, but in spite of his nerves and fear, his cock was hard. He backed out, then found the primary bedroom, dropping his stuff in the corner near Adriano's suitcase. As he stepped back, he felt a tug on his pant leg.

Jude was there, looking up with big, black doe eyes peeking through his tufts of fur. Noah picked him up and cuddled him close. "You are so much cuter than any other dog I have ever met." The dog huffed against him, and Noah stroked fingers through his coat.

He made his way back to the kitchen and found Adriano at the sink filling a large pasta pot with water. Noah stood there in the doorway, holding the dog, watching his lover as he moved. Adriano was huge but had a grace about him that most people didn't. He wondered if it was from filming, from being famous, from always being observed. But something about it was more natural than practiced.

He was smitten.

Adriano set the pot on the burner, then turned and smiled, and Noah realized Adriano knew he was there. He liked that. He liked that Adriano was aware of him. He felt his entire body soften—all but his dick—as Adriano crossed the room and put his hands to Noah's waist. He glanced down at Jude, then leaned in and rubbed his nose along Noah's, breathing in deep.

"Hi," he said.

Noah didn't respond with words or signs, but he turned his face up and initiated a kiss. Adriano groaned into it, took Noah's waist, and pulled him forward, to the side, then back until he hit the wall. One big hand lifted Jude out of his arms and eased him down to the floor before surging back up and kissing him harder, deeper.

Noah's hands went to Adriano's hair, burying in the thick, dark locks. He could do this forever. He could exist in these arms, with this mouth on his, those fingers pressing bruising shapes into his skin, for the rest of his life. He wanted it more than he had ever wanted anything.

And it terrified him and elated him all at the same time.

When had he gotten brave enough to admit it?

Adriano pulled back when he felt Noah's body poised on edge to let go, and he pressed his hand to Noah's thigh. "Do you want to come?"

Noah swallowed thickly. He wouldn't mind changing before dinner anyway, but he had a feeling the rental's washer and dryer were going to get a workout. He bit his lip and shifted toward Adriano's hand, nodding.

Adriano growled, then dragged his palm up, bypassing Noah's dick. Noah let out a sharp whine, wanting to finally feel someone touch him there, but he didn't need it. Adriano leaned in, dragging open lips just beneath his ear, and it was enough.

His body jerked with the orgasm, not as powerful as those first few but powerful enough. His hips thrust against open air, then he collapsed against Adriano's chest and let the other man gather him close. They had done this so many times, and Adriano still hadn't come. Noah's unease crept in just under the bliss and euphoria, and it must have shown in his eyes when he pulled back.

'What's wrong?' Adriano signed.

Noah bit his lip. 'Can we talk about'—he waved his hand between him and Adriano—'after we eat?'

Adriano looked hesitant. 'Are you unhappy?'

'Confused,' Noah spelled, not remembering the sign for it. Adriano showed him, and he repeated it. 'Not bad. Just need to talk.'

Adriano's entire body relaxed just a fraction, and when he leaned in again, Noah didn't reject the kiss. It was sweeter this time and soft. It was full of an emotion Noah was too afraid to name. It was over too fast, but Noah's crotch was sticky and uncomfortably wet, so he was grateful for the reprieve.

He didn't let himself think too much as he changed, didn't sink into the anxiety of what-ifs, but it was a near thing. Instead, he focused on what was to come. Dinner with his lover and a little more tenderness.

And then...

And then, he would get ready to bare all.

NOAH HAD to wonder if it was some sort of gift that all Italian men had a genetic ability to cook, though he knew that was ridiculous. But one of his first friends in college had been a whiz with a hot plate and dry noodles and cans of cheap tomato sauce. He could whip up a Bolognese good enough to make Noah want to cry with a half bottle of two-dollar wine and a jar of dried oregano added in.

Adriano's was better than that. It was dry pasta, but it tasted fresh. The sauce had a richness he couldn't describe with words, but he was happy to eat until he almost felt sick. It was an overindulgence, but Adriano's pleased grin as he watched Noah attack his plate was worth it.

When they were finished, Adriano took him by the hand, a loose grip of clasped fingers, and they made their way out back. There was an echo of the sunset's glow just along the horizon but not enough to give any real light. The yard was lit up by a handful of solar lamps, but it felt soothing in a way to be surrounded by darkness and the sound of waves hitting the sand.

Adriano led him to a two-person swing, the cushions heavy and thick, and he tucked himself between Adriano's spread legs, the pair of them stretched along the length of it as best as two fully grown men could be. Noah laid with his back to Adriano's chest and let Adriano's large hands curve over his.

"Happy?" Adriano asked aloud.

Noah nodded his fist against Adriano's palm.

"Me too." Lips pressed against his hair, nose digging into his curls. He felt more than heard Adriano take a deep breath in. "Can we talk out here?"

Noah took his hands away, then twisted around. 'Too dark?'

Adriano pulled a face, but he knew Noah was right. Neither of them seemed to want to give up this little bit of sanctuary away from both the chaos of life and what they planned to do next in the bedroom, but Noah knew he couldn't put it off for much longer.

He leaned in and stole a kiss before heaving himself up, and he heard Adriano's heavy footsteps follow him in.

They'd only taken a minute out there in the dark, but Noah's eyes struggled to adjust. They watered a little as he took the corner seat on the sofa and turned as Adriano joined him.

'If you changed your mind,' Adriano started, but Noah shook his head.

'It isn't that. I...' He hovered with his finger touching his chest, then stopped and dropped his hands for a second. 'I don't know what this is between us,' he went on. 'You like me.'

'Yes,' Adriano said, his fist's nod perfunctory and sharp. He leaned in but not close enough to touch. 'Yes,' he signed again.

'What happens when all this is over?' Noah asked.

Adriano's brow furrowed. 'What?'

'Your agent,' Noah asked, his shaking fingers fumbling over the spelling of words he didn't have the signs for. 'Your job. You can't live in Savannah.'

Adriano's brow furrowed. 'Why not?'

Noah couldn't help his laugh. 'It's on the other side of the country. There's nothing here for you.'

Adriano's face was challenging now, eyes not letting him go. 'You're here. Your family is here.'

'Your family is not,' Noah reminded him.

Adriano scoffed. 'I don't see them that often. We're not as close as we were before I started working in film. I don't let them choose for me what makes me happy.'

Noah's insides swooped like he was on a roller coaster. He craved that, wanted that. He was desperate for a moment that he could choose for himself and not out of fear for the consequences if he broke his vow. 'I don't know how to do that.'

'I know,' Adriano said. He reached out this time, touching Noah's cheek, then dragging his hand down to cup the back of his neck. He held there for a long time, letting the warmth of his palm soothe Noah's frayed nerves. 'I like it here. With you.'

'Say that in a month,' Noah replied with a laugh, and Adriano rolled his eyes.

'Two months. Six months. Ten years. I don't know where we'll be, but I like you. I want to try this with you.'

Noah glanced away, just for a second, just to give himself some reprieve from the intensity he saw in Adriano's eyes.

'Noah,' Adriano signed, and he smiled just a little bit, mostly in the eyes and at the corners of his mouth. 'I just got out of a long-term relationship. I didn't love him. I don't know if I ever loved him. I want to move slow. But I want to see where this goes. I don't want to stop when we're done with this.' He indicated the hallway, and Noah knew what he meant.

It was like Adriano could read him, those quiet, anxious parts of him he was too afraid to voice. He breathed out, air shaking in his chest, but something felt settled. 'Thank you.'

Adriano nodded, then he stood up and extended his hand. Noah didn't hesitate, even if his anxiety began to ramp up again, but Adriano held him fast and didn't hurry toward the bedroom. He paused in the doorway, pressing Noah to the hard, unforgiving wood, then kissed him hard enough to make him forget that it was painful against his spine.

He let go, then let Noah take the lead, let Noah take that first step into something that would surely change his life forever. But he realized as he stared at the small camera setup, and the turned-down blankets, and the shaded windows, it might just be for the better.

CHAPTER 14

ADRIANO DIDN'T NEED Noah to tell him he was nervous. It was apparent in the slight tremble of his fingers, and the tension in his spine, even as he led the way into the bedroom. Adriano didn't exactly mind that Noah was nervous. This was Noah's first time with all of it. No one had ever explored the naked expanse of Noah's body before him, and it was erotic, though that was such a shallow word for the way it made him feel.

Adriano had never set much value on the idea of virginity. He respected it, respected the way it made people feel, but he had never used it to measure worth. New actors who hadn't done much on-screen or with a private partner didn't hold more or less appeal when he filmed with them.

Eric himself hadn't dated much before he had gone to work for Adriano. He'd been nervous too, though not like this. He worried about pleasing Adriano, about measuring up to the scenes Adriano had on-screen. And Adriano couldn't exactly say he didn't get pleasure out of working because he did. It was fucking, and he very much enjoyed fucking. But Eric never seemed to understand that what he wanted in his life and in the privacy of his bedroom was not what he was paid to do on camera.

He hated himself a little for how often he was comparing Noah to his ex, but he supposed that was also normal. Eric had been Adriano's first real, adult relationship. He'd dated in college—a few weeks here, a month or two there, but nothing that stuck. Nothing that had substance or meaning.

Even Eric felt shallow at first. It was forbidden fruit. Sneaking around on set and fucking his interpreter, then filming a scene with Eric right there, watching, hands flying with stage direction and dialogue. He loved it.

It became more, but it never became *enough*.

If Noah never wanted more than this, Adriano wasn't sure he'd be content, and that *was* something he needed to think about. But not now.

The lights were low in the room, and everything was set up. Adriano had spent a few hours before heading to Noah's testing angles and filming a couple scenes of himself jacking off and playing with toys. He kept it active, kept himself moving, and he knew that the videos would need some editing, but not much. He didn't have expert skill in amateur videos. He had never been the guy who did the nitty-gritty tech work. But he'd picked up enough over the years, and he had friends.

He had a contract waiting for Noah that ensured he was the only one who would get paid, and he had a plan. Five videos, and then, if Noah wanted, if he was ready, a sixth. A sixth where Adriano would give something to Noah that he hadn't given to anyone else.

And Noah would take it from him and fulfill an expectation that Adriano believed was bullshit but that would most certainly line Noah's pockets nicely. Enough to pull him out of debt and cushion his way into figuring out what he wanted to do with his life next.

His mind briefly went back to the moment on the sofa,

the terrified way Noah had looked at him, how he had spelled most of his words because his fear had stolen his vocabulary. But he'd made himself clear enough.

He thought this might be a game, a way for Adriano to pass the time until all the shit with Eric and Xander either worked out or disappeared. He thought Adriano was just biding his time until he could walk away, and Adriano didn't know how to assure him he wouldn't because he wasn't sure about himself.

He had never fallen so hard so fast.

He needed time.

Noah was staring at him expectantly, not sure what to do. His hand toyed with the hem of his shirt like he thought maybe he should pull it off, so Adriano closed his fingers around Noah's delicate wrist and gave a light squeeze.

'Wait,' he signed, and Noah nodded. Adriano took a step back, then wiped his palms over the tops of his jeans. 'The plan is to film five videos to start. One per night. I have a contract for you to sign and a friend to help edit. Nothing goes live until you say it's okay.'

Noah bit his lip. 'Will you…orgasm? With me?'

Adriano blinked at him, a little startled by the question. 'This is about you. This is me making *you* come.'

'You already have,' Noah pointed out. 'More than once. And you never…' His hand hung in the air with hesitation.

Adriano hadn't realized what was bothering his lover. He'd been hyper focused on Noah to the exclusion of his own pleasure in the moment. He hadn't minded. In fact, he'd loved it. He'd taken those images—the feel of Noah's body tensing, the hitching in his breath, the hot puffs of air against Adriano's face—and he'd stroked himself over and over the moment he'd gone back to his place.

The first night he'd made Noah come with just a kiss, he'd buried three fingers in his own ass and shouted into his pillow just reliving that moment. It was erotic and gorgeous, but he'd made the mistake of not sharing that with Noah.

"Shit," he said aloud.

Noah took a step back, then stopped when Adriano held up a hand in surrender.

'No.' Adriano raked fingers through his hair. 'You *have* made me come. A lot. Just…not *with* you.'

Noah's eyes went wide when he realized what Adriano was saying.

'It wasn't on purpose. I just enjoyed making you feel good. Of course I want to come with you.'

Noah took a fortifying breath, then squared his shoulders. Courage, bravery, boldness—it looked so fucking good on him, and Adriano was already starting to swell in his jeans. 'Come with me after. I'll do it for the video, and after… you and me.'

Adriano nodded so hard his neck ached, but he crossed the distance and put his hands on Noah's shoulders. What he wanted to do was kiss him. What he wanted was to pin Noah to the bed and fuck his cock between Noah's thighs and cover them with his come.

'Do you want to look at the contract now?' Adriano asked.

Noah shook his head. 'I trust you. We can look at it tomorrow. I feel like if I don't do this now…' His hands wavered in the air.

'I understand,' Adriano answered. He took a step back, then turned the camera on. It faced the bed, so they weren't in the shot. Yet. He knew where to place Noah so his face wouldn't be seen, and the rest they could adjust in post.

He turned back to his lover and fixed him with a dark, seductive look. He wasn't sure it would work on Noah now that they knew each other so well, but he saw pink flood his cheeks, and if possible, he got harder. 'Follow my lead. I'll keep our faces off-camera. I practiced.'

Noah laughed, and Adriano wondered if it was silent or not. He took a step closer and reached for Noah's hand, taking willing fingers and sucking two into his mouth. Noah's head tipped back, and Adriano splayed his palm on Noah's chest, feeling his moan. Yes, his sweet little virgin would be good at this.

Letting one hand fall to Noah's hip, he walked him to the front of the bed. He'd be visible from chin down there, Adriano from his neck and below. It wouldn't take long for any of his fans to recognize him—his few pieces of ink, the curve of his waist, his hands. But he supposed that was what he wanted.

He supposed it didn't matter. He wasn't Sylent in this. He was Adriano—Adriano with his boyfriend, Noah.

A wave of possession hit him. For a brief, hysterical moment, he wanted to smash the camera, throw all his money at Noah, then refuse to share him with the world.

But it was only a moment.

This was sex. This was coming.

Making love would be after.

He dragged his hands over Noah's skin as he removed his shirt, letting it fall at their feet. He splayed wide palms over Noah's ribs, letting his fingertips dig in, letting them paint faint lines up to his nipples.

Noah shuddered, and he groaned again, loud enough Adriano could hear just the faint impression of it as it ripped from Noah's throat. His fingers went for the elastic waistband of his jogging pants next. They were soft grey, cheap, simple, and they had never looked better on anyone else before. His fingers had their own tremble because this was a first. This was a gift—unwrapping Noah, even for an eventual audience, but it was okay. No one was with them now. No one was seeing Noah like this before him.

He licked his lips, then nudged Noah's head up with his own lips before deepening the kiss. Noah made a noise, and it vibrated against Adriano's lips. It was maybe a protest, so he pulled back and saw the shape of *too close* curve over his mouth and tongue.

He nodded and eased his grip. Noah was tenting his sweats to the point of strained, and a wet spot had grown dark and round, the size of a quarter. Adriano waited, only a beat, then he touched him there through the fabric. Adriano heard Noah's cry louder this time. His own dick begged for more, but he would wait. It would be worth it.

Letting go, Adriano stepped behind Noah and carefully eased the sweats down past his thighs. They pooled at his feet, and then he was there—bared for the camera and for Adriano—and soon for anyone who wanted to watch. His cock was beautiful—shorter but thick, cut and swollen, and leaking a steady stream.

And that was for him. That want, that hardness, was for Adriano.

He wanted to speak, wanted to murmur against the back of Noah's ear, but that would give him away too soon. Instead, he mouthed at it, licked around the earlobe, held Noah tight by the waist and offered him no friction at all, but it didn't matter.

It would be over soon. Adriano could feel it in the line of tension in Noah's body.

His head bowed, tipping Noah's ear to his shoulder. Adriano's head was low enough that the most people would see was his profile, the top of his head, and an open mouth on Noah's neck. He bared teeth, and he attached his lips, sucking first.

And then he bit down.

Noah came like he'd been ordered to. His entire body went stiff apart from his hips that fucked uselessly into the air, straining against Adriano's hold on him. He cried out, this time too soft for Adriano to hear but enough for him to feel as the vibration hit through Noah's back and into Adriano's chest. His body went flush, and he pushed his neck against Adriano's teeth, and then his entire body went limp.

ADRIANO'S initial instinct was to throw Noah onto the bed and take him. To strip himself down completely and fill anywhere Noah opened up for him. He wanted to mark Noah with teeth, with fingernails, with his come. But he had just enough hold on his own control to reach over and stop the recording. Noah was boneless against him, back still to Adriano's front, clinging to his arm like it was the only thing keeping him up, and maybe it was.

Adriano turned Noah, then eased him onto the bed and put one knee onto the mattress. Noah spread out, arms lifted up near his head, legs spread into a loose vee. Pink flushed up from his groin, where his cock lay limp and spent in his dark hair, to his neck, which was thrumming with his pulse.

Adriano wanted to put his mouth there again to see if it would arouse Noah, but he also wanted—no, he *needed*—to take a moment and just look. He wanted to observe open, raw, uncovered skin that until this moment belonged to no one but Noah.

And now it was his.

He lifted his hand and pressed fingers to Noah's hip. Noah shifted, lolled his head to the side, and his eyes opened just a sliver.

'Water?' Adriano offered. He had a small bag with granola bars, Gatorade, and water bottles, but Noah shook his head and licked his lips, leaving them shiny with spit.

Noah held up his hand, and Adriano pushed his face against it. He took him by the wrist, turning his head to kiss each fingertip, the center of his palm, and up his arm to the crook of his elbow. He felt Noah shudder with each press of his lips, felt his body give over more and more.

Adriano's head spun with how much he wanted this man, his cock now ready to burst through the fabric of his jeans. He didn't let Noah go, but he used his free hand to pop the button and pull his zipper down. His cock sprung out through the slit in his boxers, and he groaned with relief.

Noah tensed against him, and when Adriano looked down, he saw Noah pushing up on his elbow to look at him. Noah had seen him before. He had seen Adriano's dick naked, covered in a condom, in lube, in spit, in come. He knew Noah had seen Adriano fuck more asses than he could really count anymore, but for some reason, it felt like Noah was seeing him for the first time.

A wave of guilt hit him. He hadn't meant to make Noah wait for him like this.

Adriano swore in that moment that he would die if he couldn't feel his lover's palm curl around him.

"Please," Adriano said, guiding Noah's hand down.

Noah's eyes went wide, his irises nearly consumed by pupil. His mouth was pulled into a tight line, the flush in his cheeks making his freckles stand out. He was so, *so* beautiful. Adriano wanted to kiss him again, but he held off as he watched Noah gather more of that gorgeous courage and finally—*finally*—reach where Adriano wanted him most.

His palm was cool and shaking, but it was strong. There were calluses from burns, and it was too dry, but God, it was the best feeling in the world. Adriano let out a grunt, a sharp puff of air, when Noah tightened his fingers and stroked upward. His foreskin was pulled back most of the way given how hard he was, but it started to slick up as Noah began to jack him off.

"Noah," he managed to get out. He knew the consonants and vowels were a mess, but Noah didn't look like he cared. Noah pushed up onto his elbows, pushed Adriano to the side, then climbed to his knees as Adriano watched, awed. Noah still didn't let go.

'Lie down.' His signs were sloppy, but Adriano understood them. He let Noah's free hand push him to the bed, and he fell onto his back. Noah still didn't let go. He had stopped stroking, and he was holding tighter than Adriano normally liked, but he wouldn't trade a single second of the moment for anything.

His shirt was rucked halfway up his chest, and Noah used his free hand to push it all the way to his pecs. His nipples were already tight, hard against the light friction of the fabric as it moved, and Noah's tongue drew over his lips again, then he ran his thumb over one hard peak.

"Use your mouth," Adriano all but begged. He didn't know how he sounded, if he made sense at all, but Noah's eyes met his, and he knew. He knew Noah heard him in every way.

Noah uncurled his fingers, letting Adriano's dick fall to the side. He was aching for more but content to wait and see what his lover was going to do. Bracing both hands on the bed, Noah lifted to his knees, then lowered his head. The first swipe of his tongue was hesitant, too light. But the second pass was firmer. The third had a hint of teeth, and then he closed his lips around Adriano's nipple and sucked.

Adriano had been taken to the edge of ecstasy before but not like this. Never like this. Never with such a simple touch. Pleasure shot up his spine, and somewhere in the back of his mind something asked, *Is this what it's supposed to feel like when you're in love?*

The thought was terrifying.

He was brought back to the present by Noah's hands—braver now, stronger. Noah pulled his shirt all the way off, Adriano squirming to help, the neck of it totally disordering his hair. He flopped back to the pillows just in time for Noah to attack his jeans in the same way, and seconds later, they were naked together.

Noah hovered over him, his own dick plumping up, and

his lips were parted. Noah's chest rose and fell like he was panting, but he didn't look afraid. He braced himself on his knees, then took his hands to the broad expanse of Adriano's chest. He felt around them, the curves, the dips, the thick hair in the center of his sternum. Noah trailed a touch up to Adriano's neck, gripping tight as he leaned in to kiss him with a plush open mouth and wet tongue.

He groaned against Noah, his hips seeking friction, and he found it. Noah's legs spread over him, and Adriano's cock began to drag against the groove in Noah's hip. It was too dry, it wasn't enough, and it was also everything. Noah held his own lower half still, letting Adriano take what he wanted until he was wild and nearly at the edge.

Just before he crashed over, Noah pulled back, and Adriano felt himself sob. When he opened his eyes, Noah was staring at him. He'd shifted down, straddling lower on Adriano's legs, and his hand was reaching for Adriano. Tentative fingers traced his balls, traced down closer to his hole. Then a mad thought hit him—Noah would be inside him soon.

Then Noah's hand finally curled around him, and he met Adriano's eyes with a furious look, echoing the possession that had overcome Adriano right before they'd begun. His arm moved, hand squeezing from base to tip, and he didn't stop until Adriano was spilling in hot ropes between them.

Adriano watched Noah, who watched the whole thing in wide-eyed wonder. His mouth was half-open, his tongue out like he wanted to taste. Adriano reached down with weak fingers and swiped a bit, then held it like an offering.

Noah stared, jaw tense. He swallowed thickly, and just when Adriano thought it was too much, he closed his lips and sucked the fluid off, swallowing deeply. Adriano felt something on Noah vibrate, his lips barely moving. He thought maybe he'd said something, or maybe he just moaned.

It didn't matter. What mattered was the way Noah was staring at him—with love, with wonder, with a little fear. Adriano understood. And it was okay because as he opened his arms to Noah, he fell into them, willing and without hesitation, without second-guessing.

His cock was wet and soft against Adriano's thigh, and Adriano realized he'd come again. For him. Only for him. Not for a video, not for an audience. That climax belonged to the both of them.

Adriano turned onto his side with Noah clutched close, and he nuzzled their lips together. When he pulled back, he had just enough space to ask, 'Okay?'

And Noah had just enough space to reply, 'Perfect.'

CHAPTER 15

Noah leaned against the deck, staring at the foggy haze hovering over the ocean. The sun rose behind the house, and the sky was an ombre grey stretching high above him. His coffee was warm between his hands, and he tugged Adriano's sweater tighter around his body, basking in the scent of it and the warmth. It wasn't as good as his lover, but it was close enough for the moment.

Adriano had earned his time to sleep in. For four nights, they had stayed up late.

The first night had been a revelation with Adriano taking Noah apart with the drag of fingers, the press of lips, and then being laid down on the bed and slowly taking his lover apart with his own mouth. Noah had never put much stock in the idea of being pleasured or pleasuring someone. He understood sex. He had watched Adriano in more scenes than he currently wanted to admit. They were, in a way, forbidden. They were dark, and they were erotic, and it was the way they were disconnected that Noah related to them. Pleasure without emotion.

This was so much more.

He had been feeling not quite rejected but a little

unwanted when Adriano had admitted he'd taken care of himself after he'd left Noah's apartment. Adriano had meant it as a compliment, he knew, but it wasn't until Adriano had promised himself to Noah that he became aware of what he needed.

And what he wanted.

He was desperate to know that he mattered as much, that he could make Adriano feel as much. He couldn't offer everything. Their tentative agreement that any virginity—given and taken—would happen on camera. He was fine with it. He was grateful. But he no longer felt like a virgin, and that was a lot to process.

But part of him was grateful for that too. Finally sinking inside Adriano would be more than he could have ever imagined. He probably wouldn't last long, but he would last long enough. Each time Adriano made him come, made him tumble over the edge, it took longer. By the third night, it had taken Adriano a full five minutes to coax the orgasm out of Noah without touching his dick, and it was only after he'd dragged sharp nails up the insides of his thighs and rumbled a moan against the back of Noah's ear that Noah had let go.

Part of him regretted what he was losing because it felt special that Adriano could work him up that way. But he recalled an earlier promise that Adriano would teach him restraint. Through constantly coaxing orgasms maybe, but it was working. He might last long enough to sink into Adriano's tight heat before spilling.

Adriano assured him that's all the viewers would want.

Noah knew he'd feel a little better about the video and whether or not someone like him was worth watching. He knew he wasn't unattractive, but he wasn't gorgeous the way Adriano was, His body was soft around the edges and curved rather than muscular. He, of course, had seen Adriano fuck all types of bodies and sizes, and none of them were less erotic than the others. But turning that critical eye on himself wasn't easy.

He was already struggling to balance his work life with this new personal side, and while the walls weren't closing in yet, they were starting to crumble.

Noah took a long drink of his coffee and sighed. He thought about Will's suggestion, about talking to a therapist. It might be worth it to have a safe space to talk about the way he'd grown up.

Noah dug into the pocket of his sleep pants and drew out his phone. It was nearing six, which meant he'd need to slip out and head home. Adam had been far too eager to take over the late-night and early-morning prep, and Noah knew it was, in some ways, an apology. Noah didn't know how to really start with his because he still hadn't admitted his biggest sin.

He wasn't sure his fragile relationship with Adam would survive it.

In truth, for it to make sense—for Noah's lies and the things he'd hidden to be forgivable—he'd have to tell Adam everything. He'd have to confess about his mother, about Bubbe, the full extent of his bargain with Hashem. Adam would laugh at the last one, but the first two would break his heart and shatter the illusion that their mother would have loved him, and doted on him, and made things better. And Noah wasn't sure he had the heart or the strength to do it.

But it was Noah's last day of filming with Adriano, and it was the beginning of an end. And maybe the beginning of something else too. It was the start of existing in a relationship with Adriano that didn't revolve around the debt hanging over Noah's head. At the very least, Adriano knew where all Noah's skeletons were buried and what they looked like, and he liked him anyway.

He finished his coffee, dressed, then left a quick note for Adriano like he'd been doing every morning. He was grateful starting his car couldn't wake Adriano up, and he headed all the way back into the heart of town. Adam's car was parked in the back, but Noah skipped the side door to the bakery and went up to the apartment to change. He sat with Marshmallow for a few minutes, feeling a small wave of guilt for neglecting him, and he wondered if maybe there was a better way to marry their lives together than just stolen nights behind blacked-out windows.

He didn't really want to invite Adriano to stay with him all the time. He was addicted to it now, but Adriano had been clear he needed to take things slow, and Noah knew that was only fair. He just wished it felt better.

He headed back down to the bakery after a little while and found Adam finishing up the last of the challah loaves for their final prove. He turned his head when Noah walked in, then rolled his eyes and shook his head, but he was smiling a little.

"I wish you'd done this earlier," Adam muttered as Noah grabbed a bag of flour and tipped it onto the scale.

Noah knew what Adam meant, and he bristled. "I could say the same for you."

Adam narrowed his eyes at him, then switched to Hebrew. His had never been as good as Noah's, mostly because he'd grown up here. Bubbe had wanted him to be immersed in the English language rather than standing apart the way Noah had, but Noah appreciated when Adam tried. "I'm not going to argue with you."

Noah tipped cinnamon onto the flour, then moved to the counter where the eggs and butter had been laid out to settle to room temperature. He didn't answer his brother for a while, instead tipping what he needed into the metal bowl. He watched the beater swirl through the mixture of sugar, eggs, almond extract, and butter... it was hypnotic and cathartic, and it helped keep him centered with Adam so close.

It wasn't that long ago that they were doing this every day, and yet those months they'd spent more apart than not felt like years. Adam had moved out. He had moved on in every way. Noah had been left behind, but he was trying to catch up.

"Noah?"

He turned his head and offered his brother a smile. "I don't want to fight with you anymore. I know you feel cheated out of a real childhood…"

Adam made a frustrated noise in the back of his throat. "That's not—"

"Let's call it what it is," Noah told him. "I didn't do a good job after Bubbe died."

"You were twenty," Adam argued. "I was just as responsible for ruining your life."

Noah didn't mean to wince, but the truth of it stung. He grabbed the scoop and the flour and began to slowly add it to the mixer. It smelled heavily of almond and seasoning now. He missed Bubbe more than ever in that moment. She'd at least know what to say to not make the situation worse.

"I used school as an escape, just like I used hiding here when I got home," Noah told him. "I didn't deal with any of my issues, you know. I threw myself into what I thought was supposed to be normal. It blew up in my face every time."

Adam blew out a puff of air, then hopped up on the counter where all the aprons were waiting to be folded, and he swung his feet a little. Noah's chest ached at the sight of him—how young he looked suddenly, how very much like the little boy who'd clung to Bubbe's skirts and absorbed everything she had to teach him with wide eyes and busy hands.

"She should have given this place to you," Noah added quietly.

Adam said nothing until Noah turned the mixer off and unhooked it. It tipped onto the cookie table in a lump, just firm enough to shape with his hands but still tacky. He laid out a sprinkle of powdered sugar and began to divide the dough into sections.

"Why didn't she?" Adam's voice rose over the quiet din.

Noah looked up at him and saw him now sitting in a stream of morning sun, his hair curly and long, almost aglow like it was lit with flames. Adam had the best of both parents, and for a sudden moment, Noah was overcome with another wave of frustration and anger toward his mother for not giving them a chance, for not being willing to try harder.

"Noah, why did she leave it all to you when you were willing to let it fall apart?"

Noah blinked, startled, and it only took a second to realize what Adam was saying. He *knew*. Swallowing thickly, he scooped a single ball of dough from the pile and began to shape it with his hands the way Bubbe had taught him. "You went through the office."

"I was pretty sure you were hiding something, and I knew it had to do with the bakery." Noah didn't look up, but he didn't need to to know Adam was chewing on the edge of his thumb. "So yeah, I went through it. I saw all the default notices, and I saw the loan paperwork. Were you ever going to tell me?"

Noah wondered if it was because of Talia that Adam's voice didn't have the same fight it would have had just months ago. He still didn't look up now as he placed the crescents on the baking tray. "Yes."

"When?"

"Before I had to sell." Noah let the words fall as soft as he could manage, which wasn't soft at all.

"*When?*" Adam asked again, his voice more strained. "And how long has it been this bad?"

Rubbing at his eyes, Noah sighed. "Since before she died. She handed me a sinking ship, Adam, and I did my best to save it, but I couldn't."

"And you thought shutting me out was going to work?" Adam asked, his voice going hard.

Noah turned to stare at him. "You were fourteen when I came back here, and by the time you were old enough to take over, there was no saving this place."

"So instead of giving me a choice…"

"Yes," Noah admitted with defeat. "That was my mistake, and I'm sorry for it. But I'm not sorry you met Talia and started something for yourself. You worked your ass off for that truck."

Adam scoffed. "She gave it to me. I didn't work for anything."

"She gave you the keys. You built it into what it is now. You have a partner," Noah said, praying his brother would understand how lucky he was. "You have someone who loves every piece of you, and if you fall, she'll be there to catch you."

Adam was silent, sullen, but Noah could see him working it out through the tiny frown on his face.

Noah turned toward the ovens, opening both doors and placing two trays inside. He set the timer, then swiped his hands on his apron before facing his brother. "I'll show you where Bubbe put all her financial records if you want to see them. I didn't know about them until I started getting calls from debt collectors. She was behind on the mortgage here and behind with all her vendors. I was twenty. I had no idea what I was doing or how I was going to save it." His voice cracked, and he stopped, willing himself not to think about pushing back his crushing grief to deal with the mess his grandmother had left him. "This wasn't my dream, Adam."

Adam's face was still hard, but there was something else in his eyes now. "No. But it was mine."

Noah let out a small scoff and moved back to the table to finish shaping the rest of the dough. "You were *fourteen*. I didn't know this was what you were going to want. You had lost the only mother you had ever known. You were furious at me for getting time with Ema that you never had. You were furious that I remembered Tel Aviv and that you'd been barely old enough to open your eyes when we left."

"Ema could have taken us back there," Adam said, his voice barely a whisper. "Instead of wasting away here, where she was miserable."

Noah didn't mean to laugh, but he couldn't help it. It had taken him years to remember the way his mother really was —too thin, haggard, sleepless, angry. She was sick, and she was dying. It was only a matter of time before she was gone, even if there hadn't been a crash. Noah rubbed at his sternum.

"She never got over Abba's death. Ever. She would wait until Bubbe was asleep, then creep into my room and sit on the floor by my bed and tell me how she wished the three of us had died with him. Or just you and me so she wouldn't have to sit and look at us and remember him."

The silence was thick and painful.

"You're lying," Adam finally whispered.

Noah swallowed past a lump in his throat. "I wish I was. You have no idea how much I wish I was lying."

"How old were you?"

Noah shrugged. "Eight. She started the moment we got here. First in Hebrew, then in English as we started to learn more. Then she died, and I would wake up every single night from nightmares that she was somehow going to reach beyond death and take you with her. Bubbe tried to help, but she didn't know what to do, so I just…dealt with it."

"You never told me that either," Adam accused.

Noah swiped his hand over his brow, then turned away mostly to wash but also to have a reprieve from Adam's relentless gaze. "Of course not! You were a child, Adam. You were convinced she was…something else. You were convinced I had a relationship with her that was good. I barely remember the mother who was happy, Adam, but I didn't want to take that from you."

"So why tell me now?" Adam asked. The question wasn't mean this time, just honest.

Noah turned and felt so helpless. "Because you're right. I should have told you years ago. When you thought I was a mess for the sake of being a mess, I could have told you then. I couldn't handle setting foot outside the house…" He closed his eyes. "So I begged Hashem to protect you, and that in exchange, he could have all of me. I'd give up on the idea of love and friendships and anything personal so long as he didn't take you too."

Adam made a helpless noise. "You chose to suffer to protect me, but no one asked you to do that. That's not how it works, Noah."

Noah sighed and shook his head. "I know, but I was too afraid to take the risk. Bubbe left me with this debt, with this shop crumbling beneath our feet, because I was already ruined. She didn't want to ruin you too."

"Jesus," Adam said, and though Noah wasn't watching him, he heard his brother shift on the counter. "You aren't ruined."

"I'm close enough," Noah offered with a baleful smile. "You got out, though."

"Okay, but what about you? If it falls apart now, you'll never get out of debt." Adam took a step forward, then stopped. "What are you going to do?"

Noah shook his head. "I'm…I'm going to sell it. Not the bakery but the building."

"The apartment," Adam said, his tone slightly pinched, and Noah knew it was just him trying to hide his heartache. "You're going to sell our home."

Noah nodded. He stood there, and when Adam jumped down and stormed out of the room, Noah's eyes closed, and he sagged against the counter. It wasn't worse than he imagined but not much better either. He felt Adam's anger and frustration, and he deserved all of it.

Glancing at the clock, he knew Paxton wouldn't be long. Most of the prep work was done, and Wednesdays were never a big day for them. Noah would work a few hours later than usual, feed the cat, then head back over to Adriano's for their last night.

At least the last night before Noah had to decide whether he was really going to go all the way on camera. Resisting Adriano was getting harder and harder, his restraint at an all-time low. He wanted to be inside Adriano or let Adriano sink into him. He wanted to be pulled apart in ways that made him weep with pleasure, not with anguish.

He was just so damn tired.

Turning back to the cookies, Noah shoved everything in his head into the dark shadows, then got back to work. The almond cookies were the last to bake besides the challah, and then he could focus on everything else. Adam would…well, he would either come around, or he wouldn't, and Noah…

"This." Adam's sharp voice interrupted Noah's thoughts, and he spun to face Adam, who stood in the doorway that led to the stairs. He had stacks of papers clutched in his hands, and he walked over, slamming them down onto a clean spot on the baking counter. "This is everything?"

Noah glanced at the pile, and he couldn't be sure, but he nodded anyway. "Probably."

Adam thumbed the stack, then shoved them all to the ground. "You're fucking ridiculous, Noah."

He swallowed thickly and nodded. "I know."

"You should have been a goddamn Christian."

Noah blinked at him, startled and so confused. "What…"

"You suffer enough for a Jew, but you're *such* a fucking martyr," Adam said.

The accusation was so wild, so absurd—so Adam—that the laugh bubbled out of Noah's chest before he could stop it.

And it wasn't even funny really. It mostly hurt. The honesty of it, and the fact that while Adam never felt like he'd gotten what he deserved, Noah had never felt seen, and it was all crashing down. His carefully constructed walls were nothing more than rubble as he bent in half.

He wasn't quite sure when his laughter turned into sobs, but Adam was at his side, an arm around his waist as he got him to one of the stools. Noah couldn't begin to count how many times he'd done this with the roles reversed, with Adam crying rivers into the front of his shirt when kids were mean, when his girlfriends dumped him, when he was lonely. He had bouts of sadness and rage, and Noah had held him and rubbed his back through all of them.

But it had never been like this. Noah felt small, and weak, and even a little young. It threw him off-kilter, and it felt so wrong, but there was something to be said about taking comfort in family. He liked that Adam's arms—harsh as they could be—held him tight. He liked that this was a reminder that Adam was still there, and he wasn't totally alone in the world, even if his brother hated him a little.

"You should have told me," Adam murmured as he rubbed circles on Noah's back. "Even if I was a kid, I would have been there for you. I wasn't weak."

"I know." Noah's voice was thick and muffled against the front of Adam's apron. "But you were already hurting so much."

"So were you. I love Bubbe. I'll always love her, but it was unkind and unfair of her to dump that all on you."

Noah swiped his hands down his face as he pulled back, and Adam took a step away. "It was more than just not wanting to burden you. You were a child, and I didn't want you to become like me."

"I've always been my own person," Adam pointed out, making Noah smile in spite of himself. "Even back then, I could have handled it."

"I know that now," Noah said again. "You didn't deserve to be left in the dark."

Adam fixed him with a hard stare. "You didn't deserve to hold the weight of this place on your shoulders alone. Not forever."

Noah heard what Adam was saying and understood that it was more than just anger. Adam was never great with expressing his love in words, but he was good at this. He was good at showing it. Noah had just gotten so used to not watching.

Biting his lip, Noah swiped at his face again, finding his cheeks tacky but dry. His eyes ached, and his throat was sore from how much he'd been holding back. He wanted to fall apart—needed to—but not there.

"Where are you going to live when you sell?" Adam asked him, shattering the heavy silence between them.

"So you're not going to try to stop me?"

Adam let out a put-upon sigh and shrugged. "Is there any point? Even between me and Talia, we don't have the cash to pull this place out of the debt it's in, and unless you want to ask your porn-star boyfriend…"

"No," Noah said quickly.

Adam's lips twitched, but his eyes were still heavy and sad. "Then I need to accept it's over. And I get it, Noah. Businesses fail. Sometimes even after forty-two years, they go under."

Noah rolled his eyes up to the ceiling and tried to imagine not having this place. He had no job prospects after this was finished. He knew enough people in Savannah that he'd never be homeless, never be unemployed, but his entire life since the age of twenty had been decided for him by these walls.

"I don't know what I'm going to do."

Adam cocked his head to the side. "Will you finish school?"

Noah didn't mean to laugh. He knew the question was honest, but he couldn't help it. "I'm an old man. There's no place for me there."

Adam scoffed. "That's ridiculous. Anyone can go back to school. People get their doctorates at eighty, like, all the time."

"Yeah, but I didn't even finish my undergrad. The idea of sitting in a classroom full of toddlers all joining fraternities and sororities?" Noah shuddered, and it made Adam chuckle.

"Well, there's online. There are options. We could get a new place together, you and me. I mean, Talia would be with us, but we could find somewhere bigger."

Noah smiled at him, and he felt a hundred times lighter, even if the weight of his unknown future still pressed down on him. "You need that with her, not with your pathetic brother living like a third-wheel."

He knew he saw some relief in Adam's eyes but also worry. "So tell me what your plan is because I can't sit here and worry every day about you ending up on a park bench by the damn fountain."

Noah laughed. "It's not that serious. And I'm working on something, okay?" The buzzer for the cookies went off, so he grabbed the last batch out of the oven and placed them down to cool. "Today, I'm going to try to sell everything we just baked so I can pay the damned vendors' bills. Tonight, I'm going to sleep in bed with my boyfriend and let him figure out how to make all this feel better…"

"Boyfriend," Adam echoed. "Like actual boyfriend? Because I was giving you shit before."

Noah blushed a little, but he didn't duck Adam's gaze. "Or something. It's new."

Adam chuckled and shook his head. "You *are* a fucking mess."

"I know." Noah took his apron off, then moved to the sink to wash his hands, filling his cup and rinsing each hand three times. "Tomorrow night, I'm going to set up my booth at the farmer's market. I'm going to do that for the rest of the fall. Then I'm going to put this place on the market and see what happens."

"You won't be alone, you know," Adam told him. "Even if I ever leave Savannah, I'm not…I'm not going anywhere."

"I know, Adam. And…me too." Noah smiled at him, even if the thought of Adam packing up his things and moving made his chest ache. But he desperately wanted that for him too. He just wanted his brother to be happy.

The only difference now was that he wanted to be happy too.

CHAPTER 16

ADRIANO DID his best to avoid the bake shop, but he keenly felt the absence of Noah in the hours he was gone. Adriano hated waking up alone. He'd been with Eric for longer than he hadn't by that point in his life, and even though they were barely acquaintances by the end, Adriano always woke to find him in bed.

Well, almost always. Sometimes he'd stay out late. Sometimes he'd text and say he was crashing with a friend, and Adriano never questioned it. He never thought to ask what friend or what that meant. He wondered if Eric would have lied directly to his face, but Adriano was so caught up in himself he hadn't considered that Eric might have been looking elsewhere.

As he stared at himself in the mirror, combing through his freshly washed hair, he wondered when his vanity had turned into narcissism. Eric was to blame for cheating—there was no denying that—but Adriano had let himself grow so self-absorbed, so content with their life, he hadn't considered that maybe Eric was unhappy.

Maybe Adriano was the one who was impossible to live with.

His gut clenched, and he took a breath, resolving not to let that happen again. Not with Noah. Noah was too precious to him.

He stared down at Jude, who was lying on his feet, and he smiled. He felt at home here, even in the tiny little rental with three bedrooms and a kitchen he could barely turn around in. It felt like home because Noah was there with him, and their things had sort of mingled together in the corners of the space. Adriano would have to work at it to pull them apart.

He wanted it to stay that way, even though he knew he needed to take it slow. For his sake and for Noah's.

His phone buzzed in his pocket, and he pulled it out to find Anthony's name on the screen. *Skype, two minutes.*

Adriano wanted to tell him no, to tell him this was still his sanctuary and the chaos and coldness of his previous life—or his real one, he still wasn't sure—wasn't allowed in this bubble, but he knew he couldn't do that.

Adriano padded back to the bedroom and fell onto his stomach, flipping open his laptop. Jude nipped at his heels until Adriano gathered him up and sighed as the dog tucked himself under Adriano's chin. The Skype screen sat blank and waiting, and Adriano buried his nose in Jude's fur until the call lit up.

Anthony looked tired and frustrated, and he turned to the side and said something before a younger man wearing a white t-shirt with brown skin and a mouth turned down into a natural frown stepped behind him. He had the sort of Hollywood hipster look Adriano hadn't been missing—attractive and probably hired based on his headshot.

"I found an interpreter for the afternoon," Anthony said, the man's hands working through ASL almost flawlessly. "His name is Lemorris."

Adriano's stomach unclenched. 'Great. Nice to meet you. Anthony, is this important?'

The man spoke haltingly after Adriano's hands stilled, and then he waited patiently. Where had he been when Adriano was losing his shit in Xander's office? But that was unfair, and really, that moment had led directly to Adriano wanting to leave town, and now he had Noah. There were no regrets.

"You just opened up a SinSity account," Anthony said, and Adriano's stomach plunged toward his knees.

'Are you having my email accounts followed?'

Anthony gave him a flat look. "Xander still has access to your social media, Adriano. You opened up a poster account, not viewer. He's trying to get a court order to collect."

Adriano rolled his eyes. 'I don't have exclusivity with him for Adriano Moretti. I have exclusivity for Sylent, and Sylent doesn't exist on SinSity. Besides, I have a signed contract with my co-star. I'm working P R O B O N O.' He spelled the word out carefully, watching Lemorris's lips curve over each letter.

Anthony's face got redder. "That's not going to fly."

'Then he can take me to court,' Adriano said. 'I'm not listed on the credits, though. And I fired him, so just because he can take money from me doesn't mean he can log into my email.' And really, that was his own fault. He'd been so caught up in all this, he'd forgotten just how much Xander controlled. Not his finances, but every facet of his public face. It would be easy enough to fix. For now. He just wanted to get Noah paid, and he wasn't going to let Xander ruin one more good thing.

"Why do you enjoy making my life difficult?" Anthony asked, and Adriano wouldn't have been surprised if it was said with a groan.

'Because I pay you a ridiculous amount of money for it,' Adriano answered, his face cheerful.

Anthony scowled, but Adriano didn't care. Yes, this offered a new complication to the already messy situations he and Noah were both in, but it was worth it. At least he knew Noah was worth it, and he could only hope Noah felt the same way.

Checking the clock, he saw that Noah would be in the middle of his afternoon rush, whatever sort of rush it was. Adriano had been respecting Noah's space, but Noah had been free in admitting his business was in sorry shape over the last few years. He didn't want to bother him, but he was feeling restless after ending the call with Anthony.

It was the first real conversation he'd had with his lawyer in days, and instead of anything being close to solved, there were just more problems piled on. His head pounded a little at the temples, and he pushed up from the bed, glancing behind him to see if Jude followed.

He dressed quickly, slipped his hearing aids in, and adjusted them so they'd filter out the more obnoxious sounds from being in public, then clipped Jude to his leash and jumped in the car, heading for downtown. He could see how Noah worried about him getting bored in a place like this. After a few weeks, it would be easy to exhaust what little there was to do.

He was a California boy, born and bred. He grew up with his toes in the sand, with his feet on a board, with saltwater in his ears, nose, and eyes. The Atlantic wasn't the same as the Pacific. It was calmer, greener, softer.

Savannah was by no means temperate. The high noon sun was hot on his bare arms, and the humidity was pressing, but there were enough trees to keep him shaded as he moved toward Forsyth Park. He turned the corner, the way he'd gone when Noah had taken him to the market, and he saw the stall skeletons still set up with rolled tent flaps and pinned signs.

Tomorrow night, he'd be back. Noah had reluctantly agreed to let him help out both in the kitchen and at the booth, and he felt a sort of thrill to be allowed to step into

Noah's world. He felt the pressure to prove himself too. To prove that he was more than a spoiled rich diva.

He glanced down at Jude, then looked around to see if there was anywhere that might sell water for the dog. The fire station was across the street, and he half considered peeking into the building when he saw a familiar white truck with the metal shutters propped open and a handful of people eating at folding card tables.

The Lofty Latke food truck was the mark of Noah's official split from his brother—and maybe his self-sacrifice. Adriano knew he had never loved his brothers with the same intensity that Noah loved his, and he wasn't sure if that made him a bad person or not. But he did take comfort in knowing that they felt the same way about him.

Pietro had been worried, and Luca had stepped in when Adriano needed him, but neither had bothered to text and check in. The rest of his siblings had scattered after college, and being the baby, he hardly remembered any of them.

As he drew closer, he saw Talia—Adam's girlfriend—lean out of the truck and hand something down to a little girl, who grinned and moved back to her table. Adriano softened. Talia had a hardness to her which Adriano noticed first, but that wasn't the only thing. It couldn't be.

A hand tapped Adriano on the shoulder, and he startled, turning to find a familiar face standing a few feet away. He'd met Oscar when he was perusing the streets, standing outside of his snack shop holding a tray of samples, and Adriano had stopped for a quick chat. Oscar was a lot like the other people around the area, friendly and oddly eager to get to know him, even with a communication barrier.

Adriano couldn't help his grin as he dropped to his knees, giving the Golden Retriever a thorough scratch before smiling up at the guy.

"Taking a walk?" he asked.

Oscar shrugged. "Needed to think," he said. Or something

like that, but Adriano had only caught part of it. 'This is Paisley,' he spelled.

Adriano grinned and gave the dog another scratch before he stood up. "Do you think the food truck has water for Jude?" Adriano signed water, and Oscar copied him, then nodded and gestured for Adriano to follow him. Jude trotted right alongside Paisley, obviously excited to make a new best friend, and Adriano kept his gaze mostly fixed on the truck.

Talia noticed them first, her eyes widening, then going narrow. She elbowed Adam and leaned in to say something, which had Adam spinning in place, gaze fixed on Adriano as they came to a stop at the window.

Adam dragged his tongue over his bottom lip, then with shaking hands and in signed English said, 'How are you?'

Adriano snorted and repeated the signs in ASL. "I'm fine," he added and signed along with his voice. "Just need some water for the dogs."

Adam took the lead and came out of the truck and around with two bowls of water for Paisley and Jude, setting them up in the shade.

His eyes were on Adriano the entire time. Adriano saw all the similarities and all the differences between the brothers. Adam was classically good looking—sharper cheekbones, well dressed, his hair just as curly but left wild and long. His eyes were a richer brown than Noah's, whose eyes were more like honey, and his lips were held in a half sneer when at rest, which Adriano knew many people enjoyed. His own was much the same.

But he lacked the homeliness that Adriano had become obsessed with in Noah. The curved jawline, and the soft belly, and the sprinkle of freckles. Adriano knew he'd probably grow to be friends with Adam if Noah wanted to keep him, and he also knew he'd never regret his choice to pursue Noah, even if it started on a whim.

Adriano was vaguely aware that there was a conversation

going on around him, but before he could try to participate, his phone buzzed. His heart leapt a little in his chest when he saw his lover's name on the screen.

> Noah: I hate to ask, but I need a favor. There's a bar near Central Ave called the High Street Tavern, and I need a six-pack of OU Blue Moon. I already called Rose, and she said she has it ready for me. No worries if you're too busy.

> Adriano: nvr 2 busy. OU?

> Noah: means Kosher. It'll have an O with a U in the center of it. Just double-check for me, and if you don't mind, could you bring it here?

> Adriano: drunk on job. Lol. B there soon.

He set his phone down and waved his hand at Adam until he looked at him. "High Street Tavern?"

Adam looked surprised. "Um."

"Noah needs beer," Adriano clarified, though he didn't ask for what, and Adam didn't seem like he was going to ask.

After a beat, Talia tapped him and pointed at Adriano, then at herself, then down the street. Adriano wondered for a moment if she would ever learn enough ASL to converse like two grown adults. He'd done the pantomime thing more than he wanted to think about, and it wasn't under his skin yet, but he could feel it starting to itch.

All the same, he knew what Talia was saying, and he nodded. He turned to Oscar and affected puppy-dog eyes. "Keep Jude for a little while?"

Oscar rolled his eyes, but he nodded his fist then spelled, 'OK. Give me your number, and you can text me when you're done.'

Adriano did, quickly tapping his number into Oscar's

phone before sending himself a text. Jude seemed more than content to continue biting on Paisley's ear and didn't seem to notice when Adriano stood up and headed down the sidewalk after Talia who had taken up a brisk pace. Adriano knew it was probably awkward for her too. Communication barriers often made him want to put his fist through the wall. Hell, he was confused why Talia wanted to come along in the first place.

But she had, and she led the way across the street and down another until they were stepping into a bar that looked old and rustic. There was no one inside, and it took a moment for Adriano to realize the place was closed.

He followed Talia to the bar, which looked like any one of the trendy bars Eric dragged him to in Malibu, apart from the sort of ageless feel of the wood walls and floors. It was quiet, though—no thrumming vibrations of music—and he didn't see movement anywhere.

Talia seemed to know the place well enough, though, because she bent over the marble top and came back with a server pad and a pen. *Rose's in the back. She heard us come in and said she'd be out in a second.*

Adriano smiled and signed, 'Thank you,' mouthing it, and Talia caught his meaning, nodding back.

She bent over the pad again and wrote for a while, then looked hesitant as she pushed the pad over toward Adriano. *Adam was on my case the other day about learning sign language. Stuff like that is hard for me. I barely passed Spanish with a C-. But I'll try if you plan to stick around.*

Adriano realized the note for what it was—a sort of third-degree. *What are your intentions with my boyfriend's brother?* He smiled a little and shrugged. "I like him. We haven't talked about the future much, but if he wants me to stay, I'd like to."

Talia worried her bottom lip between her teeth. *We don't get along. Me and Noah. I'm trying, though.*

Adriano nodded and gave Talia's shoulder a pat in solidarity. He didn't know the situation well enough, and he could also easily see why Noah would conflict with others. His body was soft at the edges, but his wit and temper weren't. Adriano loved that about him, though, and he hoped it wouldn't change.

We heard what happened with your ex. That's shitty. Were you together long?

Adriano had a feeling that note was a bit of espionage on Adam's part, but he didn't mind. His entire business with Eric had been fully public, even if most of the world only had Eric's side of things. "We were together since I was in college. We split up a few times, but I think it was fifteen years total."

Talia's eyes went wide, and Adriano felt the breath she released. *So is Noah a rebound thing?*

Adriano felt his eyes narrow, his hands itching to sign instead of having to voice all this. It was an unfair question for how he felt about Noah, but he reminded himself no one there knew him, and a lot of these people didn't seem to know Noah either. "Eric and I fell out of love a long time ago. Years. But he was my interpreter, and being together was easier than being apart."

Is it true he's engaged to your former agent?

Adriano's eyes went blurry as he stared at the note. He'd been deliberately avoiding all social media but maybe to a fault. He blinked again, and Talia had written more.

Shit. Did you not know? He posted it on Twitter.

Adriano curled his fingers into tight fists to avoid them shaking, and he licked his lips before he tried to speak again. "I didn't know." The words felt heavy and misspoken on his tongue, but he didn't care. He was saved for the moment when the kitchen doors swung open and a short, slight woman walked out.

She had a round face and wide eyes, her dark hair piled in a messy bun on top of her head. There were strands of silver glinting in the overhead light, but she looked young for greys. Her smile was friendly, and her full mouth moved a mile a minute as she spoke.

She stopped abruptly, though, glancing over at Talia, then Adriano watched her eyes zero in on his hearing aids, and she blushed high on her cheekbones as she set the beer down in front of him. "Sorry," he saw her lips shape.

Adriano waved her off. He was grateful for the distraction, but he'd have to face this and soon. "Kosher?" he asked.

She blinked then turned the case to the side and pointed at the little OU symbol Adriano had seen plenty of times but had never wondered about. He gathered the beer to him, then tipped a nod at Talia and Rose before hurrying out. It was rude—probably unforgivably rude—to run out like that. Hell, she might have even needed payment. He might have just stolen product.

But Talia's reveal had shaken something in him, and he didn't know why. He didn't want Eric back. That wasn't it. It felt like something deeper, more profound. Like maybe he'd wasted fifteen years on a man who had just been waiting for someone better to come along.

It was probably normal, wondering what Xander could give Eric that he couldn't. Adriano was more attractive, and he was better in bed. He didn't even have to fuck Xander to know that. But then he thought about Noah, about how simple things like kissing and touching felt more passionate than any sort of bondage or kink or role play or romantic setup he'd ever been in, while filming or not.

Just Noah's fingers on him alone got him more worked up than Eric's acrobatic tricks ever could.

And maybe that was it. Adriano could offer Eric money, and popularity, and an easy lifestyle. He offered him permanent work and someone to come home to at night. A warm body to fill their bed. But nothing else.

Certainly not love. At least not real love.

He was shaken, but maybe it wasn't from pain. Maybe it

was from the realization that he'd been holding himself back from something like this, something so good and so fulfilling he was ready to give up anything if Noah asked him to.

Then there was the calming, warm, quiet knowing that Noah would never ask him to give up anything. And that alone told him it was right.

CHAPTER 17

Noah had sent Paxton off, flipped the open sign to closed, then propped open the side door before he got to the sufganiyot dough. It felt different and a little wrong but sort of decadent to veer from Bubbe's recipes. He had a list of fillings scribbled out to his right, and he'd finished all of them except the Belgian ale, which—with any luck—was on its way along with his boyfriend.

Or...lover. Whatever they were.

Noah didn't really want to think about things with Adriano beyond the present moment. He was wrung out and exhausted from his long cry with his brother. Adam had wrung every bit of Noah's energy from him in the best way. It was cathartic to finally be unburdened and to know Adam didn't hate him.

But Adam knowing changed nothing. It meant Adam had more time to prep, to go through the apartment and take the things he wanted and the things he needed. He'd be around to help Noah strip the place down to bare bones when it was time.

That was months away, but it felt like he could blink, and it would all be over.

More than anything, he wanted to finish up this night and get back to Adriano's. He wanted to lose all sense of self, all sense of awareness, except the places where Adriano dragged pleasure from him. He just wanted to not *think*.

Noah startled when the door opened, and he looked up at Adriano. His hands froze where they were kneading the dough. Adriano looked shaken. His face was a little pallid, his eyes half-lidded, mouth in a deeper frown than usual.

His gaze locked on Noah, then he set the beer down hard and crossed the room, sweeping Noah into his arms, floured apron and all.

"Hey," Noah soothed, pulling back.

Adriano's palm cupped Noah's cheek, and his thumb trailed a path under Noah's left eye. 'Crying?'

Noah let out a small sigh, and he knew there was no point in lying. 'Yes. This morning. Adam was here.'

Adriano scowled. 'He hurt you?'

Noah took a step back and tried for a smile he hoped was soothing. 'No. I told him the truth about my grandmother leaving me the bakery while it was in massive debt and about it going under. I told him I was selling the building and the apartment.'

'He was angry?'

Noah shook his head. 'Sad. He was frustrated I didn't tell him before. We don't communicate well.'

Adriano snorted in amusement and gathered Noah close again, kissing him, though it lacked the passion of the last few days. When he pulled back, he didn't step far away, just enough so he could drop his head down to rest against Noah's.

They stayed that way for what felt like forever, then Adriano stepped back and let Noah get to the dough. 'How can I help?'

Noah raised a brow at him. 'You can tell me what's wrong.'

Adriano looked a little put-out, then glanced back at the door he'd shut when he'd come in. 'Personal stuff.' Noah winced, and Adriano looked immediately apologetic. 'My ex is getting married.'

Noah's eyes went wide, and he pushed the dough aside to let it rest for a minute. 'Eric?'

Adriano's eyes darkened. 'Yes. To Xander.'

'Your agent?' Noah clarified.

'E X,' Adriano spelled, his fingers sharp. He pulled out his phone and opened his Twitter app. It was already loaded to Eric's Twitter. Noah had followed it once. Eric was a funny guy, witty and sharp. Adriano had more followers, but Eric had enough for a verification check, and he was always responsive.

Noah had been jealous, but he'd also liked the guy before he knew what he was capable of doing to someone Noah cared about.

@ChaddicusRex: sometimes when life closes one door, three more open. Can't wait to make @XanderBlessingame an honest man, though neither of us are innocent enough for that. I wish I could invite you all to the wedding, but you'll be there in spirit.

Noah read it, then reread it, then looked up at Adriano and searched his face. He was angry—that much was obvious—and maybe a little hurt. Noah didn't blame him for that. He felt some measure of relief, though, when he didn't find heartbreak, but he wondered if that was cruelly selfish, considering how long Eric and Adriano had been together.

'What can I do?' Noah asked.

Adriano made a soft noise and brushed his thumb over Noah's lips, then leaned in to kiss him before stepping back. 'Teach me how to bake something. Give me something I can beat up.'

Noah laughed, then gestured to the mixing bowl, which was full of dough for his second batch of sufganiyot. 'Flour and knead that. Do you know how to knead dough?'

'I've done it before,' Adriano said. He washed up, dried his hands, then gathered the dough onto the floured table and began to work it.

Noah watched him for a moment, briefly worried that Adriano's mood was going to ruin the dough. But Noah had probably thrown out a mortgage payment's worth of ingredients in his lifetime, taking his aggression out on what would have been sweets and breads, so he couldn't judge.

Only Adriano didn't ruin it. He was careful and methodical with precise hands that were strong but delicate. Noah felt his cock harden, and his mouth watered, and he wondered if the door had locked when Adriano closed it.

Breathing out, he turned toward his own task again and began to roll everything out into a neat square. The sharp-edged sufganiyot stamp—just a biscuit cutter—slipped through the dough to make perfect rounds, and he carefully placed each circle onto the tray for the second prove. By the time he was done, Adriano was leaning against the counter, staring with dark eyes.

'I like watching you work,' Adriano told him.

Noah was already flushed, and he felt himself grow hotter and harder between his legs. 'It's more practice than skill.'

Adriano hummed softly as he came around the side of the counter. 'What do I do now?'

'It needs to rise,' Noah told him. He was aware his hand had a faint tremble of want, and with the way Adriano's eyes flickered from his face to his fingers, it was clear he'd noticed too.

Adriano brushed past him, a deliberate motion, and took the already greased bowl. He didn't break eye contact as he set the dough inside, then draped the discarded towel over it and set it aside. Noah swallowed so loudly it clicked in his throat, and he couldn't stop the faint whimper when Adriano moved in close again.

'Noah.' He didn't spell it this time. He mouthed Noah's

name with something totally new. His name sign, fingers curling down from his chin.

It meant precious.

Noah's breath rushed out of his lungs, and he barely had time to suck it back in before Adriano was on him, pressing him to the baking counter, one thigh roughly parting Noah's legs and lifting him up onto his toes. Noah ground himself against his lover, his head tipped back as Adriano devoured his neck, and Noah was so, so close.

And not just because he had no restraint or control but because it was Adriano. Adriano wanted *him*. Only him.

"Noah," Adriano murmured against Noah's flushed skin. "Noah." His hand dragged between them, then his fingers ducked under Noah's apron, and the heel of his palm began to stroke Noah through his jeans.

His head swam, all the blood flooding into his dick and making his balls tight. He was going to spill right there, right in his kitchen. An absurd thought—this ancient, archaic law about being punished by Hashem for spilling seed onto the ground—hit him. He felt a rush of panic, but it only lasted a second because Adriano was hoisting him up onto the baking counter, his large hands fumbling with Noah's button and zipper.

"Want to taste you. Please," Adriano begged. He looked into Noah's face, into his eyes, asking for consent.

Noah touched his cheek lightly with the tips of his fingers, basking in the rough growth of Adriano's facial hair. He hadn't shaved in days, and Noah wanted to feel that rough burn on his bare legs. 'Yes,' he signed.

Adriano's gaze went possessive, predatory, hungry. Noah braced himself, leaning backward, his hands inches from the unused dough. He scraped his nails along the wood as Adriano nosed his hard cock, then sucked the tip into his mouth, letting it rest there, fat and swollen against his tongue.

Noah had gotten his wish. He felt nothing, could think of nothing except how Adriano's lips were stretched around him, just holding him there. Pleasure was shooting through his limbs in short starbursts, whiting out the edges of his vision, but everything about Adriano was still clear.

'Please,' his flat palm circled his chest, and with that single plea, Adriano sank down, and Noah's dick hit the back of his throat.

That was all it took. Adriano had done more than touch him. He had consumed him, devoured him. He sucked Noah dry as Noah's hips pumped up off the table, his balls spasming in time with his pulse, and Adriano groaned like it was the best thing he had ever tasted.

When it became too much, Noah tapped him, and Adriano pulled away with a wet pop. His lips were slick with spit, and when he dipped his tongue into Noah's mouth, Noah could taste the faint tang of himself. He kissed Adriano back harder than he meant to, but Adriano didn't seem to mind.

He was hard in his own jeans, his erection pressed to Noah's thigh, but he didn't seem in a hurry to do anything about it. He just held Noah close, kissing him until they needed to breathe properly, then he pulled away and nuzzled his nose against Noah's cheek like he couldn't bear to stop touching as many places as possible. Then he thrust his face into the crook of Noah's neck and just stood there.

As Noah's pulse returned to normal, he felt Adriano pressing soft kisses against his skin before he pulled away. 'Did we break some major religious laws?' he asked, his hand still shaking a little from the adrenaline. 'That probably wasn't kosher.'

The cool air against his limp dick brought Noah back to reality. His face flushed with what he'd just done. He didn't think there were any specific laws in the Talmud about having your dick sucked in your bakery, but he didn't think even the most liberal rabbi would condone it either.

It felt...decadent. Maybe not a sin. He had never bought into the belief that enjoyment and pleasure were wrong.

Noah laughed, and it felt freeing. 'No laws about eating come, so I think we're fine. As long as it didn't get in the food, which isn't a religious thing, but the health inspector would have an issue.'

Adriano licked his lips, then looked behind Noah at bits of the dough, which had been ruined by his scrabbling fingers. 'Maybe don't use that. And sanitize.'

Noah rolled his eyes, but he let Adriano help him down, let Adriano crowd him against the counter again and kiss him until his toes curled and his heart filled his entire chest. *I love him.* The thought came barreling in, unrepentant, refusing to be ignored. He didn't say it, not yet, but he wasn't sure he'd be able to hold out for long.

For now, he gave Adriano's side a pat before zipping his jeans back up, then moving to the sink to wash up. Adriano joined him, and after they dried, Noah pointed at the beer. 'You still want to help?'

'Yes,' Adriano answered, and he squared his shoulders and set his jaw.

Noah grinned at him. 'Then let's get to work. We can finish everything else'—he let his hand hang in the air for a moment—'when we get home.'

Home.

It shouldn't have felt so right, but *oh*, it did.

THE PAIR of them parted ways after storing everything they could for the market on Thursday. Adriano headed back to the island while Noah went upstairs to change his clothes and feed Marshmallow.

He was looking forward to being home or at least in a space that was his, but he wasn't looking forward to the emptiness that came with it. For as tight as he'd held him and for as desperately as he'd kissed him, Adriano had made no promises to him. Noah knew they needed to talk, but he wanted to delay the possible answer that Adriano wanted to back off.

Noah took his time showering, then ate a little of the leftover soup Adam had brought over the other night. He gave his cat affection and attention, even though the little beast didn't seem to care whether or not Noah was actually there, and he headed out when Adriano sent him a text letting him know he was finished with whatever business he needed to take care of.

The night air was cooler, just a hint of lingering humidity. The rains were winding down, but the season was far from finished. Most of the storms would shut down the market and events, and part of him was looking forward to the excuse to stay in and watch the streets flood. They didn't get hit as hard as some places, but they usually had one or two tropical storms that killed the power all day.

He used to love it as a kid. He'd take Adam's chubby hand in his and drag him through the puddles once the thunder and lightning had moved on. They'd catch little frogs that seemed to spring up from the ground, and they'd smile at the old man who had a barbershop and used to hand out what he'd called *penny candy*. He'd died before Noah came back—when he realized the entire city had not existed in a bubble.

His old enemies had moved on, the people he'd envied now holding positions of power. He saw Ronan with his dark eyes, and Fitz with his never-ending smile, and he realized he'd never be like them. But maybe that was okay—at least it felt okay now. It felt like maybe they didn't mind so much that he was never going to be social the way they were.

Maybe Birdie's apology and admission had proven something. Noah had only believed what he wanted to because it was easier than dealing with the stuff he had going on inside.

He tapped his foot on the ground in an absent rhythm, then perked up when he heard Jude's soft yips. Adriano came around the corner not long after, and he smiled, gathering Noah into his arms for a kiss.

'Ready?' he asked when he pulled away.

Noah nodded, then led the way to his car. Jude perched on the console between them, and the drive to the rental was almost too short. Noah wasn't as anxious as he was the first night, but knowing this was an ending had him on edge. There had been a sort of humming desire between them since Adriano had sucked his cock, and Noah wanted to get this over with because, as much as he wanted to drag this last night out, he also wanted Adriano to get off. Adriano's pleasure had become just as important as his own if not more. Things felt unequal and strange, and Noah wanted to be back on even footing.

He startled out of his thoughts when Adriano touched the side of his neck, and he offered a smile of apology when he felt his lover's rough thumb brush against his jaw. 'Sorry.'

Adriano shook his head. 'Do you want to eat or watch TV? Rest for a bit?'

Noah bit his lip. It sounded nice, even if it was procrastination. But no. That wasn't what he wanted at all. 'I want you.'

Maybe the ferocity of his need was all these years of being deprived, not just of sex but of touch. He'd steadfastly avoided even the most casual affection from anyone but Adam, and even his brother was stingy. But he didn't think he'd react with anyone else the same as he did with Adriano. Noah wanted to believe—no, *needed* to believe—that only Adriano could make him feel this way.

Adriano took slow, deliberate steps toward Noah, and when they were touching, he backed him up against the wall.

He held him, achingly similar to the way he had at the bakery, one large thigh parting Noah's into a wide vee before lifting him high onto his toes.

Adriano's head dipped low, his nose brushing along Noah's cheeks, followed by parted lips, hot breath ghosting over Noah's oversensitive skin. He groaned, and Adriano moved one hand to circle his throat, just resting lightly there with fingers pressed to his pulse point.

Noah's heart raced, and he let his head fall back against the wall as Adriano laid waste to the crook of his shoulder with tongue and teeth. There would be marks. Oh, there would be evidence left behind beyond empty balls, sweat, and a few tears.

"Precious," Adriano murmured against his clavicle, and those three words rushed to the tip of Noah's tongue, but he held them back. Even if Adriano wouldn't hear them, Noah refused to utter them just then. Not yet, though he would be a fool to think he could hold out much longer.

Noah's temperature rose another degree before Adriano finally let him go, sliding him to the ground before taking both hands in his. He walked backward as he led the way to the bedroom, and he flicked on one of the low lights. The camera was where it was before, poised on the stand that would keep their faces out of the frame, and Noah stared at it for a long time.

There was no preamble for this one, no discussion. Adriano set Noah in the middle of the room, then pushed the button. The red light glowed, a beacon, a reminder, of what this part was. Then there were hands. Large fingers tugged at his clothes, pulling his shirt over his head, dropping his jeans to the floor. Normally, Adriano remained dressed. At best, his throbbing erection was seen tenting his pants, but this time, he took Noah's hands and set them at his waist.

He said nothing, signed nothing, but he didn't need to. Noah worked, driven by instinct and desire to have all of

Adriano naked in front of him, to be the one to control the moment when the rest of the world would see him naked.

There were pieces of this Noah wanted to keep for himself, but having this control was filling him with a desperation he wasn't expecting.

Adriano looked around, then he turned Noah away from the camera. His hard cock pushed between Noah's thighs, thrusting into the dry heat only for a moment. Adriano let out a soft grunt, then pulled away and used his hands to ease Noah down onto all fours.

They hadn't talked about this, they hadn't discussed what Adriano planned to do with him during this last filming, but it didn't matter. He trusted Adriano. He dropped his forehead to the bed, feeling both shameless and a little scared to be on display. Adriano was sitting off to the side, and Noah knew his ass was fully exposed.

Adriano's hand curved over it, squeezing, kneading. His other hand joined, and Noah felt hot air over his hole when Adriano suddenly spread his cheeks wide. Then there was a finger or maybe a thumb. It was huge, and a little rough, and wet because Adriano had licked it. It swirled through his whorls of untamed hair, then pushed just enough to remind Noah he could slip inside before it was gone.

Noah let out a sharp moan at the loss, but the empty feeling didn't last. His body was zinging with pleasure, but he wasn't close. Just days ago, he would have come by now. He would have come downstairs when Adriano was sucking hickies onto his neck, but now...it was more. He was ready, restrained.

His cock hung thick and weeping between his legs, but it would take effort this time. Adriano didn't seem to mind, though. He let out a low chuckle as he pressed his finger against Noah's hole once more, then, without warning, a tongue replaced it.

Noah let out a shout of surprise, of ecstasy, of need. His

elbows shook and gave way, and his whole upper body fell to the bed. Adriano kept his lower half up with firm hands bracketing his hips like parentheses as his tongue devoured him from the inside out.

It was too much and not enough, and perfect and imperfect all at once.

It was as close to Hashem as he might ever feel—the way his heart soared, and his head spun, and his heart raced.

"Please." He wasn't supposed to talk, mostly because it wouldn't matter, Adriano couldn't hear him, and being on all fours like this, he couldn't sign. But he couldn't stop himself from begging anyway. "Please."

He was close. He was close. He was...

He was coming. He was fucking backward against Adriano's face, the orgasm almost wrong because he wasn't full enough, but he couldn't stop it. He sobbed as Adriano plunged his tongue deeper, swirling it around, leaving him sopping wet with spit.

As he shook, Adriano laid soothing hands on his back, painting them downward with firm strokes, kissing the small of his back as he made soft, humming, soothing sounds.

"Noah," he realized Adriano was saying. "Noah."

Noah gathered the strength to turn, and with a sloppy, single hand signed, 'Turn the camera off.'

Adriano didn't hesitate. He was up in a flash, the light dimmed, then flickered out. The quiet hum that Noah always forgot to listen for was gone, and in its place was an utter absence of sound. He swallowed thickly, his breathing too loud in that shallow space.

He wasn't done. He needed something else.

"Fuck me." He said it, then spelled the letters on a clumsy hand. "I need you inside me."

Adriano's eyes were half-lidded but fierce as they watched Noah's fingers like he couldn't quite believe him. His hand rose to his chin, and he signed Noah's name again.

'Fuck me.' Noah's hand was stronger now and steady. He rose to his knees and turned, but not completely. Adriano's thigh was still molten hot against his own. 'I want you to fuck me. I need you to fuck me. I need you inside me. Come inside me.'

Adriano shivered, and for a moment of wild unease, Noah thought his plea was going to be rejected. Then Adriano let out a noise almost like a wounded animal and gathered Noah to him. He pulled Noah astride his bent thighs, back to his chest. His rock-hard cock slid between Noah's cheeks, and Adriano's mouth attached to the back of his neck in a painful, sucking kiss.

"Say it again," Adriano demanded, not letting go.

Noah lifted his hands. 'Fuck me. Come inside me.'

Adriano didn't let Noah go. He shuffled forward, then reached for the nightstand drawer and took out lube and condoms. Noah knew it wouldn't be bare. Adriano was a porn star, and it was the only way to be truly safe, no matter how often he was tested. And that was fine. Noah wanted it messy, but more than that, he wanted it however Adriano could take him.

Adriano's eyes slipped shut, then he leaned in and put his mouth to Noah's shoulder before speaking, unclear but understandable. "If you want me to stop, tap my thigh."

Noah nodded hard enough Adriano could feel it, and he liked that Adriano trusted him enough not to open his eyes then. Noah followed him into the dark. It was soothing and calming, even though he didn't know what was coming.

He heard the snap of the bottle, then two fingers were between his ass cheeks as a large arm wedged itself between their bodies. Adriano didn't waste time. Noah's hole was still spit-slick and a little open, and Adriano's finger slid all the way in without much resistance. Noah shuddered from head to toe, his eyes still squeezed shut. He lolled his head back, and Adriano attacked his jawline with kisses as he added a second finger.

This is it, Noah thought. *This is it*. He wanted to think there was no going back, but that line had been crossed the moment he'd sent Adriano that first message. This was simply the inevitability—the end of that road—and maybe the beginning to another.

Bodies were made for pleasure. A rabbi at the temple had said that once when he was younger. Some of the teens were lost, and even Noah didn't understand what he was willing to give and what he was willing to take.

Hashem gave us pleasure for a reason.

Such a simple answer. Noah knew even then he liked men, but he was too afraid to voice that. He thought it applied now. Maybe. He wanted to believe such a large, all-encompassing God wouldn't condemn him to a life of suffering for what his body wanted. For this thing he had no control over.

But oh, *he* had the power now. He felt it as Adriano's entire body pushed against his, frantic with his own need to bury himself in Noah's ass.

There would be more for the camera. Noah would perform again later and give something—and take something—that he never had. But he hadn't realized how happy he was to have this moment, this experience, knowing it was just them.

That it would always be just them.

"Are you ready for me?" Adriano asked.

Noah nodded, squeezed Adriano's arm, and lifted onto his knees a bit higher so Adriano could get the condom on. He felt it—the slight, uncomfortable press of latex, but it was slick with lube and rock-hard and throbbing with Adriano's desire.

Adriano's desire for him. For Noah. No one else.

Noah went pliant as Adriano started to push inside, and

the pressure and the stretch was so much. He swore he felt like he would split in half, but he wouldn't have given it up for the world. His hands grasped the sides of Adriano's thighs as his lover finally slid all the way inside.

"My precious Noah," Adriano said against his ear.

Noah's eyes rolled back in his head, and his heart constricted as Adriano began shallow thrusts. He grunted with them, spreading his legs farther, leaning back. He wanted this, wanted to spend every second filled up with Adriano.

And then, the angle changed, and Adriano hit something that made Noah cry out and lurch forward. Adriano started to stop, but Noah shook his head frantically and pushed up, searching for that angle again. When he found it, he shouted and bounced harder, and Adriano laughed as he joined in the motions with harder thrusts.

"That's it, that's it," Adriano coaxed.

Noah was hard, ready to spill all over again. He didn't dare touch himself. He just rode the waves of pleasure until he crashed over the edge, and he was dimly aware of Adriano following behind. His seed was hot, even encased in the condom, and Adriano's dick felt bigger as it pulsed.

Noah's entire body was trembling like he was cold, but he took breaths as he came down, and he let Adriano hold him tight as he started to soften. Noah let out a small noise of protest when Adriano moved him to the bed. He pulled away with a wet squelch, and when he returned to spoon up against Noah's back, his dick was slightly tacky and bare.

Adriano's mouth found the sore spot on Noah's shoulder where he'd sucked a mark earlier, and he ran his tongue over it before tracing it with soft, open lips. "Are you okay?"

Noah turned over and shuffled back, though he kept their legs tangled together. 'I hope I didn't ruin anything. The video.'

Adriano shook his head. 'The video was beautiful, but

this…' His hand hovered, then fingertips traced around Noah's lips. 'You are everything. I'm falling for you.'

Noah closed his eyes a long moment, just basking. There was truth in Adriano's eyes—and affection. Maybe even love. He looked back at him after a second and lifted his hand between them. 'Me too.'

It wasn't quite a confession, not yet. But for now, it was close enough.

CHAPTER 18

Thursday late morning started hot, not a cloud in the sky, the sun beating down on the back of Adriano's neck causing him to break a sweat in spite of the low-key work he was doing. Noah was working a half day at the bakery, so Adriano volunteered to head over to the park to meet a man called Fitz. Noah explained he was the fire chief and one of the lead organizers of the market.

'He's nice,' Noah promised, then smoothed hands down the front of Adriano's t-shirt like he couldn't help but touch him. 'I don't know if he signs, but he'll do what he can to make it easy on you.'

Adriano grinned, knowing it looked hungry and predatory. He was starving for Noah in all ways, and he wondered when this feeling would be sated. He cupped Noah's cheeks with both hands, then dragged him into a deep, wet kiss. 'I'm not worried about it,' he replied when he pulled back. 'It sounds like fun.'

Noah's grin softened, his eyes a little heated, but he wasn't as overwhelmed by Adriano's touch as he had been. Adriano thought he might miss it, but he also knew it didn't take much to work Noah up, and that was enough. 'It won't be. It's work.'

Adriano shrugged, then dragged one hand down Noah's back as he gathered him close, stopping to cup his ass. 'Sore?'

Noah laughed with his shrug. 'Yes. But I like it.'

Adriano groaned, then kissed him again before tearing himself away. He took Jude's leash in hand, hooked his bag over his shoulder, then began the slow trek over to where the market was going to set up. It didn't take much to spot Fitz. Noah had described him well, though Adriano was instantly aware Noah had left out the fact that Fitz's entire right side from the neck down was shiny and tight with scars. He held his arm at an awkward angle like he couldn't straighten it completely, but that didn't seem to stand in his way as he hauled large boxes from the back of a pickup to the ground.

He was almost as tall as Adriano and almost as wide. His hair lay in soft brown waves that fell over his forehead, and his eyes were bright and friendly. His CCFD shirt—navy-blue with a logo on the pocket—stretched over his pecs, and Adriano knew if he wasn't so head over heels for Noah, he might have been interested.

Fitz took notice of him right away and waved him over, bending down to pet Jude first, which Adriano loved. There was something to be said about a town where everyone greeted his baby before him. When he righted himself, he extended his hand, and Adriano shook it, feeling calluses on his palm.

'Hi,' he signed. 'My name Fitz.'

Adriano couldn't tell if it was early education sign or something he'd picked up from YouTube. The grammar was wrong, and his movements were jerky, but it was something. 'Adriano,' he spelled before offering his sign name.

When Fitz pulled out a small pad of paper, it became obvious he was uncomfortable. *I only know a little sign from when I met Birdie's mom. Sorry.*

Adriano waved him off and scribbled beneath Fitz's neater writing, *No worries.*

Noah said you were coming by to help?

Put me where need me. Jude OK here?

Fitz frowned at the paper, then looked over his shoulder at the parking lot before shaking his head. *I don't know who that is.*

Adriano scratched his nose, then realized the mistake. 'Dog.' He pointed down at his little baby who was perched on one of his feet, staring up with his tongue lolling out.

Fitz had a loud, booming laugh, which Adriano both heard and felt, and the guy clapped him on the shoulder before he wrote again. *That little puffball? Brilliant. He can go hang out with Isaac and the cats.* Fitz pointed across the way at a little traveling paddock halfway through being set up. Two slender men were leaning against the half-standing fence post with their heads close together. *Isaac and Liam. They'll watch Jude.*

Adriano nodded, feeling a little apprehensive about turning his baby over to a paddock with a bunch of other animals, but Liam had been great with Jude at the cat café, so he trusted him. He straightened his shoulders, then turned to Fitz and pointed to the notepad. "Can I borrow that?"

Fitz blinked then grinned and nodded, handing it over. Adriano signed a quick thanks, then turned on his heel and crossed the grass toward the men who had gotten back to work. Liam noticed him first, and he said something to his companion who stopped and looked over his shoulder. Adriano watched as his eyes went wide, as his tanned skin went a bit pale, then pink around his ears.

The man recognized him.

Adriano held up the hand not holding the leash and notepad in greeting, then stopped a couple feet away to scribble on the paper. *Helping Fitz. Fitz say u watch Jude 4 me?*

Liam took the note, his tongue darting over his lips

nervously as he read, and Adriano was pretty sure he let out a nervous laugh before he looked back up and pointed to his companion. 'This is my boyfriend, Isaac.'

Adriano offered his sign name. 'Do you sign?'

Isaac flushed all over and made a see-saw gesture with his hand, then rubbed a circle around his chest with a fist. 'Sorry.'

Adriano waved him off, then took to writing again because he just wasn't in the mood to deal with half signs and pantomime. *It's fine. Writing good. Jude OK here?*

Isaac, who was reading over Liam's shoulder, looked up and nodded eagerly. He nudged his partner out of the way before dropping to his knees, and Jude wasted no time at all endearing himself to the total strangers. In seconds, he was on his back baring his stomach for pets.

Liam laughed and rubbed the back of his neck before tapping his chest with his thumb and wiggling his fingers. 'Fine.'

Adriano nodded. 'Thanks.' He pointed to himself, then over to where Fitz was unloading, and Liam gave another nod. It wasn't much, but it was something. Adriano watched Jude trot after Isaac, then pause by one of the small crates to sniff before scrambling back. Probably an irritated cat, and Adriano didn't blame the thing. He hated the feeling of being closed in and locked up.

It was strange how a life of freedom to live however he wanted had started to feel like a cage. And part of it was being Sylent. Part of it was being a publicly consumed celebrity with no real right to privacy. But part of it was also letting himself get lost in the *idea* of himself rather than the man he was.

How a small town with barely thirty thousand people managed to break down those walls was beyond him, but he felt like he could breathe for the first time. When he got back to Fitz, he had a smile on his face as he was put to work. The boxes were heavy, and he was sweating even harder. He was surrounded by people he couldn't really speak to, most of whom didn't know who he was from Adam. And he felt something like home.

THE ANTI-CILANTRO FOOD truck rolled up to the market around noon, so Adriano headed over to the window with Fitz and ordered a couple of burritos to take back to the bakery. They got along okay with Fitz's poor signing and the notepad, but Adriano was relieved to see that he was trying, that he was working on picking up more ASL.

His right hand was the only thing that gave him trouble, his thick fingers stiff, and he apologized for them repeatedly until Adriano touched his arm, then wrote a long paragraph in his best English to ease his worry.

I didn't know a lot of Deaf growing up, but in college there was club with diverse group. There were Deaf missing hands, Deaf with CP, Deafblind...not all equal, you know? ASL hard language, and I'm glad you try. I can't read lips well, and HAs only help me hear traffic or dog barking. I don't want you to keep working with your hand if uncomfortable. Notepad is fine.

Fitz's smile was sheepish as he scribbled out his reply. *I was burned in a fire when I was twelve on a Boy Scout camping trip. I'm right-handed but had to relearn everything with my left. Therapy helps. I do knitting and crochet to help flexibility. I just know how much it sucks to not have access. I'm not ashamed of my arm, but I'm sorry I'm not better for you.*

Adriano shook his head and patted his shoulder again. *You will be. Sign Language can adapt to the way you need it.* He liked the way Fitz went soft around the edges, the way his smile reached his eyes. These people were good people, genuinely good people. They cared in ways Adriano hadn't seen in years. Hell, maybe *ever*. They weren't looking for any and every opportunity to step on someone else to climb a rung higher on the ladder leading to absolutely nowhere.

They just wanted to exist, and that was enough for them.

And God—*God*—he wanted that to be enough for him too.

Fitz tapped him, then nodded to the food truck where a guy was leaning out the side offering out Adriano's bag, so he got up and grabbed it, tucking it under his arm. Glancing over his shoulder, he saw the paddock was up, and Isaac was sitting in the middle of it with two small goats and Jude who were all running after a ball.

"Do you think he'll mind if I take these to Noah?" Adriano asked aloud.

Fitz shook his head and wrote a quick note. *No, but if he does, I'll take over. I'm glad you like Noah. He's been through a lot.*

Adriano stared at the note until the words blurred. Normally, that kind of pressure would terrify him or send him running. He didn't want to feel like he was responsible for someone's happiness, but it was wholly different with Noah. He didn't want to be Noah's whole world, but he wanted to be part of it. And he wanted to be more than a man who worked him up and got him off. He wanted to be someone that made Noah smile the moment he walked into a room. He wanted to be one reason of many that made Noah's life feel complete.

"He's a good person."

Fitz nodded, and there was a ferocity in his eyes Adriano didn't quite understand. He was missing a lot, he knew. Noah had suffered as a kid—for his funny accent, and bad English, and strange customs. Too much like Adriano. Adriano's Deaf identity came first above all things, so it wasn't often he met someone who had assimilated less than he had, but Noah had all but cut himself off from everyone.

He was slowly stepping out a bit more, though. And

Adriano felt a wave of gratitude that he could be there to see it.

He tipped a wave at Fitz, signed a promise to be back later, even if Fitz didn't catch all of it, then he hurried down the street. He was glad it wasn't far, and he smelled bread baking as he turned the corner, a smile lighting up his face at the sight of the bakery window.

Pulling the door open, Adriano saw Noah's employee, Paxton, standing behind the counter. They hadn't officially met yet. Paxton was usually on his way out when Adriano arrived, so he offered a smile, which was returned, though there was something in Paxton's eyes that Adriano didn't much like.

Paxton lifted his hand in greeting as Adriano got closer, then he formed a C with his hand and rubbed it up and down his throat a few times. 'Horny?'

Adriano choked and felt a bit of rage bubbling up. Just because he was an adult-film star didn't give people the right to talk to him like that. Doing porn didn't mean his body or his sex life was on display at all times for anyone to just take.

Before he could fully unleash on this kid, however, Adriano noticed his eyes were fixed on the bag he was holding, and it became clear. He bit his lip, then set the bag down, held up his hands in surrender and shook his head. 'Hungry,' he spelled. He formed the C with his hand, then started at the top of his throat and dragged it down once. 'Horny,' he spelled slowly, to make sure the kid got it, then he repeated the earlier sign.

Paxton's eyes went wide, cheeks pink. His mouth began to move frantically, and Adriano could only imagine he was fumbling his way through an apology.

He didn't have the energy to ask him to repeat it or write it down, so he waved it off, then grabbed the food and pushed past the swinging door and into the kitchen. Noah was there at the baking table, his head bobbing in a rhythm that told Adriano there was music on. It wasn't loud enough for him to feel it, but the way Noah moved—the sway in his hips, the tapping feet—it was probably upbeat.

Adriano loved him. God, he was *so* in love with him.

He cleared his throat, and Noah peered over his shoulder, his face flitting through a few expressions before he settled on happiness. He swiped hands over his apron, then crossed the room and dragged Adriano into a kiss. There was the faint sweetness of jam on his tongue, and flour on his cheek, and his nails were crusted with drying dough, but he was the most beautiful thing Adriano had ever held in his arms.

Pulling back, Adriano cupped Noah's cheek for a long moment, then held up the bag and shook it. 'Lunch. Also, your employee just asked me if I was horny.'

Noah's eyes went wide, his mouth parted. 'He *what?*'

'I think he meant hungry,' Adriano offered, and Noah slapped a hand to his forehead.

'He can fingerspell, sort of. He asked me to teach him a few basic customer service signs, but I didn't teach him that one.'

Adriano grinned and put the bag of food down before laying a hand on Noah's waist. 'Is that part of the services here?'

Noah gave him a flat look and smacked him lightly on the arm, but he didn't stop Adriano from backing him up against the baking table and stealing another long kiss. When they pulled apart, Noah looked vaguely dazed and happy. 'What did you bring me?'

'Burrito. Isaac and Liam,' he spelled, 'are dog-sitting right now. Fitz says he'll watch Jude this evening until I get back.'

Noah's grin was soft again as he broke away from Adriano, took the bag, and led the way upstairs. It felt good to be back in the little apartment, even if he knew Noah wasn't going to be there forever. It still felt like he was being given pieces of Noah that so few people had the privilege of knowing.

They sat on the sofa, Marshmallow instantly joining them at their feet, and Noah pulled a face when Adriano tore his burrito in half and offered a bit of chicken to the beast weaving around his feet.

'You spoil him,' Noah accused.

Adriano shrugged, not sorry. He took a huge bite, then set his food down. 'Have you known Fitz long?'

Noah blanched, and he aborted the bite he was about to take. The burrito sat, untouched, over his legs. 'We were in school together. He was always…' Noah dropped his hands and took a breath. 'He didn't bully me like the other kids, but he never stopped them.'

'And the others?' Adriano asked.

Noah nodded, then spelled the names. 'Ronan and Aksel were a lot like him. Not cruel but never particularly kind. It's different now. Ronan is the park ranger working out at Lake Mayer, and he handles tours at both cemeteries. He started those jobs before I came back to Savannah. We haven't seen each other, though. I didn't leave the house much before last month.'

Adriano reached over and brushed a light thumb over Noah's cheek until he had his full attention. 'Eat,' he ordered, and Noah's chest heaved with a sigh before he obeyed. 'Do you not want me to be friendly with Fitz?'

'I like him,' Noah answered with a shrug. Adriano liked the way his cheeks bulged with food, the way he didn't seem to care how he looked as he devoured his lunch. 'I don't think I gave them the benefit of the doubt.' The letters of the last four words were clumsy on his hand, but Adriano followed them. 'I'm trying to be better.'

'I know,' Adriano told him. He leaned in to smudge a kiss on Noah's cheek. 'You're amazing.'

Noah shook his head, but he looked pleased, and the two

of them finished their lunch in relative silence after that. When Adriano got everything put away, Noah was on his feet and near the door, so Adriano crowded him against the wood and pressed their bodies together from chest to groin.

"I want you," he murmured, then leaned in to kiss Noah's neck. He grinned when he felt Noah get hard, then grinned wider when he realized Noah wasn't near the edge. Pulling back, Adriano cocked his head to the side. "I want to take you on a date."

Noah's eyes went wide, and he freed some space to sign. 'A date?'

Adriano nodded. 'A real date. We're dating, but we haven't gone on more than one date. I want to romance you.'

Noah bit his lower lip to hide his smile, though it didn't work. 'Okay.'

Adriano smiled big enough to show teeth. 'When? Friday?'

'Shabbat,' Noah signed apologetically.

Adriano shook his head. 'Sorry, forgot. Saturday night. After sunset.'

Noah's smile was back, and he nodded shyly. 'Okay.'

'Okay,' Adriano echoed before kissing him again. 'Meet you at the market soon?'

Noah dug his phone out of his pocket, looked at the time, then nodded. 'I'll load up the car and text you when I'm on my way.'

Adriano nuzzled their noses together, kissed him again, then stepped back fully. 'I'll have the booth ready.'

Noah's eyes met his, and Adriano held his breath. They were on the edge of something he was afraid to admit—aloud or on his hands—but it passed. Noah stood on his toes to kiss him one last time, then led the way back down the stairs.

CHAPTER 19

NOAH SHIELDED his eyes against the last full rays of the low-set sun. Behind him, Adriano was hauling the bins that held most of the stuff he'd baked the night before and into the afternoon. Boxes of cookies, babka, and sufganiyot filled with an array of creams and jams. It was nothing like he'd done before but everything Bubbe would have appreciated, and he liked to think she'd be happy for him, even if she might not have fully approved that he was falling for an adult-film star with a chaotic life.

Bubbe had wanted Noah to be happy, and *b'ezrat hashem*, he was.

Reaching into the bin at his feet, Noah swallowed back his nerves as he pulled out the sign he'd made after Adriano left and turned toward him. He waited until Adriano was done unpacking the breads, then he gently tapped his elbow. 'Can I show you something?'

Adriano smiled at him and stepped back toward the edge of the booth. 'Everything okay?'

It was—mostly. Noah couldn't shake the fear, especially now that filming was over, that Adriano wouldn't have a reason to stay. Savannah wasn't posh like Hollywood. It didn't have things to do the way Adriano was used to. The people here were either tourists or locals without a lot of worldly experience.

Adriano had been relaxed that afternoon, but Noah recognized the strain of communication in him, and he wondered now how long it was going to take for Adriano to get tired of putting in all the effort. Noah couldn't be with him all the time, and he knew deep down that Adriano didn't want another lover as an interpreter. And frankly, Noah didn't want to fill that role all the time either.

He'd been struck with an idea when Paxton had asked him to help with a few basic signs, and he'd run with it, but he felt fear gripping his throat and his hands felt frozen. What if Adriano was offended? What if it was a stupid idea?

Adriano brushed a touch to Noah's cheek. 'Noah.'

He'd never get tired of seeing his sign name on Adriano's big hands. Licking his lips, he nodded and held up the sign. 'I thought we could try this tonight.'

Adriano looked at him, then down at the words printed in block letters Noah had colored in with red Sharpie.

Learn A Sign, Get A Cookie

'What is this?' Adriano asked.

Noah jutted his chin toward the plastic bin near the front table that was full of small butter cookies. 'I made those, and I thought we could give them out for free to anyone who learns a sign. We could…I don't know. Teach them the basics? Hi, how are you, please, thank you, favorite animal.' Noah couldn't read Adriano's expression, and he started to feel panicked. The poster board lowered in his one hand while the other signed. 'Sorry, it was a dumb idea…'

Adriano was on him then, backing him up against the flimsy tent walls, mouth devouring his. "Perfect. Precious.

You." The words rose to Adriano's lips, spoken against Noah's as he kissed him.

Noah flushed and allowed it for a moment, but with all the people around, he felt his anxiety spike, and he gently eased Adriano away. 'It's okay?'

Adriano brushed a thumb over Noah's kiss-swollen lips. 'Yes. Thank you, and sorry if I made you uncomfortable.'

Noah's flush was heavy enough to make him dizzy, but he shook his head and gave Adriano's hand a squeeze before letting go. 'We can take turns manning the sign booth.'

Adriano nodded eagerly and set it up on the far side of the tent, propping up the sign with tape against the wall facing the main walkway, then he took the cookies from Noah and laid the bins out in neat rows.

It was messy—nowhere near as put together as Bubbe's— but for the first time, the mess didn't bother him. It felt like something he'd created and not like a thing that had been dropped on his shoulders with crushing weight.

The sun dipped even lower into the horizon, and the traffic started to pick up. Somewhere in the direction of the fire station, Noah heard music start up and just above that the bleating of Will's goats. His first customer arrived—a woman and a child he didn't recognize. They eyed the breads, and the little girl's hand tapped on the little plastic bin holding the chocolate filled sufganiyot.

"Are they like normal doughnuts?" the woman asked.

Noah bristled at the word normal, but he offered a smile just the same. "They're an old Jewish recipe, so I like to think they taste better than what you find in the supermarket...but they're similar."

Her mouth quirked as she read the signs. "Okay, one chocolate and one of the Blue Moon."

Noah felt a small surge of vindication. He'd reduced the beer and used it to infuse the custard, and he had a feeling it would go over well. He had a feeling Adam would be a mixture of proud and annoyed when he finally saw it.

"What's that over there?" the woman asked as she handed over a twenty.

Noah made the change, then followed her gaze to where Adriano was leaning against the table and teaching three teenagers how to sign something. The angle wasn't enough for him to see, but by the grins on their faces he didn't think it was a favorite color.

"My market partner is Deaf, so he's teaching everyone signs for free cookies," Noah explained.

The woman frowned, but the little girl jumped on the balls of her feet. "I learned that at school! I can…I can say this!" She widened her stance like she needed the balance, then signed on her small little hands, 'My name Melody.' She spelled her name with the careful, slow fumble of a new learner.

Noah waved his hands in applause. "Very good," he said, then signed it. "Do you want to go learn something else? My friend Adriano is very nice."

The mom looked dubious, but the girl was too excited and took off ahead of her. "Does he live here?" the mom asked, inching toward the end of the table.

Noah's heart sank a little, but he shook his head. "No. He lives and works in LA, but he's taking time off." Though, in truth, he didn't really know how long Adriano planned to stick around. He glanced over to see that Melody had gotten Adriano's attention, and she was showing him the handful of signs she knew—her name, age, a couple of the colors.

Adriano beamed, then squeezed his body through the gap in the tables and knelt down in front of her to teach her something else. 'My favorite animal horse,' he signed very slowly, murmuring the words along with his hands.

The woman softened a bit. "He's good at that."

Noah couldn't help his smile as he watched the girl copy him until she had it right. "Yes, he is."

"You come back and show me what you remember, and you can have more cookies," Adriano told her as they finished.

Melody's cheeks were puffy, crumbs on her lips, and she signed, 'Thank you,' before her mom took her hand and they wandered off.

Noah stepped back as Adriano eased back into the booth, and this time, he didn't feel worried as Adriano stepped in close. 'You're cute when you're teaching little kids.'

Adriano rolled his eyes, but he put one hand at Noah's waist and dug his fingers in. 'You're cute all the time.' He brushed a kiss over his lips, then turned back to rearrange the cookies as another customer approached, and Noah got back to work.

BY SEVEN, Noah's stomach was growling, and the last thing in the world he wanted was something that came out of Bubbe's kitchen. He was entirely sold out of the beer and chocolate sufganiyot and only had two of the raspberry left. Their cookie supply had dwindled down to almost nothing, and the sign booth had shut down when Adriano had given the very last one to Melody who returned to show him she had remembered everything he taught her.

'Food?' Adriano asked.

Noah nodded. 'Yes, please. Something with greens, though. No more junk.'

Adriano chuckled and leaned in to kiss his cheek. 'Be back soon. I'll find something good for us.'

'Thank you,' Noah told him, then leaned on the counter as he watched Adriano bob and weave through the slowly dwindling crowd. He checked through his wares one last time, then the cash box, which was overflowing. It wasn't enough. It would never be enough to make up for the hole he was in, but it was something. Adriano had already sent the first five videos off to his friend for editing, and they'd be back this week for the pair of them to watch and approve.

Then…then the first one would be posted.

Noah had reluctantly signed the contract accepting sole rights over the content. He'd added in his bank account, he'd accepted all terms and conditions, and had tentatively agreed to a trip at some point in the future to visit Adriano's lawyer to sign a better contract that would protect him from what Adriano's ex-agent might do.

But for now, Adriano assured him it would be fine. After all, Xander owned Sylent, not Adriano.

'Adriano is for you,' his lover assured him late Wednesday night after their hearts began to beat slower, and their heavy breathing began to ease. 'He can't have the piece of me that's here with you.'

It was an almost I love you. It was something more than just I like you, at least. Noah had been on the verge of confessing then. He was deliciously sore and sated in more ways than he could have dreamed. And he was…he was happy. He was romanced. He was content. The more he got to know Adriano, the deeper he fell.

There was no glass shattering with him.

Noah startled when someone cleared their throat, and he turned to see Adam and Fitz standing at the edge of the table. Adam's face settled into a smirk. Noah knew he'd been caught, but he didn't much care anymore.

"You know, until right this moment, I thought Fitz was a fucking liar," Adam said. "I didn't think you'd actually show up."

Noah bit his lip and decided whether or not he'd take it personally. He earned the hurt, he knew, but Adam's tone was a soft mocking, the way brothers should be. He reached under the counter and pulled out the paper bag he'd been saving. "I tried a new recipe."

Adam stared, then he bent down and pressed his hand to the grass before standing back up. At Noah's frown, Adam shrugged. "Just checking to see if hell freezing over made it up here yet."

Noah rolled his eyes, but he shoved the bag at Adam. "You can eat it later and text me about how much you hate it."

Of course Noah's slight plea went ignored. Adam was a man of little patience, just like he'd been as a boy. He was the kind of kid who tore wrapping paper to shreds, who ripped tape off boxes, who never understood the meaning of wait. That same enthusiasm had him reaching into the bag and biting into the sufganiyah hard enough to send part of the custard oozing out over his hand.

"Holy shit," he said, voice muffled by the soft dough. "Is this *beer*?"

"Blue Moon," Noah answered softly. "Rose was stocking some of the OU cert cases for me."

Adam looked Noah directly in the face as he chewed, then shoved the rest at Fitz who took it with a fumbling hand. "Eat the rest of this." At Adam's command, Noah's heart sank. "It's too fucking good, and I'm so full I'm going to die."

Noah's entire body shuddered with a wave of relief. "It's not awful?"

"No, and if I didn't love you, I'd beat the shit out of you for holding out on me like this. You *can* bake," Adam accused with a slightly powdered finger leveled at him.

Noah turned his gaze away. "I didn't learn nothing from Bubbe. It's just…I didn't love it the way she did. Or you do."

Adam softened, and he reached past Noah for a napkin. "I'm glad you did this."

Noah shrugged. "I'm glad you pushed me."

Fitz smiled because he had to know the comment was

directed partially at him. "Can we add some of these to our bagel order?"

"Yes," Noah told him, then he felt a small pang of grief because he'd have to break the news to him eventually. No matter how much people loved this, it was coming to an end. "Just remind me on Sunday."

Fitz nodded and gave him a quick salute before he turned away, leaving Noah and his brother alone. The tension was thick between them, but Adam didn't look angry. "People are going to miss the shop when it's gone."

Noah bowed his head. "I know. But a weekly bagel order —even adding doughnuts to it—it's not going to make a difference."

Adam let out a bone-deep sigh. "Yeah. I went over all the books while I was there on Sunday, and…and I get it. And I'm still not happy you kept it to yourself, and I don't love that you took out a fucking loan, but…"

"I'm not going to apologize for that," Noah told him firmly. He held Adam's gaze. "I had to take the pressure off you. That's all I wanted," Noah told him. "And I'm going to be fine."

"If you're not…" Adam warned, but Noah waved him off.

"I am. I promise."

Adam nodded, opened his mouth like he was going to say something, then stopped. "Give me the rest of your cookies." He dug into his pocket and slapped a wad of cash on the table. "You're almost out anyway, and I was going to put together a couple of meals for Dr. Alling to take to some of his long-term patients."

Noah was surprised he knew who Adam was talking about, but Aksel Alling had moved to Savannah a year after Noah's family had. Noah only took notice of him back then because anyone with differences stood out in this town whether they wanted to or not, and everything about Aksel had been a sore thumb. Aksel was in Noah's grade—with one arm and a thick accent just like Noah had.

His English had been a little better, but he was still different. Aksel hadn't taken the teasing lying down, though. Not like Noah. He won and lost a few fistfights and gained the respect of the other kids in his class long before Noah had the courage to say two words when the teacher called on him. When Noah came back from LA, he found out Aksel had gone off to medical school. He returned a few years after Noah with MD attached to his name, and he started his own practice, which was sorely needed in Savannah.

"You two are friends?" Noah asked as he scooped what was left of the cookies into a paper bag.

Adam shrugged. "We ran into each other a few months ago, and he told me he does meals for some of his long-term patients. Over Purim, I threw together some stuff for his charity thing, and he liked it, so…I guess we have sort of a contract now? He's better friends with Fitz than with me."

Noah raised his brows as he threw the cash from Adam into the cash box. "Which means…"

"They never dated," Adam said, scooping the bag into his arms. "But they hooked up when they were bored or horny."

"Adam," Noah breathed out.

"Dicked down and still a prude. How very much like you," Adam chastised, then laughed when Noah's cheeks went pink. Adam gave him another intense look, then shook his head. "It looks good on you."

Noah frowned. "What does?"

Adam grinned. "Love." He winked, then turned on his heel and walked off.

Noah stood there like a fool for far too long before remembering he had to close up shop. He checked his phone and found a text from Adriano saying the lines were impossibly long, but he really wanted pizzas from Enzo's truck, so he was going to wait. Noah shot back a thumbs-up emoji, then began to pack everything up.

He was lost in his thoughts when he heard someone knock on the table, and Noah lifted his head, his eyes going wide in surprise because he most definitely recognized the man standing in front of him. He'd followed him online for years, enjoyed his videos for years.

He'd even hoped for the best when the guy swore he was madly in love with Adriano.

"Hi," he offered. Eric was as pretty as ever and smaller in person than he seemed in his selfies with Adriano. He was lithe and thin but well defined in his tight designer shirt and jeans. He had sunglasses on his head, pushing his hair back, and his smile was straight, and white, and perfect. "You're not sold out, are you?"

Noah licked his lips. "Um. Yes, actually. Sorry. My brother has a truck down the road, though, if you…"

"The latke place?" he asked. "I saw it, but everyone was talking about your doughnut thingies."

Noah's guts were twisting in on themselves. "Ah. Sorry…"

"You don't need to be shy," Eric said. He splayed long fingers over the table and leaned forward. "You can't hook Adriano by playing coy. That's not his thing."

Fear and confusion rippled up his spine. "Are you looking for him? Does he even know you're here?"

Eric's smile went wider. "So you *do* know who I am."

Noah shrugged. "I guess so."

Eric gave him a calculating look, then lifted his hands and began to sign so swiftly Noah had no hope of following. He caught a few words here and there—*week…not pretty…last night…mine*. But nothing else. When it was obvious Noah couldn't follow, Eric sighed and shook his head, his face full of pity. "So that's a no on Deaf speed?"

Noah felt like collapsing in on himself. Adriano had never once made him feel like his signing wasn't good enough or fluent enough, even if he knew it wasn't perfect. He never felt like there was a barrier, but now…

"I mean, of course he doesn't care with his flavor of the week. It's not important since this isn't long-term," Eric said with a laugh. Noah's eyes went wide, and Eric shot him a look of pity again. "You know that's what this is, right? He does this every fucking time we break up. God, he took this little twink model who didn't know his ABCs to the Caribbean a couple years ago when I threatened to move out. Spent a month making that boy's dreams come true before he came home. He's *such* a diva."

And, well…that wasn't a lie. Noah had known that about Adriano since before they met. He'd seen the pictures on Twitter, had watched a couple of videos. But Adriano hadn't looked at that guy the way he looked at Noah. He needed to believe that, even if his resolve was slowly cracking. "I'm not going to speak on his behalf, but it seems weird that you're here a few days after posting your engagement on Twitter. To his agent."

Eric drew his bottom lip between his teeth. "Adriano and I are both impulsive, and we can both get a little mean. He knows it's not serious."

"Does he?" Noah asked.

At that, Eric laughed. "When he got home from his little island getaway, he bought me a Porsche, sweetie. Then he sucked my dick until I cried, told me I was the most beautiful man he had ever seen, and *begged* me never to leave him again. It's just…our thing. It's not personal. You seem really nice, and this whole thing is so unfair. He shouldn't dick you around like this."

Maybe if Noah was a better person—or less anxious, or if he had managed to start therapy sooner—none of what Eric was saying would have mattered. But the guy was smart, and maybe…God, maybe he was *right*. Maybe this was all some sort of game for Adriano to make himself feel better until Eric apologized.

It's not like Noah had anything on the guy. It was obvious that between them, Eric was Swarovski crystal, and Noah was a dandelion growing between spaces in the sidewalk. Eric was rich, and beautiful, and he understood the world Adriano lived in. And he spoke his language better than Noah could hope to. He felt like such an idiot.

"Adriano's getting pizza," he heard himself say, startled that it wasn't obvious in his tone that this man had taken an atom bomb to is entire life. "If you really think he's interested in hearing your apology, you can go find him."

Eric lifted a brow. "He can't hear it. He's Deaf."

Noah snorted before grabbing his keys and backing up. "If you think ears are the only thing used to hear what people are saying, you have a lot to learn. It was nice to meet you, Eric. I hope you enjoy the market."

He didn't text Adriano after that, he didn't look up, he didn't run, he didn't stop. He just walked. He walked until he reached his car, and then he drove. He made his way into his apartment, and locked the door, and managed to reach the sofa as Marshmallow found him and curled up in his arms.

He didn't cry, despite the way it felt like he'd been flayed open. If he closed his eyes, he knew he'd picture Eric approaching Adriano—the fight, their hands flying, the passion simmering between them.

And Adriano would hold Eric the way he'd held Noah, wouldn't he? And he'd kiss him the same. He'd forgive him. He'd go home.

Right?

His phone buzzed, so he turned it off.

He didn't really know what Adriano was going to do, but at the moment, he wasn't brave enough to ask. It was easier to close his eyes, hold his cat tight, and wait for the world to pass him by.

CHAPTER 20

ADRIANO MADE his way back through the sparse crowd, knowing Noah was probably ready to pack it all in and head home. The stall had been nearly cleaned out before he'd gone for food, but more than that, he could see it in Noah's face.

They hadn't gone too deep into Noah's past, but Adriano knew enough to know that his boyfriend probably suffered from at least complex PTSD if not something else that triggered his anxiety. Noah had been dipping his toes outside his world of baking and holing up in his apartment just before Adriano had arrived in Savannah, but he knew it was a process.

He knew doing the filming, and going on dates, and running a booth wasn't going to cure Noah. He was well aware his boyfriend would never fit into the life Adriano lived back in LA. The best part about that, though, was that Adriano liked the idea of abandoning ship. He liked having this escape, and he felt absolutely no draw to head back to the total chaos of his past. He wasn't ready to give up his job, but he had options, and he was more than willing to commute once his shit with Xander was sorted out.

Adriano reached the booth, then paused with a frown

when he realized it was empty. Noah's bag and the cash drawer were gone, but the empty, leftover bins were still stacked along the side. Setting the pizza and drinks down, Adriano dragged a hand through his hair, then spun around and narrowed his eyes at the crowd.

He didn't see Noah, but the blacksmith, Birdie, was watching him from across the way with a look on his face like he might know where Noah was. Adriano didn't waste any time walking up. 'Did you see Noah?'

Birdie bit his lower lip. 'He took off. Some guy walked up to him, and Noah looked…' Birdie's hand wavered in the air. 'Afraid,' he finished. 'The guy started signing something really fast, then laughed at Noah. Noah took off after that.'

Adriano blanched. 'What did he look like?'

At that, Birdie laughed. 'Pretty. Nice clothes, dark blond hair, sunglasses. Attractive.'

Adriano didn't want to believe it, refused to even consider that Eric would actually show up here, but there was no other person that could send Noah rushing off without a word to Adriano.

He pulled out his phone and shot him a quick text, *Are you at home?* He said thanks to the other man, then walked back toward the booth and stared at the remnants of what had been such a successful night. He had signed with strangers and with some of Noah's acquaintances. People were interested, and they were excited. He gave away cookies, then hugs when he ran out of sweets. Noah had sold his booth empty.

And now he was gone because maybe Eric was there—or Xander. Maybe they had shown up to fuck everything up all over again. Adriano pulled out his phone a second time, opened his contacts, then stared at Eric's contact. He hadn't bothered to communicate with him since Eric had dumped him on social media, and he didn't want to start now, but he was worried. He thumbed up a few letters, then down, and tapped on Luca's name.

> Adriano: can u do me favor, see if Eric in Savannah?

He shoved his phone into his pocket, abandoned the pizzas, then gathered up the bins and walked across the lawn toward the petting zoo where Jude had spent his day. Isaac was there, but Liam was nowhere to be found, and in his stead was a very tall, broad man with greying brown hair and a thick beard. He had both arms around Isaac's waist, and he was speaking into his ear, making the younger man smile.

God. Adriano's heart ached. He wanted nothing more than to hold Noah like that, but he could only imagine what Noah had been told if the man really was Eric.

Isaac saw his approach and broke away from the older man, walking over to the little pen off to the side. Jude was there, sleeping on a pillow, and he rose obediently, his little tail wagging as Adriano approached.

It was like being able to breathe, cuddling his dog close, and he stood, taking out his phone to tap on his notepad app. *Thanks 4 watch him. Need 2 find Noah. U take these bins? Belong 2 bakery.*

Isaac read the screen, then nodded and looked behind him at the older man who was watching the exchange. When he realized he had Adriano's attention, he walked over and motioned for the phone.

I'm Will, Noah's friend. You must be Adriano. Everything okay?

Before Adriano could type, he saw Isaac's lips move, presumably in explanation, and Will's frown deepened.

Let me call him, Will offered, and Adriano nodded, feeling a rush of relief as the man pulled out his own phone and pressed it to his ear. It lasted only a second, though, and he tapped on the keyboard. *Straight to v-mail. He must have it off.*

Fuck. *Fuck.* There was no way to deny who had done this. If they were back home, Adriano would know who to get in touch with. He'd have an army of pissed off friends behind him to kick down Eric's door and make him pay for fucking up the one good thing Adriano had managed to get out of the whole mess. But he had no idea where Eric could even be. He might not even be staying in Savannah, though if he was, there was only one place.

His phone buzzed, and he jolted before lighting up the screen and finding his brother's name there.

> Luca: He went on a road trip, so yes, he's probably on his way to you. Need help?

> Adriano: Nope. Talk 2U L8R.

Adriano signed his thanks to Will and Isaac, then held Jude tight as he walked back across the grass toward the food trucks. He knew Adam was probably still there, and with any luck, Noah. He was single-minded and ready to fuck some shit up, and that's when he almost tumbled headfirst into Oscar, who was walking Paisley on her leash.

It might have been funny if Adriano wasn't half out of his mind with anger and worry. 'Sorry,' he signed.

Then he realized Oscar was the exact man he needed. He held up one finger, and when Oscar nodded, he pulled his phone out of his pocket and thumbed through his photo album. It wasn't hard to find a full-faced shot of Eric, and he felt his stomach clench at the sight of him.

With a breath, he showed Oscar his screen, then waited to get the other man's attention again. He pointed to the screen, then spelled, 'My Ex.' Oscar nodded when he understood. 'You see him around here?'

Oscar mouthed along with the letters, then shook his head and circled his fist over his chest. 'Sorry.'

Adriano tapped open his notepad. *If u c him, pls tell me. His name Eric and I think here. I think he said something 2 Noah bc he left and can't find him.*

Oscar's look was full of sympathy but no real knowledge, and that did make him feel a little better that Eric had only inflicted his bullshit on one person, but he hated that the one person was Noah. Oscar gave him a firm nod, then reached out and squeezed his arm.

He waved a goodbye to Oscar, stopping to give Paisley a quick pat, then started on his way to the bakery. With any luck, Noah would be there, but if not, he was happy to stand vigil until his lover got back.

Adriano was shut out. The door that led to the stairs up to the apartment was locked, and as much as he wanted to think he could wait all night, he had Jude to think about. He rang the buzzer enough times that he knew it would irritate anyone inside, but when no one threw anything from the windows and when no one came down, he realized his plan was futile.

If Noah was up there, he wasn't going to see him.

The not knowing was going to drive him crazy. It was under his skin, and the only thing in the world he wanted was to take Noah in his arms and kiss him until he unearthed every seed of discord Eric had planted. He said a little prayer into the universe that Eric wouldn't be brave enough to come near him soon, though, because Adriano was pretty sure he'd risk jail to get a few good punches at his perfectly shaped nose.

He let out a groan, then set Jude on the ground and turned to head home when there was movement behind him. Noah's name was on his lips when he turned, but it was Talia, looking somewhat sheepish as she let herself out of the bakery and shut the door behind her.

Fuck, fuck, *fuck*.

Talia was holding a note, and she flinched when Adriano snatched it out of her hands. *Noah doesn't want to talk right now. Adam is up there with him, and Noah said he'd text you in the morning. He asked me to give you a ride home.*

Adriano bit his lip and swallowed past a lump in his throat. But at the very least, he loved Noah enough to comply with his wishes. It was only fair after all. He handed the note back and nodded, but he was in no mood to have a full conversation with the woman, and he was in no mood for an awkward drive back to the rental.

"Tell Noah I'll speak to him soon. I'm going to walk." He committed an act of impoliteness that he used far too often on his brothers and turned his back. He had no idea if Talia called after him, but no one tried to stop him as he made his way to the main street and began the long journey back to the empty house.

His feet ached by the time he got there, and Jude put up no fuss at all when Adriano ordered him into the crate. He set the latch and pulled a blanket over his baby, then collapsed in the primary bedroom, lying on his stomach as he pulled his laptop close.

His entire body craved comfort. It craved the warmth and softness of Noah against him—the one thing he wasn't allowed to have right then. He wanted to stomp his feet and raise his voice and throw a full tantrum until he got his way, but he knew better.

If this had been Adriano in a different life, even a year ago, he might have considered it. He might have pouted outside the door or wheedled Talia to let him up, then threw everything he had at Noah until the man gave in and let him in.

But he was trying not to be that person. Noah made him want to be better, to explore the depths of himself he'd left hidden for more shallow waters that had gotten him fame and money. He'd had the potential to be more than just a rich brat once upon a time, but it was just easier to give in to the lifestyle of the people around him.

Now he felt unfulfilled. Now he felt like those years were wasted.

With a sigh, Adriano curled his legs up and logged into his email to find a note from Anthony. *Making progress, and if you lie low, we might be able to have a settlement ready. You'll have to pay the fee, but due to Eric's post on Twitter about the engagement that went viral, I'm pretty sure we can get them to dissolve any obligation between you and the firm because of conflict of interest. You can thank Eric for his fuck-up.*

Adriano read the email once, then twice, then a third time. It made sense. It made absolute and total sense why Eric was there. He'd fucked up, and he'd cost Xander money. He was either under orders to make nice with Adriano, or Xander had dumped his ass for someone not so impulsive. Either way, Adriano wasn't interested in what either of them had to say.

He'd pay the stupid fucking fee to dissolve his contract with Xander's company, he'd give them double middle fingers as he backed out the door, and he'd get on with life. Hopefully—presumably—with Noah in it. If it meant living here and flying to California to film, he'd do it.

He had weeks to decide, maybe even months, though. He wanted to woo Noah. He wanted to romance the shit out of him until Noah couldn't imagine being with another man. He wanted to turn his world upside down and make him fall as hard and as fast as Adriano was falling.

He just...wanted Noah. He could be patient until morning, but he knew between now and then, it was going to be a damn long night.

CHAPTER 21

Noah was well aware he was sulking like a child, and he was well aware Adam was on the cusp of a full-on meltdown. He half expected his brother to throw a punch after the fourth time he refused to say anything.

It was only when Adriano wouldn't lay off the buzzer, and Adam threatened to let him up, that Noah relented. "His ex is here," Noah told them both. His voice was hoarse from holding back tears, and he hugged himself tight around his middle. "He showed up at the fucking market and cornered me in the booth."

Adam looked murderous, but Talia—startlingly enough—look worried. "Is this guy violent or something?"

Noah gave a weak shrug. "I don't know much about him. I don't know how he even knows. I mean Adriano must have told him he was here. Which means they've been talking."

Adam shook his head. "Maybe, but Noah, I can tell you from experience that Adriano doesn't seem like that kind of guy."

"He wasn't lying about what he said, though," Noah blurted. He remembered Adriano's Caribbean trip with some faceless guy. And how after it was over, he was publicly romantic and fawning all over Eric's Twitter feed. Eric was a lot of things, but Noah didn't think he was necessarily a liar. Adriano's world was just so different, and Noah wasn't sure he even belonged on the fringes.

The buzzer continued to sound through the apartment, and Adam sighed, pressing fingers into his temples. "Talia, can you go down there and tell Adriano that Noah will call him tomorrow?"

"Call him?" Talia asked.

Adam rolled his eyes. "Text him. Whatever. You know what I mean. Just...tell him Noah needs space, but it won't be forever."

"Adam," Noah started, but his brother cut him off with a sharp shake of his head.

The door slammed after a couple of minutes, and then the buzzing stopped. The brothers let out matching sighs of relief, and Noah laid his head on the cushion. Marshmallow had abandoned him when the noise began, and he had no idea where he'd run off to, but he could use the comfort.

"What exactly did this ex say to you?"

Noah ran a hand down his face. "That...that I was a fling Adriano was using to make himself feel better. That he's done it before, and he has. I've been following him on Twitter since I signed up. I've seen him do this."

"That doesn't mean he's doing it now," Adam pressed. "That man is in love with you."

Noah peered one eye at him. "How the hell do you know? You're not an expert on love just because you fucked your way through your culinary class, Adam."

Adam gave him a flat expression. "I *know* because it's the same expression on my face when I look at Talia."

The words hung between them for a moment, then Noah shifted to look at his brother fully. "There's no reason for him to love me, Adam. I'm a mess. I can't even handle some bullshit confrontation with his asshole ex. *Hashem yishmor*, I could barely handle the market without losing my mind!"

Adam leaned forward in the chair and laid his hand on Noah's knee. "But you did it. And you had a good time until that asshole showed up, right?"

Noah grunted his reply, but he couldn't bring himself to deny it either. "I need…I need help. Therapy. Something."

Adam chuckled and drew his hand away. "*Yes*, you should definitely see a therapist."

Noah hated that he was right, hated that his stomach was closing in on itself. "Why am I such a mess?"

"Because our mother was terrible and threw shit on you that no child should have to bear, and Bubbe wasn't much better at helping." Hearing Adam admit it—hearing him not absolve their mother based on Noah's word alone—made him feel something, though he didn't have words for it. "But you still deserve love, to be in love, to be loved back, and that man is head over heels. I'd bet my relationship with Talia on it."

"High stakes," came Talia's voice as she walked back into the room. She perched on the armrest of Adam's chair and offered a soft look to Noah. "Adam is right, though. Adriano is head over heels in love with you. He was on the verge of tears when I told him to go."

Noah, if possible, felt worse. "I just need to…I don't know. Process?"

"You're allowed that," Adam told him. "I can't stay here all night. I have to go pack the truck in and prep for tomorrow. And I'm guessing you're not going to be any good for morning prep…"

"Actually," Noah said, pushing himself to sit up straight, "that's exactly what I need."

Adam looked dubious, but eventually, he nodded. "Fine, but promise me you will contact him in the morning. He deserves at least that from you, and you deserve to know the truth."

Noah nodded. He rose and followed Adam to the door, then let out a small, startled sound when his brother grabbed him close and squeezed him tight enough to rob him of breath. "*Todah*," he whispered.

Adam pulled back and shook his head, giving the side of his face a pat as his mouth fell into a soft grin. "*Tipesh*."

Noah tried for a scowl, but the would-be insult was spoken with such a tone of affection that he almost started to cry. They stood there another moment, then Adam turned and reached for Talia, who was reaching for him at the same time. And Noah saw it then. It was impossible to miss. The light in Adam's eyes, the light reflecting back in Talia's. The way they fit, their perfect orbit around each other. He hadn't missed it before. He just hadn't been paying close enough attention.

But it mattered now—it was important now—because Adam was right. Adriano had looked at him just like that, had reached for him just like that. And Noah could not deny he had reached back.

CHAPTER 22

ADRIANO DIDN'T SLEEP. He tried to let Talia's promise soothe him and his lawyer's email settle the anxiety in his gut, but it didn't help. Noah was still not speaking to him—had been radio silent all night—and Eric was still around town somewhere just waiting to fuck everything up.

Adriano lay on his back with Jude at his side as the sun crested over the ocean horizon. The sky was a grey blue, and there was humidity in the air with a promised storm. He missed Noah with a fierce ache he hadn't expected, and he wanted to get out of bed and take action, but he couldn't.

It wasn't fair.

When his phone buzzed, Adriano nearly jumped out of his skin, and he fumbled for the device, swiping his screen with shaking hands. When he saw Noah's name there, his eyes blurred with tears. He wasn't sure what it would say. This was a make-or-break moment, he was pretty sure. But he couldn't wait.

> Noah: Sorry I freaked out. I want to talk later. Do you still want to spend tonight with me?

> Adriano: I want 2 talk. Miss u.

> Noah: I miss you too. I was an asshole, and I hope you forgive me. Bubbe's closes at four, but I think I might lock up at noon. I want time with you before sunset. Meet me?

> Adriano: I cook u dinner. C U then xoxo

> Noah: xoxo

Adriano laid back on the pillow, his heart beating hard enough to almost worry him. Jude had jumped off the bed, so Adriano turned onto his side and stared at the message thread. *Noah* apologized. *Noah* thought he was being an asshole, and maybe freezing Adriano out was kind of a dick move, but Adriano couldn't blame him for it.

He knew what Eric was capable of. He knew he was good at creating chaos when he wanted to. Noah was still fragile, was still figuring things out. Having done the market was huge for him, and to have that tainted and destroyed by Eric's vindictive plans...

Noah wasn't the one who needed to apologize.

Fatigue consumed him suddenly, and Adriano found himself drifting, his phone clutched to his chest. Somewhere in the back of his mind, he warned himself not to let go, but the relief was too strong, and it stole a couple of hours.

Adriano woke near ten, bolting upright, and he swayed on his feet as he tried to stand. Gripping the wall, he regained his equilibrium, then stumbled to the shower, taking less time than he ever had in his life. He started to worry about his looks, but he realized that nothing about his appearance mattered to Noah.

Maybe at first. Maybe it was the way he looked, the way he moved, the way he fucked. But Noah wanted him, not Sylent, not some public figure.

He put a little product in his hair, finger-combed it backward, then moved to the kitchen to start a cup of coffee. It was less than ten minutes before he was out the door, caffeinated and with a granola bar sitting heavy in his gut. He sat in his driveway, then pulled up Oscar's number on his phone.

> Adriano: Can I pay u 4 dog sit pls?
>
> Oscar: You found Noah?
>
> Adriano: Yes. Know you barely know me, so sorry 2 ask.
>
> Oscar: Bring him by. If I'm not around, Liam will do it. I'm glad you found him.
>
> Adriano: TY

HE HAD JUST enough time to drop Jude off and get to the store before Noah was expecting him. Oscar was out front when Adriano pulled up to Oscar's snack shack, and he gathered the dog and his things into his arms.

Oscar offered a sympathetic smile as he took over the leash and hooked Jude's bag over his arm, then lifted his hand. 'You okay?'

Adriano shrugged. "Long night. Noah and I have to talk it out. Thanks for helping."

Oscar waved him off, so Adriano climbed back into the car and headed into town. The parking lot of the only supermarket was mostly empty, and he breathed a sigh of relief as he grabbed a basket and stepped into the cool air. The afternoon was getting warm, and the pressing humidity of the oncoming storm was making him sweat. He swiped a hand over his brow, then moved to the pasta aisle and went for easy.

A box of dried lasagna noodles, a couple jars of sauce from a passable brand. He strolled toward the cheeses and loaded up on the freshest mozzarella he could find, then a chunk of cut parm. He was in the meat section, perusing the selection of ground beef when a hand touched his arm, and he glanced up to see Talia raising a brow at him.

"Cooking?" Talia asked, a word easy enough for Adriano to understand.

"Noah texted. I'm spending tonight with him, so I thought I'd make lasagna." He started to put the ground beef into his cart, but Talia caught him by the wrist and shook her head. Adriano frowned, but set it back, and when he looked at Talia, she was holding out her phone.

Meat+Cheese=Not kosher

Adriano's cheeks burned. He didn't know nearly enough and understood only a fraction of what he had looked up online. He didn't want to fuck this up, but he didn't know if he'd ever be good enough to get it right.

Adam and I aren't observant, but we do our best to be careful with Noah. No bacon, no shellfish, no meat mixed with dairy. He'll bend on kosher certified foods, but he prefers not to.

Pursing his lips, Adriano nodded, then signed his thanks. He could do it with vegetables just as well. He had learned a few things standing at his mother's knee in the kitchen. But more than anything, he wanted Noah to know that regardless of whether or not the food was good enough to write home about, it was for him. It was all about him.

Talia didn't try to say anything else, but she strolled with him to the vegetable section. They pantomimed a couple of things almost like small talk. He wasn't sure Talia would ever really put in the effort to learn his language, but he had to admit the company was nice. After the night before, Adriano was still reeling a little.

He'd spent half the night questioning whether or not he really should be there. If Noah had wanted to end things, it's not like Adriano had any ties to Savannah. But Talia being there with him felt like some sort of connection or maybe an olive branch. It felt like other people were making an effort to help him feel at home, and that mattered.

Adriano started to lead the way toward the bakery, but Talia grabbed his arm and gave her head a firm shake before pulling out her phone again.

Adam will MURDER you if you bring Noah store-bought dessert. He'll make it for you if you want it.

Adriano couldn't help but laugh at the realization he was stepping into a family of bakers—one with a shop, for now, and one with a truck. He glanced back at a pile of strawberries in boxes, then signed it. "Strawberry," he clarified. "And whipped cream?"

Talia raised a brow, then flushed, and Adriano realized the food kink possibilities. Not something he'd ever been into off-camera, but with Noah, anything was possible. And everything. Not tonight, though. He didn't want this to be about sex. He wanted this to be a moment where he showed Noah—with more than words—what he meant when he said he was falling for him.

He grabbed two boxes and a little spray can of cheap whipped cream, then started toward the checkout. He was eyeing a small bin of single-serve applesauce packets when a person came around the corner, and Adriano's entire body froze.

Eric's smile was too familiar, the glint in his eyes a painful reminder of what he'd walked away from. Adriano had wondered since he got to Savannah what he'd do if he came face-to-face with Eric again. How could he not? But he felt nothing at first, then simmering resentment over so damn many years wasted.

'I was hoping I'd run into you,' Eric signed.

Normally, Adriano would have been able to breathe easier with someone as fluent as Eric, but now he just wanted to break his fingers to silence him after what he'd done to Noah. 'Why? You could have texted instead of creeping around town and lying.'

Eric's brow raised. 'Is that what your little boy toy told you I did?'

Adriano's entire body was thrumming with furious energy. 'No. He didn't tell me anything.'

Eric looked mildly amused until Adriano saw Talia say something out of the corner of his eye. Eric snapped back, and Talia laughed.

'What did she say?' Adriano demanded.

Eric gave him a mean look. 'Not your business.'

He was doing it to be cruel, to leave Adriano out, to remind him that he had the power of hearing. Eric had rarely used that against him, but this wasn't the first time. It was, however, a reminder of why Eric had never been a good person. He had never been a person worthy of Adriano's love. Adriano had just spent years ignoring that part of his ex.

'You need to leave,' Adriano told him.

Eric scoffed. 'You don't have the right to demand that.'

Darting a glance at the checkout, Adriano realized they'd gained an audience. Chances were, he was being loud. He rarely bothered to control whether or not he made noise anymore, especially when he was angry, and right then, he was furious.

Talia tapped him on the shoulder, and the look on her face was one of concern.

"Can you pay for me?" he asked. "I'm going to have a word with Eric outside."

Talia nodded and took Adriano's offered card before fixing Eric with a hard look and pushing toward the line. Adriano didn't bother to wait and see if Eric followed. He just marched out and around the corner, where they could have some semblance of privacy.

'Look at you,' Eric signed when Adriano stopped and turned to face him. 'Voicing for the hearies.'

Adriano took a step closer to him, and the rage on his face finally gave his ex pause. '*You* are a hearie. You're worse than them because they don't withhold communication to make themselves feel powerful.'

Eric blanched, but he made no move to tell Adriano what it was Talia had said, which meant it was an insult. 'Come home, Adriano. Stop being an asshole and just come home.'

Adriano scoffed. 'I am home.'

Eric's look was one of disbelief, and he rolled his eyes. 'This is some shitty little town in fucking *Georgia*. Our condo...'

'*My* condo,' Adriano corrected. 'My condo in LA, my cottage on Coronado. My name, my homes. I'm selling them, Xander is fired, and I'm through with you both. Enjoy your engagement.' He glanced down and saw Eric's bare hand. 'Or not.'

Eric's cheeks were flaming, splotchy red. 'I didn't want him. I was trying to make you jealous. I was so tired of you not giving a shit about me.'

'I still don't give a shit about you,' Adriano said. It was time to be hurtful with honesty because he didn't care what happened as long as Noah was with him. 'I'm in love with someone else.'

'That chubby guy with freckles? The one you want to film with? Some college drop-out whose business is going under?'

Adriano became profoundly aware of how far Xander had been able to dig into Noah's background before he cut Xander's access to his email. 'He had no right to my personal information once I fired him. I hope he enjoys the lawsuit. I hope you both do since you were also no longer employed by me when you went into Noah's personal information.'

'*Precious?*' Eric signed.

Adriano couldn't help his grin as he spelled Noah's name, then signed it again. 'He is everything to me, everything you never were and never could be. I'm through. And I'm sorry you never felt like you were enough. That was proof we should have stayed broken up years ago. The first time.'

Eric's eyes went wide and watery. 'Adriano…'

"No!" He slashed his hand through the air, felt his frustrated grunt rip up his throat. 'I can't. We're done. Please just go home and pack and move on.'

'Are you really going to sue me?' Eric asked. He looked scared now, and it was obvious. He and Xander had fucked up. And they knew it.

'Yes,' Adriano said, and he felt no remorse. Eric had been bleeding him dry for years, had broken up with him and crawled back, then treated him like shit and begged for forgiveness all because Adriano had been providing. He was not a boyfriend. He was never a boyfriend. He was a bottomless meal ticket.

Eric grabbed his arm to stop him from walking away. 'What am I supposed to do?'

Adriano scoffed. 'Beg Xander to take you back. Sell the Porsche and buy an apartment. I don't care. But don't ever let me see your face again. We're done.'

Turning on his heel, Adriano walked away from him and found Talia standing near the front doors. He came to a stop a bit closer than he normally would have, then leaned his head in. "Is he still behind me?"

Talia glanced over Adriano's shoulder, then shook her head.

Adriano let out a breath, then dragged a hand down his face as he turned it up toward the sky. The sun was behind the clouds now, heavy and dark with rain. "Thank you. I'm sorry to drag you into that."

Talia touched his arm, then shook her head again.

"What did you say to him that pissed him off?"

At that, Talia laughed, then dug into her pocket and pulled out her phone. *I said, oh I know who you are. Eric the choad, the guy too terrible in bed to make it as a porn star so he had to fuck one to live his dreams.*

Adriano laughed hard—mostly out of stress, and relief, and acceptance. He laid a hand on Talia's shoulder. "Thank you," he said again.

Talia squeezed Adriano's wrist, then typed, *Noah and I are working on our friendship, but I like you. You're good for him. I hope it works out.*

'Me too,' Adriano signed back, mouthing the words. He took his cart from Talia and appreciated that she didn't follow him to his car. He needed the moment to regroup. He still felt like crying, which was new. He hadn't cried once during the mess with Eric and Xander, but nearly losing Noah over it had him damn close.

Swallowing thickly, he loaded the bags into his car, then sat behind the wheel and breathed until he could take air into his lungs without choking on it. After a beat, he grabbed his phone to send Noah a quick text.

Adriano: b there soon.

Noah: Good. I can't wait.

CHAPTER 23

Noah wanted to pretend like he had even a modicum of chill, but he was trying his best not to lie. The single phone call from Talia warning him about what had happened at the supermarket sent him to the street, pacing in front of the closed shop as the minutes ticked from one to twenty.

Then he heard the faint roar of Adriano's sports car's engine, and his heart leapt into his throat. He saw when Adriano noticed him, saw the way the car wavered a bit as it pulled into the empty space Noah had left for him. Adriano barely had his feet on the ground before Noah threw himself into Adriano's arms, and his giant boyfriend let out the smallest grunt as he gathered Noah close.

Warm lips brushed over his forehead, his temple, down his cheek as Adriano's mouth made its way to Noah's. They kissed with panting breaths and desperate tongues, Adriano turning and pressing Noah hard against the door of his car.

Noah didn't want to exist anywhere else but there again, except he still didn't love being watched. He felt eyes on him, and he pulled back, though no one seemed to be around. 'Come inside?'

Adriano nodded, then reached into the back for his

bags. When Noah tried to help, Adriano grunted and shook his head, holding them away until Noah gave up. So he led the way inside and waited impatiently as Adriano carefully put all the cold items away and left the dry ones on the table.

A moment passed between them as they stood two feet apart in the kitchen, Adriano's feet bare and in a patch of afternoon sunlight. Their eyes locked first, and Noah felt a warm sort of buzzing course through him. He wasn't sure who took the step first, but the distance between them faded to nothing.

They didn't kiss again. They were barely touching, Adriano cradling Noah's face between his large hands in a hold so light he could barely feel it. And yet, in spite of the gentle touch, he felt surrounded, held, consumed.

'Talia told me,' he finally managed to sign.

Adriano's fingers tightened just for a second, then his hands dropped, and he glanced away. 'I figured she would call.'

Noah drew his top lip between his teeth, feeling his nose stretch with it, then he gestured to the sofa, and Adriano followed him. They sat close, facing each other, knees pressed together. Noah wanted to be back in his arms, but he also wanted to talk this out.

'My brother thinks I have PTSD,' Noah began. 'I looked it up last night after I finished my prep.'

Adriano's brow furrowed. 'Do you agree?'

Blowing out a puff of air, Noah shrugged. 'Some of the stuff fits, some doesn't. There's definitely something wrong with me.'

Adriano shook his head, reaching for him before he stopped himself. 'No. There's nothing wrong.'

Noah couldn't help his laugh. 'Well, there's something happening in my head that I can't control. A single bad date in college shouldn't have made me terrified to try another one, but it did. And I didn't have sex until you came into town.'

Adriano grinned a little salaciously. 'I don't mind that.'

Rolling his eyes, Noah smacked him on the knee. 'Of course you don't. But it's still not...typical.' He was struggling to find words and signs that felt right. 'Hiding like that isn't something that should come naturally to me, but it does. It didn't always.'

'Tell me about the bad date?'

Noah licked his lips nervously, but he didn't look away. 'He was a guy in one of my classes, and he asked me out. I thought we were having a good time. He was my first date ever, and I was nervous. I tried to kiss him and...' His hand wavered, but when Adriano laid a hand on his knee, Noah felt brave and loved. 'He laughed at me, and mocked me, then he left me there.'

Adriano's face darkened. 'What's his name?'

At that, Noah threw his head back and laughed. 'I promise I don't remember, and it doesn't matter. Most people would just be embarrassed, but I spiraled out of control and became too terrified to ever try again until you invited me to that event. But we both know how that went. So I came home a virgin, and I stayed that way until you showed up to find me again.'

A pained look crossed Adriano's face. 'I'm sorry.'

Noah shook his head. 'It all happened a long time ago. It wasn't the bad date, though. That was just a symptom of whatever I have up here.' He tapped his temple. 'I sent a couple of emails to therapists here in town.'

'Why did you shut me out last night?'

Noah couldn't help his wince—mostly out of guilt and a little out of the fear that hit him again just remembering the things Eric told him. 'Eric was making sense. He knew all the things I was afraid of.'

Adriano lifted a brow. 'Tell me.'

The last thing in the world Noah wanted was to look Adriano in the eyes as he signed all this, but he owed Adriano the truth. 'I'm a nobody. I'm a small-town nobody that caught your eye on a vulnerable day. You wanted a distraction while things in your life got sorted out, then you'd go back home to your big life with all your famous friends, and I'd still be here thinking I meant something to you.'

'Noah.' His name sign hadn't changed, and Noah's heart thudded in his chest.

'I know it's not true, but in that moment...' Noah stopped and stared at his hands—at the flecks of dried dough stuck to his skin, at the way none of his body was shapely or fit—and Adriano liked him anyway. Adriano wanted him just like this. 'He laughed at me because I can't sign Deaf speed...'

'Yet,' Adriano spelled, making sure Noah understood. 'You don't sign Deaf speed *yet*.'

Noah nodded. 'I hope. But he...he laughed. He said you do this. He said you took some twink to the Caribbean when you broke up the last time, then you came home and bought him a car and begged him never to leave.'

Adriano rolled his eyes so hard it looked like it hurt. 'I took our friend who had just finished his last round of chemo. Eric was supposed to come with, but he thought the islands weren't going to have all his usual comforts. We fought, and I left without him.'

'Did you beg him to stay with you when you got home?' Noah asked, though he wasn't sure he wanted the answer.

Adriano shrugged. 'Maybe. Our relationship was toxic, and I was shallow. I didn't want things to change because I didn't want to deal with change. What I have with you isn't the same, and I know now that I don't love Eric. I don't think I ever did.'

Noah bowed his head, breathing steady, and nodded. He stayed that way a minute, until Adriano hooked a finger under his chin and drew up his gaze, and Noah found he never wanted to look away. 'I'm sorry I didn't just talk to you. I just…I thought he was right. How else would he know where to find you?'

Adriano's expression went stormy as he pulled his hand back. 'Xander, my agent—*ex*-agent—still had access to my email accounts. He saw when I made our account on SinSity and he tracked you through Twitter. He was trying to sue me for rights to our videos, but because he was no longer my contracted agent, there's going to be a countersuit.'

Noah's eyes widened. 'Seriously.'

Adriano's expression didn't lighten. 'Yes. And one against Eric. He had no right to come here, no right to harass you. He was hired in a professional capacity, and using my personal information to aid Xander…He's not going to get away with it. I'm just sorry they put you through it.'

'Are they going to leak my name?' Noah asked.

Adriano heaved a sigh. 'They might. I don't know. We don't have to post the videos. We can find another way.'

Noah bit his lip and considered it because it was a lot. He'd gone from someone who wouldn't leave the storefront to filming amateur porn, and it was likely some of the town would see it. He'd have to tell his brother so Adam wouldn't stumble on it. He'd have to come clean if people asked.

Because even if Eric or Xander didn't release his name, eventually people would know it was Adriano, and then they'd know it was him.

'I want to do it,' Noah told him. 'I want to have a therapist to help with my anxiety, but I want to do it.'

'Do you still want to fuck me?' Adriano asked him, and Noah blushed furiously.

But he didn't look away. 'Yes. And…and it can show my face. Our faces.'

Adriano looked mildly surprised. 'You don't need to do that.'

Noah felt oddly emboldened, and he shifted closer, letting

their legs tangle. 'I want the world to see your face when I sink inside you.'

Breath coming out in a hard rush, Adriano licked his lips and leaned in. 'Yes,' he signed with a nod of his fist.

Noah grinned. 'Good. Now kiss me.'

It was an order Adriano was happy to follow.

THE REST of Shabbat passed in the same comfort it had the week before. They didn't talk about the videos that were still with the editor. They didn't talk about work, or about Eric, or about Noah's anxiety. They read a lot and tangled up with each other on the sofa, in the armchair, in bed.

Adriano stood behind Noah when he prayed and wrapped arms around him when the Shabbat ended and he lit the Havdalah candle, and he laid a hand on Noah's chest to feel the vibrations as he sang the final blessing. Then they kissed as the flame sent shadows flickering across the walls, and Adriano drew him into the shower and spent ten minutes dragging a soapy sponge over every inch of his body.

They still didn't get each other off, and Noah finally felt in control of himself, even at Adriano's hands.

'I promised you a date,' Adriano said, flicking through Noah's closet until he found a nice shirt and a pair of trousers. Adriano was dressed much the same, just more expensively, but Noah realized he never felt unequal with him. Even when he was a virgin who couldn't keep his dick under control, Adriano never made him feel less.

It was heady. And it was wonderful.

And he loved him.

He let Adriano lay him out on the bed, and he opened his entire body to the man's lazy kisses. It felt intense and wonderful to hold Adriano against him, to feel his mouth in unexpected places like the curve of his ribs, the hollow of his knee, the bend in his elbow. There was no destination this time, just existing together.

Eventually, Adriano propped up on his elbow and hovered over Noah, his free hand tracing lines up and down Noah's soft belly. 'Happy?' he asked.

Noah's smile was answer enough it seemed because Adriano leaned back in to kiss him for short, eternal seconds. Eventually, they made it out the door. Adriano drove, and Noah enjoyed the cool night air on his skin and the feeling of being somewhere new and different, even if it was just minutes from his front door.

Mangia e Zitto was still busy, even after nine, and Noah let his hand slip into his boyfriend's as they made it inside and were shown to a table in the corner. It was dark, candle-lit, and more romantic than Noah imagined it would be.

'I always thought fancy dates would be cheesy,' he admitted after they ordered wine.

Adriano chuckled and shook his head. 'They are, but that's not a bad thing, is it?'

Noah's grin widened. 'No, I guess it isn't. There's a place for it.'

Reaching across the table, Adriano took Noah's hand in his and rubbed his thumb over Noah's knuckles. They locked eyes, then Adriano brought Noah's hand up and kissed him there. It was almost too much, but it was also just enough.

'I wanted to tell you something,' Adriano said after taking his hand back. 'It's going to sound stupid maybe? Or...maybe not the right time? But I feel like if I don't say it now...'

Noah's heart leapt in his chest, and he knew—of course he knew because Adam had made it so obvious. The love he held for Adriano was reflected right back at him in the way Adriano's eyes locked onto his, and in the way his mouth went soft, and in the tender way he handled Noah.

And the way he made Noah feel like enough, even if he still needed work.

"Listen, asshole! I fucking see them right there, and if you don't let me in, I'm going to blast this place so hard online you'll never recover. Do you even know who I am? Do you know who I *know*?"

Noah's eyes went wide as he recognized the voice. He'd never forget it. He snatched his hand from Adriano's and turned in his seat to see Eric wavering in the alcove in front of the dining room. Eric's eyes locked on his, half-crossed, but he recognized him.

"He's right fucking there with his little virgin whore."

Adriano clamped his hand on Noah's wrist. 'What did he say?'

'He's drunk,' Noah told him. 'He called me a virgin whore.'

"Can't even sign properly. God, I'm not drunk, you *whore*. I'm pissed off!"

Noah interpreted, then started to rise, but Adriano shook his head. 'Let me. Give me five minutes. Tell the server I'm sorry.' He dug into his pocket and took out his wallet, sliding a sleek, black card toward Noah. 'Ask them to pack up our food.'

Noah's heart sank, realizing that this moment was ruined. He felt cursed. The man he was in love with was currently walking his drunk ex out the door as the manager came over, looking both angry and apologetic.

"I'm sorry," Noah all but whispered. His face was burning, and everyone was staring. Everyone was staring. They were whispering. He heard the faint tittering of laughter, just like before, even if it wasn't his date this time, and his ears started to ring. His vision started going white, and his breaths began to hitch in his chest.

He hadn't had a full-blown panic attack in years, but there was no stopping this one.

"Hey." A warm, strong arm curled around his waist, and

another body slid up next to him. Noah's eyes were blurred, but the voice was familiar as a hand plucked the card from his fingers and handed it off to the manager. "I think his date would like their stuff packed to take with them."

The arm holding out the card wasn't organic. It was sleek and black with mechanical fingers. Noah turned his head fully and saw Aksel Alling smiling at him. Beside him, the larger man, Ronan, looked gruff as ever with his heavy brows and scowl.

"Let's head outside," Ronan said, his voice roughened even more since high school. He used his hold on Noah to propel him while Aksel stayed behind to take care of the bill, and Noah let Ronan lead him to a bench under a yellow flood of lamplight. Noah's legs went weak, and he sat as Ronan stood back a few paces. "Are you okay?"

Noah's laugh was high and tight. "I don't know?"

"You were having a panic attack."

Noah laughed again. "Uh…yeah. How did you know?"

"I'm pretty familiar," Ronan said, then let out a small huff that might have been something like a laugh. "Was that your boyfriend who dragged that guy out?"

Noah studied Ronan's face, searching for the awkward teen boy he'd last seen up close during their senior year. He was there, beneath the beard, beneath the receding hairline and the wrinkled forehead. He was there in the way his eyes were still soft, even if he always looked angry.

"I think so," Noah admitted. "That guy was his ex."

"What a dick," came another voice. Aksel was walking back with bags of food in his hand and the card pressed between two fingers. Noah took them from him, then laid the food at his feet and bowed his head.

"Sorry. That was mortifying."

Aksel's prosthetic hand landed on his shoulder and squeezed with an unexpected gentleness. "For him," Aksel insisted. He still had the barest hint of an accent from learning English as a kid, a lot like Noah had. He'd shown up in Savannah with both of his parents straight from Norway, though he'd taken to English a lot faster than Noah. "He was the jerk who interrupted your date."

Noah bit the inside of his cheek, then stood up and straightened his back. What he wanted was Adriano. What he wanted was his boyfriend to hold him and tell him that this wasn't ruined, that he wasn't cursed. He found Adriano's car parked right where it always was, but he didn't see him anywhere.

"I saw him go around back," Aksel offered with a half smile.

Noah scrubbed both hands down his face and groaned. "This is a nightmare. This was my second date with him, and it was just…a nightmare."

"You and your boyfriend haven't gone on a date before this?" Ronan asked.

Aksel gently touched the man's elbow. "I think he means ever."

Ronan's eyes widened a fraction. "You're serious?"

"Well, I had one date in college, but it barely counts." Noah's blush was furiously hot in his cheeks, and he glanced away. "It's not that weird."

"No, just…" Ronan said with a huff. He'd never been great with words, and after the fire—after the trauma of almost losing Fitz—he was even quieter. "You're attractive. Really attractive. I'm just surprised."

"He's allowed to be picky, Ro." Aksel smiled at Ronan softly, then turned to Noah. "For what it's worth, I don't think it's ruined. I think he's trying to save it still."

Noah only regretted that he couldn't see what was probably a furious ASL fight, wherever they were. But he wanted to give Adriano space to deal with whatever was left of Eric. "You two should get back to your date. I didn't mean to mess it up."

Aksel shook his head. "*This* wasn't a date, just a good meal after a long day."

"Still," Noah insisted. He didn't have the heart to tell them he just needed a minute, but they seemed to get it because Aksel nodded and started to back away.

Ronan followed at his heels for a minute, then he stopped and turned, facing Noah. "I'm glad to see you tonight. Maybe…I'll see you around? Soon?"

If the night hadn't been such a shitshow, Noah might have felt better. As it was, he still felt elated and surprised. He nodded and licked his lips nervously. "Yeah. Yes. Maybe stop by Bubbe's."

Ronan nodded. "I will. See you." His voice was still gruff, but that was just him, and Noah was starting to understand that maybe people were more nuanced than just friends or enemies. He had wasted a lot of his young life not realizing that.

The pair disappeared, and not two minutes later, a cab pulled into the parking lot and around the corner. Noah sat back down on the stone bench and listened to Eric's voice rising in protest, then to him crying softly. A door shut, and then the cab was gone.

For a single, impossible second, Noah worried Adriano had gone with him. Then he saw him coming around the corner, picking up speed when he saw where Noah was waiting. Noah was on his feet, exhausted by the emotions the drama had pulled out of him but grateful to have warm arms pulling him in.

"Sorry," Adriano said, holding Noah's face up to kiss him and kiss him and kiss him. "I love you. I was trying to say I love you." Adriano pulled one hand away to make the three-fingered sign at him, then he pressed it over Noah's heart. 'I love you.'

Noah closed his eyes, then held his own sign up in reply. 'I love you.'

Adriano curled his fingers around Noah's wrist and kissed the place where his middle and ring finger sat curved against his palm. Noah's eyes closed after that. The night was bound to be even longer, but it didn't matter. Adriano was with him, and there was some sort of happy ending right there in that empty parking lot, with tears in his eyes, and a kiss on his lips.

It was all absolutely perfect.

CHAPTER 24

ADRIANO WAS NERVOUS, and he hadn't expected to be. He had bottomed before, just never on camera and not often. Once or twice, when Eric was a little drunk and feeling needy, Adriano had given in. But it hadn't ever been pleasant. Eric was selfish and sloppy and quick. There was something erotic about being filled, but he felt used rather than cherished, and it wasn't something he wanted to encourage in their relationship.

This time was different. This time was Noah's intense gaze, and his clever, skilled fingers, and the mouth Adriano could spend hours kissing. The camera was on now, pointed right at them. It had been six weeks, and the first two videos had gone just as viral as Adriano had predicted. Noah's royalties were racking up fast and beyond what Adriano could have hoped, though he knew in part it was because he'd been found out.

But the best part was watching people love Noah and reading the comments about how hot his lover was, how erotic, how desperate the audience was to *be* Adriano instead of *with* him. It was a powerful feeling to know Noah was his.

He and Noah had watched the final videos together all at

once, then devoured each other with the last of them playing in the background. They were hot, and Adriano could jack off to the image of Noah coming all over himself without even touching his dick for the rest of his life, but having Noah's body to himself was so much more.

Now he lay on the bed, Noah kneeling over him, two fingers shoved deep in Adriano's ass. He spread his legs wider and moaned for the camera, but he also moaned for Noah. He let the vibrations ripple through him as he arched and thrust himself against Noah's hand, and he lost his breath when Noah added a third finger.

'More,' Adriano begged.

Noah's heated gaze met his. His freckles stood out against his wanton blush, making him look deliciously debauched, and it took all Adriano's strength to not pull Noah by the hips until he was buried balls-deep in Adriano's waiting hole.

'Please,' he added when Noah made no move to comply.

There was more lube suddenly, shocking and cold, then a fourth finger. He felt split apart on Noah's hand, and he never, ever wanted it to end.

'Ready?' Noah asked with one hand.

They had agreed to no voicing. Not for this. Not between them. Adriano's language was enough, and they'd met a nice guy in town who did captions and was happy to agree to add them.

'Are *you* ready?' Adriano threw back. 'Are you ready to lose everything to me?'

'You already took my heart,' Noah told him, and Adriano's head fell back against the pillows. 'I want the world to see me give the rest of myself to you.'

It was terrible, cheesy dialogue, but before their night had been viciously ruined by Eric's meltdown, they had agreed there was a place in their lives for things like that. And Adriano also knew Noah meant every word.

'Fuck me. Fuck me, please.' Adriano's shaking hands were not an affect for the video. He was goddamn desperate.

Noah didn't need more coaxing. The condom was on, he was slick with lube, and he used one hand to push Adriano's leg up toward his chest. The perfect view for the camera, and the perfect angle to take every inch of Noah in one, slow thrust.

Adriano felt mad with desire, every fiber of his being on edge, primed and poised to lose total control. He had no restraint. None. He was gone over Noah and had been from the first moment he watched his soft, careful hands sign out their sympathy.

Now those hands were his.

Adriano felt himself groan as Noah pushed all the way in. He angled himself so the camera could keep the shot, but it was enough to send Noah's dick grazing his prostate, and a sharp, "*Oh*," ripped from his throat.

His dick gave a vicious throb, and he sat up halfway on his elbows. He had to see Noah, to look him in the eye, to be as close as they could get. The movement had Noah lurching forward, their chests pressed together. He sank deeper, fucked him harder, hips slapping against Adriano's ass.

His orgasm was cresting from the barely there pressure of Noah's stomach against his cock. "God," he whispered, the word jagged in his throat. "God."

Noah squeezed his eyes shut, his dick pulsing and thickening farther.

It was enough. God, it was enough.

Adriano fell back with a heavy shout, his upper body curving toward the ceiling as he spilled all over himself.

Untouched.

He rode the waves of pleasure as Noah's thrusts stuttered, and he rolled his hips as he chased the last bits of pleasure. When Adriano was brave enough to open his eyes again, he found Noah staring down at the mess on Adriano's stomach, eyes wide with wonder at the sight of it.

'From me,' he signed with one unsteady hand.

Adriano nodded, then pulled Noah's fingers to his mouth and kissed the pads of each one. 'From you. For you. I love you.'

Noah's fingers curled into the shape, then he pressed them against Adriano's heart. 'I love you too.'

'Precious,' Adriano added, letting the word take on every meaning—cherished, important, beloved. Noah.

Their gazes settled together, gentle and never breaking, and Adriano knew that no matter where they went from this moment on, he was home.

NOAH CHECKED HIS WATCH, staring across the market pathway at the slick grass and puddles littering the sidewalks. The air was rich with the scent of ozone from the rain but growing hotter and more humid every minute after the storm had passed.

It was a typical storm, though it felt like anything but. He had a meeting in twenty minutes with the guy who was going to lease Bubbe's building—a favor to Nellie, the realtor, who was in a parent-teacher conference. In all honesty, Noah didn't mind. Where he would have once shrunk back at the idea of socializing with a stranger and involving himself in business like this with the apartment, with the bakery, he wanted to know that it was going to be as loved and cherished as it had been since it opened.

The decision had been made months ago, long before Adriano had even set foot in their little town, but this felt final. Signing an agreement to lease the place out felt like a bookend, even if there was still more room on the shelf. He and Adam would make a little money off it, though, which would help Adam's business, and it would ease Noah's conscience knowing that he wasn't staying.

Because he wasn't.

When Adriano suggested he reapply to school in LA, Noah had laughed at him, then kissed him for being sweet and thoughtful. But Adriano hadn't been joking. 'You have one semester to finish. All your credits are there. You left on good terms due to a family tragedy. It can't hurt to try, can it?'

The cost of an application fee and the weeks of anxiety that followed were the highest price he had to pay, but Adriano was very good at distracting him.

Noah had tried to forget, losing himself in the last weeks of being able to bake in Bubbe's kitchen, the last weeks of setting up the market stall and actually mingling with neighbors. He never did take Ronan and Aksel up on their offer for dinner, but he had dragged Adriano out to Will, Liam, and Isaac's house, where they'd shown off their terrible signing skills. And Adam started coming back around on Saturday nights to cook.

Then Noah got his acceptance letter and a potential lessee all in the same week, and it was a sharp slap to the face by reality's unkind hand. It felt good, it felt right, but it wasn't supposed to be forever.

Noah fiddled with his phone as he waited for the minutes to tick by. Adriano was still in LA dealing with the last vestiges of his lawsuit with Xander. Or well, his company really. Xander had been fired and had issued a public apology. His name had been tarnished, though Adriano didn't think the blacklisting was going to last too long. But he didn't care.

The suit against Adriano had been dropped, and the suit against the company for breach of privacy was coming to a close. After two months of having Adriano all to himself—in his bed every night, arms around him, waking with kisses at each sunrise—Noah missed him. It had been eleven days, and *hell*, he missed him.

It had been five hours since Adriano had texted, saying things were a little busy but he'd be in touch soon. Noah tried not to worry, but he always would at least a little. He'd worry that Adriano would miss the glamour of his old life, that this quiet, subtle thing with Noah wouldn't be enough.

He knew that wasn't reality, but it was hard to accept when Adriano was so damn far away, when he couldn't just reach out and touch him.

"Excuse me, sir. How much for the hot baker?"

Noah didn't need to look up to recognize the voice, and his heart leapt into his throat as he scrambled around the counter and straight into Adriano's arms. He heard Adriano chuckle, low and deep, and he buried his face in his lover's neck. Adriano smelled like airport, like stale air and bad coffee and other people's cologne. And he smelled like him. And he smelled like home.

'You're early,' Noah accused as Adriano set him back down.

Adriano didn't answer, instead cradling Noah's face with his big hands as he crowded him up against the table for a long kiss. When he broke it off, he let out a contented hum and rubbed their noses together. 'It was over. I won. They have to pay a settlement, and I didn't want to be gone any longer than I had to. I missed you.'

Noah felt those words like a physical ache, and he dragged Adriano into another kiss until his phone started to buzz with his alarm. "Shit," he murmured, pulling back. 'I have to go meet Wilder at Bubbe's.'

Adriano shrugged, then pulled the closed flap over the stall and took Noah's hand. 'I'll come with you.'

Noah wasn't about to argue. He didn't want to let go for a good, long while. They made the slow walk over, and Noah saw the man standing in front of the building, pacing a little, tapping away on his phone. He felt a rush of fear, of panic. *I can't do this*, a small voice whispered, but Adriano's hand in his told another story.

He could absolutely do this. He could move on. None of this had to be forever, and no change would have to alter the person he was.

Wilder glanced up when they approached, and Noah grinned at him. They'd exchanged two emails, and the most Noah knew was that he was moving from across the country, and that he wanted to open up a cupcake shop that specialized in gluten-free baking.

Noah hadn't expected him to be so good looking—tall with rich black hair styled back away from his face and wearing jeans and a button-up. He had long-fingered hands, one of which reached for Noah's, and as he turned, Noah saw a hearing aid nestled against the back of his ear.

He blinked, then turned to Adriano who had also noticed. 'Do you prefer sign?' Noah offered.

Wilder's eyes went wide, but not on Noah—on Adriano. It was the too-familiar expression Noah had picked up on as Adriano socialized more and more with the town. After a beat, Wilder cleared his throat, then offered his hand to Adriano.

'Sorry,' the man signed after pulling away. 'You're…'

Adriano nodded, then spelled his name before offering his sign name. 'Adriano. ASL okay?'

Wilder grinned. 'Perfect. Is there a strong Deaf community here?'

At that, Noah's face fell. 'No, not really. They've been great about learning, but there's not a lot of opportunity here without more Deaf people. But they do try.'

Wilder didn't look bothered. 'I'm CODA and HoH. I think I'll be okay.'

Noah grinned, then turned to unlock the shop and flicked on the lights. His footsteps echoed, and he knew it was because a lot of the place had already been packed up. He hadn't shut the doors—not yet—but it was starting to look empty. His heart ached a little bit, but at the sight of wonder and promise on Wilder's face, the pain eased.

'This is amazing,' Wilder signed after a few minutes. 'This is…exactly what I was looking for.'

Noah took a breath, and ignored the twist in his chest when he asked, 'Do you want to see upstairs?'

Wilder's smile widened, and he nodded.

CHAPTER 25

Noah lifted his curled fist to the door, hesitated, then dropped it. He took a breath, then forced himself to knock, shifting from one foot to the other until it opened, and his brother stood there looking sleepy and disgruntled.

"Did I wake you up?" Noah asked.

Adam narrowed his eyes at him, but instead of answering, he turned on his heel and walked back into the apartment, leaving the door open. Noah only waited a moment before following him in and moved into the kitchen at the smell of coffee.

"Talia always fucking wakes me up when she has an early shift," Adam grumbled. He shoved two mugs into the microwave as he pushed the button on his espresso machine. A rich smell filled the air, and Noah saw the little pot of steamed milk sitting already frothed and ready. "I know you're not here to tell me someone's dead since we have no family and I follow everyone you do on Twitter."

The microwave beeped, and Adam took out the mugs, adding in the milk, then the espresso before passing one to Noah. He stared down at the milky liquid, swirling with the caramel color of espresso foam Adam had perfected by the time he was thirteen.

"I don't want to go." Noah's words came out soft and hesitant, almost like he was betraying his own secrets.

Adam made a small noise, then slid up to him, resting his back against the counter, hip pressed to Noah's. "It's not forever." His voice echoed the words Noah had been telling himself since he'd told Nellie to approve Wilder's application, but they didn't bring any comfort.

"No." Noah took a drink of the coffee and burned his tongue. The café hafuch—a taste of home, which was the closest Adam had ever been to Israel—was comforting but not enough.

The silence stretched on so long Noah wondered for a moment if he'd made a mistake coming to Adam. "Why aren't you with Adriano?"

Noah let out a small scoff. "He's sleeping off jet lag." Not a total lie but not entirely the truth. Adriano was sleeping, but Noah was there because he needed his brother. He took a fortifying breath, then turned to face Adam. "I've known for a long time that you were ready to move on with your life and stop living...the way I was living. To stop living with someone like me."

"Noah," Adam started to protest, but Noah held up a hand.

"I was ready to let you go, but I also made all these big decisions without..." He stopped. He'd gotten Adam's blessing before he put the bakery on the market, but right now, it didn't feel like enough. "It was still yours. Whatever those fucking papers said, Adam, it was still yours too."

Adam set his coffee down and crossed his arms. "I know."

"I don't want you to hate me." The admission came softly, barely above a whisper, but Adam flinched like Noah had shouted. "After all these years of not being able to stand me, I need to know that I can walk away, and you'll want me to come back."

"I'll always regret not telling you I loved you more after…" Adam swallowed, and Noah knew what he meant. After Bubbe died. Before Bubbe's death, Adam had been sweet. He'd been a pain in the ass, but he'd been affectionate, and he looked at Noah like Noah was his whole world. Then Bubbe was gone, and Noah had to be someone entirely new, and Adam changed because Noah had changed.

"It's okay. I still knew," Noah told him.

With a sigh, Adam reached out and curled his hand around the back of Noah's neck, drawing him close. Adam had outgrown Noah by the time he was fifteen and was now at least three inches taller, but until this moment, Adam had never felt bigger than him. "I'm not entirely ready to let go, but that's okay."

Noah shook his head. "Is it?"

Adam squeezed his fingers tighter, and it was painful but comforting, keeping Noah present. "Yes. If I've learned anything from being with Talia, it's that discomfort can be… cathartic. And necessary." He let up on his grip, and Noah looked up at him. "Letting this go doesn't mean letting me go."

Old habits died hard, though, and Noah's vow to keep Adam safe in exchange for everything he was still rang in his ears. "Bubbe would have done this, right?"

Adam laughed a bit. "She might not have rented to some guy who could put her favorite grandson out of business, but"—his mouth softened—"yes, she would have done this. She would not have done everything you did, though. You're braver than she was. You're braver than I am."

"I don't know," Noah started, but Adam shook his head.

"Nothing's changing. Nothing real is changing," Adam told him. "And that's because of you."

Noah swallowed thickly and nodded. "Thank you."

Though he didn't know if he believed Adam, but maybe he would. Eventually. "I should get going. I want to grab breakfast before Adriano wakes up."

Adam nodded, then moved to the end of the breakfast bar and swiped up one of his pastry boxes, handing it off to Noah. "The brie and raspberry are on the left, strawberry and rhubarb on the right."

Noah wrinkled his nose but took it anyway and fought back a too-large grin. "Thanks."

"Tell your sugar daddy I said hi and that I'm glad he's home."

Blanching, Noah turned away, but he smiled in spite of himself. "You know, he's not the only one now, right? You should see my bank account."

"Shut the hell up, or I *will* watch your porn, Noah. I will have a porn party and invite the whole town."

At that, Noah did laugh, big and hearty and full of life. He let Adam show him to the door, then turned and nodded at his brother. "You'll help me pack?"

"*Elohim yishmor*, yes," he said, exasperated but grinning. "Now get the hell out of my apartment."

"Say hi to Talia," Noah called back as he started away from the door. He heard the echo of Adam's chuckle as Noah headed to his car. He didn't feel entirely better, and he probably never would. This was almost his entire life that was being packed up in small boxes and either stored or moved across the country.

And he was saying goodbye—for now. Maybe for a little while. Maybe longer.

But it was time.

EPILOGUE

NOAH SWIPED a hand over his forehead before walking to the window and pushing it open farther. It wasn't just the late-August heat but the dust in the air, scattered from old boxes, that was making it hard to breathe. And the fact that it was happening. Noah's bank account was full, his loan paid off, a nest egg sitting quietly, and life was okay.

But he was still selling. He was still packing away these bits and pieces of his life—his childhood, his teenage years, the tortured adulthood he'd nearly withered away behind until Adriano entered his life like a hurricane.

He felt raw some days. Therapy was helping, but there wasn't really a cure for his condition. There were meds he wasn't taking just yet. Keeping them on hand felt better than actually starting. He was managing okay on his own with the help of the soft-spoken woman in an office downtown who also had a few recommendations for when he got to LA.

But he knew anyone would be sad doing this. He glanced over at Adam, who had been sitting with the same box for half an hour, and he plopped down next to him, peering over the edge. It was some miscellaneous box Bubbe had thrown together—some of Noah's old matchbox cars, a tattered dinosaur stuffie Adam had carried with him when he was three, then abandoned by four. Beneath that looked like old report cards and a stack of photos.

Adam had one in his hand, a shot of Noah and Bubbe on the beach. Noah barely recognized it now—the shores of the Mediterranean on the coast of Tel Aviv. He was standing with his feet in the water, and the sea behind him was faded in the photograph, but he remembered how sharply, impossibly blue-green the water shone in the afternoon sun. He could almost smell it there, almost taste it on the sides of his tongue.

"Do you ever want to go back?" Adam asked quietly.

Noah touched the edge of the photo. "Sometimes, yeah. I mean, Abba's grave is there. It might be nice to lay some stones."

Adam nodded, chewing on his lower lip for a minute. "It never did feel real to me. I mean, I was born there, but it was never mine."

"You'd like it," Noah told him. "I hated it for a long time after we got here. I was angry. There were days like this, but there were raids, and bomb threats, and people dying all the time. And the conflict killed Abba. I never understood it." Noah closed his eyes and could just picture his father—the spitting image of the man Adam was now—the same smile, same eyes, even the same laugh. It didn't hurt him the way it hurt their mother, though. Adam was a way of getting to keep those pieces he'd lost.

Adam sighed. "Do you think he would have liked me?"

"I don't know." Noah wanted to lie just to make Adam happy, but that's where all his problems had started with his brother. "He wasn't around much. Sometimes I thought he'd rather be doing anything else besides being home with us and Ema."

Adam closed his eyes in a slow blink. "Then I'm glad I got you instead of him."

Noah's insides hurt, deeply and profoundly. He'd never felt like enough, but this was Adam's way of telling him it was okay. He glanced over, and Adam was holding another photo. Noah was twelve. He knew because of the cast on his leg and stitches in his cheek from the crash. He was reclined on the sofa, and Adam—the chubby-faced toddler—was fast asleep on his chest. In the photo, Noah's eyes were closed, and he held on possessively.

Adam made a small noise in the back of his throat. "You loved me."

Noah laughed, the sound a little harsh. "Yes, Adam."

"You loved me more than she ever did."

Noah closed his eyes and breathed. The answer was yes. Yes, he loved Adam more than their mother had and maybe even more than Bubbe. He loved Adam as an extension of himself, though that wasn't quite true. He loved his brother more than he'd ever loved the reflection that stared back at him in the mirror.

Clearing his throat, he looked down at his hands. "Did you find everything you wanted to keep?"

Adam sighed, then dropped the photo back into the box. "Yeah. The apartment doesn't have a lot of room. You sure you don't mind storing it all?"

Noah laughed. "I'm not taking a lot with me. We're only staying four months."

"Until people recognize you for the star you are," Adam said, and Noah's face erupted into a blush. Adam swore he and Talia hadn't watched the videos, but he wouldn't put it past his brother to peek just to be a shit. "Promise me you won't be gone forever?"

Noah gave him a flat look. "I don't want to be gone at all, but I wanted to do this. I don't know what the hell to do after, and please don't say porn."

"What?" Adam defended as he climbed to his feet. "It makes good money. Though I guess you have your sugar daddy for that." Noah scoffed and turned away, but Adam caught him by the arm and turned him slowly. "Let's go see them."

"It's not time, Adam. It's not…"

"Noah," Adam breathed out. "Don't. You'll be in LA for yahrzeit."

"You know I was planning to come back for it," Noah started to argue, but Adam gave him a flat look.

Noah knew the truth. He knew he was deflecting because standing over the graves of his mother and grandmother was always a lot for him. But he'd been collecting stones over the past few months, and he knew Adam had done the same. He detached himself from Adam's fingers, then walked into the kitchen and opened the one drawer he hadn't packed. One of the stones looked almost black, polished by the little stream out by Will's house. The other was in the shape of a crescent for Bubbe.

He clutched them in his fist, then showed them to Adam who nodded, jaw set. "I brought mine. I want to do this with you in case, for whatever reason, you don't make it back."

"I will," Noah told him fiercely. It was a promise he intended to keep, even if he did stay away longer than four months. He'd been thinking of doing some traveling, and Adriano wasn't opposed. "But just in case," he added.

"What time do you have to meet the squatter?" Adam asked.

Noah narrowed his eyes at his brother. "Please don't make Wilder feel unwelcome. I like him. He's nice."

"You like him because he's hot, and Adriano likes him because he's Deaf, and meanwhile, I'm going to lose all my damn business to this hipster."

Noah laughed and pulled Adam close. "He'll be here at four. We have time to drive down and back. And he sells gluten-free cupcakes. You'll have plenty of people who want your brie croissants and Blue Moon custard sufganiyot."

Adam wrinkled his nose, but he didn't argue as he followed Noah down the stairs—for one of the last times together—and to the car.

The drive to the cemetery was almost an hour long. Bubbe insisted their mother be buried in an all-Jewish cemetery instead of the Jewish section in Bonaventure, and finding one had taken some time. But both his mom and Bubbe had been permitted, and Noah had never worried about the cost because Bubbe had been nothing if not thorough before her death.

He knew Adam came more often than he did, and Noah liked to blame it on his faith, but in truth, he was never able to divorce himself from the grief of losing them both. He wanted to be better about it, and maybe Adam was on to something when it came to facing what hurt most head-on. But he was about to put thousands of miles between him and what was left of his ragged past.

The grass was freshly wet beneath their feet as Adam led the way, and Noah held the stones so tight they cut into his palm, feeling skin almost give way when he laid eyes on the names of the two women he had loved most in the world.

"They'd be horrified at the way I've lived," Adam muttered, putting the stones in his left hand before laying them down—first for Bubbe, then for their mom. "They'd take one look at Talia and ask me what the hell she's doing with a bastard like me."

"I'm with a porn star," Noah reminded him. He laid the black stone down for his mother but held the crescent a bit longer. "Anyway, they'd see the way you two look at each other, and that would be more important than anything in the world."

"Do you think so?" Adam looked so young, sounded so young. He was suddenly the person of fourteen, holding Noah's hand, wanting to know why Hashem saw fit to take both his mother and his grandmother away from him.

Noah had no answers then, just like he didn't have one now.

But he had faith. He'd always have faith.

"I think so." He felt Adam take his hand just before he bent over to lay Bubbe's stone for her, and he pressed his fingertips to the cold, stamped concrete. He didn't feel her there. He didn't feel her anywhere. Not anymore. But he missed her.

"Does it get easier for you?" Adam asked, his voice thick.

Noah didn't want to risk speaking, so he shook his head. They stood there, hand in hand, the last of their family. It was a little bit alone, but it wasn't so lonely anymore.

"We should head back if you don't want to miss the squatter."

Noah let out a tiny sigh, but he knew Wilder would grow on Adam. Or he wouldn't. He'd still find a home in Savannah like so many had. They made their way back to the car, and Noah took just a moment for himself to breathe again. When his lungs felt clear, he tossed a smile at his brother, then started back up the street.

ADRIANO WAITED at the rental for Noah to finish up his day. He'd gotten a text from Noah, letting him know he was dropping Marshmallow back off with Isaac, then heading back to the shop to give the new guy the final tour. The leasing agency would handle the rest, and Noah would be free.

Or something like it.

He gave Jude a scratch and felt a sort of profound loss, looking around at all their things packed in neat boxes and bags. He didn't want to leave—but Noah needed this. He needed to set foot out of the cage he'd created for himself. First it was school, then the world.

Adriano startled when he saw headlights, and he was on his feet and near the door when it opened. Noah looked a bit ragged and red around his eyes like he'd been crying. He pushed into Adriano's arms easily, quietly, at least as far as Adriano could tell.

His back ached from not moving, but he was still content to stand there and hold the love of his life, just like that, as long as he needed. Noah, of course, didn't make him wait an eternity. Just five minutes before he pulled back and cupped Adriano's cheek, taking a kiss for himself before he moved to the sofa.

'How was it?' Adriano asked.

Noah shrugged. 'Good. I think the place will do well. People need something new.'

Adriano nodded. 'And the rest?' He meant the cemetery—he meant the time with his brother—and the last moments they had with their childhood home.

Noah's chin trembled a little, and he licked his lips before a few tears seeped out. Adriano brushed them away, but more replaced them, so he simply let Noah cry. 'It's over. It was hard. I miss them so much, but it was time, you know?'

Adriano didn't know. He might, eventually, in some way. But he'd never know what it was like to lose his country and his language, to lose everything important to him and be stuffed into a tiny box the way Noah had been. He was grateful for it and still profoundly sad for his lover. But Noah wasn't suffering all the time.

Adriano made him smile.

It felt...worth it.

'Take me to bed?' Noah asked after a short silence.

Adriano stood up and offered his hand. Noah slipped his own fingers between Adriano's larger ones, and they made their way down the little hall to the primary bedroom for the last time. They'd wake up with the sun, they'd put the rest of their bags in the car, and they'd head west.

For now. Maybe for a short while. Maybe a lot longer.

But that didn't matter right then. Right then, they had tonight.

And then, after that, they had forever.

The End

ALSO BY E.M. LINDSEY

[Broken Chains](#)

[The Carnal Tower](#)

[Hit and Run](#)

[Irons and Works](#)

[The Sin Bin: West Coast](#)

[Malicious Compliance](#)

[Collaborations with Other Authors](#)

[Foreign Translations](#)

[AudioBooks](#)

ABOUT THE AUTHOR

E.M. Lindsey is a non-binary writer who lives in the southeast United States, close to the water where their heart lies.

Printed in Great Britain
by Amazon